The Silverwood Chronicles

Guardian of the Silverwood

Wm. Matthew Graphman

THE SILVERWOOD CHRONICLES
GUARDIAN OF THE SILVERWOOD

Copyright © 2014 Wm. Matthew Graphman.

All rights reserved. No part of this book may be used or reproduced by any means, graphic, electronic, or mechanical, including photocopying, recording, taping or by any information storage retrieval system without the written permission of the publisher except in the case of brief quotations embodied in critical articles and reviews.

This is a work of fiction. All of the characters, names, incidents, organizations, and dialogue in this novel are either the products of the author's imagination or are used fictitiously.

iUniverse books may be ordered through booksellers or by contacting:

iUniverse
1663 Liberty Drive
Bloomington, IN 47403
www.iuniverse.com
1-800-Authors (1-800-288-4677)

Because of the dynamic nature of the Internet, any web addresses or links contained in this book may have changed since publication and may no longer be valid. The views expressed in this work are solely those of the author and do not necessarily reflect the views of the publisher, and the publisher hereby disclaims any responsibility for them.

Any people depicted in stock imagery provided by Thinkstock are models, and such images are being used for illustrative purposes only. Certain stock imagery © Thinkstock.

ISBN: 978-1-4917-5532-7 (sc)
ISBN: 978-1-4917-5534-1 (hc)
ISBN: 978-1-4917-5533-4 (e)

Library of Congress Control Number: 2014921785

Printed in the United States of America.

iUniverse rev. date: 12/12/2014

Dedication

This books is for Kathryn and Ethan. Thank you for encouraging me and leading me through this project. Your feedback and great ideas helped make this book come to life. Love, Your Dad.

Special Thanks

My Wife - Wendy Graphman
April Easter
Peggy Strader
Mary Whitney

Chapter 1

An arrow whizzed by, just missing her silver hair; Taya took a deep breath before peering around the corner. Her keen elf-green eyes clearly saw through the twilight as if it were day, and the upper portion of a dark skinny monster was pushing its way through the barricaded door.

"Guntharr, they're starting to break through," Taya called out behind her. "We need to get out of here!"

On the far side of the room behind her, a tall warrior who had seen his share of battle stood facing what appeared to be an average door.

"I'm working on it." Guntharr replied in a slightly irritated tone. "Hold them off for just a few more seconds." With that, the warrior lifted up a massive stone hammer and brought it crashing down on the door. Any average door would have shattered into a million pieces with the blow, but his weapon simply crashed with a resounding boom that shook the entire room.

Taya wrinkled her nose and reached back into her quiver to pull out one of the few remaining arrows she had. Knocking her arrow, she twisted around and spotted the lead monster attempting to pull itself free from the pile of boxes, chairs and furniture that they had used to block the door.

Almost without thinking, she released the arrow. It streaked through the dark and found its target without difficulty. It slammed through the monster's chest with such force that it picked it up and hung it on the doorframe. The creature let out a terrific scream and fell silent as it hung with its feet dangling off the floor.

"I guess I'm not getting that one back," Taya moaned. She reached back and took a quick inventory of her arrows. She counted three. This was not good. If Gunthar wasn't able to get that door to the back alley opened very soon, they would be flooded with creatures like the one she had just posted on the wall.

"I've only got three arrows left," she called over to him.

"I'm working on it." The warrior replied. "This door is magic. I'm going to have to try something else. Make those last three arrows count."

Taya's eyes narrowed at him as she studied his words. Any other person within earshot of their conversation would have taken that last remark as a criticism or a slight, but Taya learned very quickly after she had been left in Guntharr's care that he only wanted the best for her and had always been very kind. He wasn't being terse, but he was giving her a clue as to how to make the best use of the arrows.

He knew that the arrow heads had been fashioned out of some of the finest Elven steel in the five realms and that the shafts had been shaped from the branches of a Dagmoor tree. This wood was as hard as steel, but still light and flexible. Arrows like this would cost a commoner a week's wage for a single arrow. Taya had been provided thirty of them by Guntharr long ago, and now she was down to three. This saddened her as she had always been so careful to retrieve and take care of the arrows and now they were gone. With only three left, she had to make them "count" as Guntharr had said.

The noise and commotion coming from the barricade had intensified, so Taya decided she needed to have a look. Instead of peering around the corner at eye-level, this time she crouched down. This put her in a disadvantaged position. She needed to get a reading on where the monsters were; but she didn't want to reveal her location in the same way, in case they were waiting to get off a shot.

Her instinct was correct. Because, as she looked around the wall, a small dagger thudded into the wall just above where she had been standing a second before. Her eyes made out two monsters now that had pushed their way through the barricade. They were almost perfectly lined up. Quickly, she reached back and pulled one of the three remaining arrows and knocked it in her bow.

The lead monster had a clear bead on her now and was fumbling to grab another throwing dagger out of his belt, but the press of the creature behind him kept him off balance and he struggled. That delay was all Taya needed. Winking with one eye so she could locate the perfect spot, she adjusted her aim slightly and let the arrow fly. With expert precision, the arrow buried itself into the two creatures. The lead creature looked down at the small stub of an arrow sticking out of this mid-section and looked back at the surprise of the second. Both let out a groan and slumped forward onto the barricade creating more obstacles for the creatures behind them to overcome.

Taya stood upright and listened as the commotion behind the barricade increased, but no apparent attempts were being made to push their way into the room. "Well, that worked out better than I thought," she said half to herself.

"What worked better?" Guntharr asked, eyes closed and concentrating on something.

"Are you sure you're not part elf?" She asked in response. "Because, you have better hearing than some elves do."

"Training and concentration," was his response.

Guntharr stretched out his hand toward the door and straightened out to his full towering frame. Whispering a prayer, a light began to glow around the door.

Taya always marveled at this exercise of his. While she knew that Guntharr was not a magic user in the normal since of the term, he had the ability to communicate with his God, and more often than not, whatever Guntharr asked, it always seemed to be done. The light grew in intensity and the cracking sound of wood could be heard. Guntharr lowered his hand and opened his eyes as the light grew to an almost blinding intensity. Suddenly there was a loud explosion as the door burst into shards out into the alley behind the building.

"You must teach me your magic, someday," Taya marveled as she walked up to him.

Guntharr smiled over to his young elf ward. "No magic here, Taya," he held up a hand, "only faith."

She bowed in respect to his correction. "After you," he ushered her out into the back alley.

Guntharr had known in his gut that they were walking into a trap when they had entered the inn, but he couldn't imagine that there would have been an ambush in wait for them. Whoever it was that was after them, this was starting to get serious. The minions that they faced were starting to increase in number and the inclusion of a magically bound door in the only known escape route was definitely a step up from the types of traps that have been placed before them.

The real question that stood out in his mind was, why? While he had made his share of enemies along life's road --how could he not, being a soldier and guardian -- he couldn't think of anyone that hated him enough to come after him with such ferocity and persistence. He glanced down in both directions of the alley. While they were safe for a moment, there was no doubt that the gang of thugs that were trying to take them out in the inn would figure out where they'd gone.

"Taya," Guntharr looked over at the elf, "call for Raskin. We need his eyes to figure out the best way out of here."

Taya nodded and immediately cupped her hands and begin to whistle a melodic tune. "He should be here momentarily."

Guntharr nodded, "Great, how far can you see in that direction?"

Taya's eyes had been trained to see in nearly total darkness farther, than any human could see in normal daylight. "It looks clear. I only see a couple of small rats and a stray dog."

"Rats and a stray dog," Guntharr chuckled, "that's all you see down there?"

Taya smiled. "That's all that is of interest. If you need more details, I can try to provide them."

Guntharr pulled out his war hammer and trotted in the direction that Taya had spotted the residents of the alley. Taya followed close behind the huge man, trying to keep a close eye on the path behind them as they quickly moved toward the next intersection.

Passing by the lazy dog that had made this alley its home, they failed to see any rats, but that was not a big surprise, as most rats, even the ones in Hydesvalley, didn't like people.

Suddenly the sound of large flapping wings drew closer to them. Guntharr and Taya stopped abruptly to try to identify which direction the sound was coming from. Reacting quickly, the two spun around as a large hawk-like bird glided to a perfect landing on top of a heap of trash that was pushed up against the wall.

"Where have you two been?" Squawked the hawk.

Taya rushed up to bird and threw her arms around it and gave it a big hug. "It's good to see you too, Raskin."

"Easy, easy, bird bones are not as sturdy as people bones," Raskin fluttered.

Taya stepped back and admired the bird's almost three feet in height.

"I was starting to worry," Raskin continued, "I had lost sight of you when you entered the inn. When I saw the mob of ruffians come barreling in, I knew that you were in trouble, but there was nothing I could do but hope you would bring the fight back out into the streets."

Guntharr stepped forward, "You may get what you wished for, if we don't hurry. I need a scouting report for the surrounding alleys to find the least obstructed way toward the north quarter."

Spreading its mighty wings, the hawk began to ascend. "I'll be just a moment," and Raskin vanished into the night sky.

"Guardian," Taya began to address Guntharr.

"I wish you wouldn't call me that," Guntharr replied.

Taya's head turned slightly, "but you won't allow me to call you Father."

"That's because, I'm not your father." Guntharr started moving on down the alley.

Taya smiled, "I understand, but if you won't let me call you Father, which you are not, or Guardian, which you are . . ."

Guntharr held up a hand to stop her, "Guntharr, will do."

Taya shook her head in disapproval, "I cannot. That title is too informal for one in my standing."

"It's better than, 'hey you,'" Guntharr joked.

"But Guardian," Taya tried to persuade him.

"Can we continue this after we make it out of this mess, please." Guntharr looked down with tenderness.

Taya's smiled, "Of course."

In the distance, they could hear sounds coming from the back room that they had left.

"Come, this way." Guntharr commanded.

The two took off at a full run down the alley looking for any clear means of escape. A loud cry from behind them confirmed what

Guntharr had feared; they had spent too long planning their next move and the creatures had gotten through their barricade.

The creatures, while not extremely bright, were in fact much faster than Guntharr and his ward. The alley that they were in seemed to have no end, but also did not seem to tie into any other avenues for escape.

The pulsing of wings overhead could be felt by the two running and Raskin called down to them, "Just ahead, the alley ends at Boar Avenue."

Guntharr's mind raced as he revisited his mental map of the city. If they were indeed near Boar Avenue, they would soon be out in the clear and able to choose from many different escape routes. They would just need to delay the creatures a few more seconds so that they could get lost in the city.

"Raskin," Guntharr called over his shoulder, "Can you distract our friends for just a moment?"

All Guntharr heard back was a loud squawk that resembled a battle cry more than anything Raskin could have said.

"Please, don't get hurt," Taya added, but the hawk had already disappeared from earshot.

At Guntharr's directive, Raskin ceased gliding over them and instead soared straight up. Once he had reached what he deemed was a reasonable height, he twisted in mid-flight and pulled his wings in. Diving down faster and faster, Raskin targeted the leading two creatures that had quickly gained on his friends. He counted ten creatures already in the alley and more were literally falling out of the back of the inn every second. He had a plan. He didn't know if he would have enough velocity to pull it off, but he had to try in order to give Taya and Guntharr a chance.

Every second that Raskin fell from the sky his speed increased. He opened up his wings slightly just so that he could level off and navigate down the alley. Just another second and he would be over his target. Dropping his feet from his body, he stretched out his talons. Traveling at the speed of an elvish arrow, Raskin's talons grazed the tops of the lead creatures with such force that it sliced a gash in their heads the depth of an axe blade. Not only did the attack kill the first two creatures, it sent them hurling back into the creatures that were following close behind. The result was a tangled pile of arms and legs. The third set scattered as the front four rolled to a halt.

Raskin extended his wings and began to gain altitude as several of the creatures struggled to swat and pull down the massive bird. With a loud squawk of victory, Raskin spun around in the night sky and headed back to rendezvous with his friends.

Out in the street, Taya faintly heard Raskin's victory squawk. Guntharr must have heard it too as he quickly pointed to a side road that would lead them to a place of cover. "Hurry, this way! Raskin's bought us a few extra seconds."

The two took off with renewed encouragement down the street past several closed up houses and shops. Boar Avenue, which was one of the lesser travelled streets in Hydevalley, bordered the edge of the city along with many farms. Guntharr spotted a promising stable and pulled Taya in that direction.

Circling around to the back, they found the door unlatched. Quickly, they entered and latched the door. Finding a sturdy pitchfork, Guntharr slid the it into the door handle and latched it, locking the door tight. Putting his hand up to his ear; Taya nodded and closed her eyes, concentrating on the sounds around her.

It took her a second to settle down and filter out the sound of her and Guntharr breathing. Stretching out with her senses, she was able to hear the beating of Raskin's wings just overhead. The second set of sounds was that of a group of feet, that she was sure associated with the ones chasing them. A smile slowly spread across her face as the sound of those feet started to fade into the distance.

Taya opened her eyes slowly and looked over at Guntharr, "They're heading away from here."

For the first time in the last several hours, Taya saw Guntharr drop out of battle mode and relax. Guntharr started to hook his war hammer, when he suddenly snapped back into battle mode. Taya reacted at his sudden change, "What is it?"

"Shhh," he put his finger to his lips. Nearby, in the darkness, Guntharr heard the deep breathing of a very large creature. Taya looked confused at her guardian. "What . . ." but Guntharr held up a hand to silence her.

"Stay here," Guntharr commanded and hoisted his warhammer back into his hand.

Slowly, he walked through the dark to the back of the barn. Thin strips of moonlight stretched throughout the barn, but failed to create enough light for the man to see. As he neared the far corner, the breathing grew slightly louder and Guntharr pressed himself against a large post. Focusing on the sound, Guntharr judged the distance and placement of the creature on the other side of the partial wall. With focused resolve, he spun quickly around the corner and came face to face with an average horse.

Taya, clearly seeing what was going on due to her enhanced vision, let out a musical giggle.

"I suppose you knew it was a horse all along, eh, Taya." Guntharr hooked his warhammer on his belt and began petting the nose of the friendly beast.

"You know," Taya moved closer to him, "in this low of light I can also see certain elements of ambient heat, and I'm seeing your face glowing just a little bit right now."

Guntharr turned to watch her approach and then she began whispering to the horse. "I suppose it is," he replied.

The horse let out a few brief snorts and a slight whinny.

"We should probably try to get some rest." Guntharr began walking back to the front of the barn. "It will be light soon, and we'll need to get back on the road as quickly as we can."

"I don't understand," Taya followed behind him. "What were those creatures back at the inn and why did they try to attack us?"

Guntharr settled down into a resting position against the door. He patted the ground beside him and waited for Taya to sit down. "To answer your first question, I'm not exactly sure what they were, although I have a guess." Guntharr paused. "As for the second question, I'm afraid you're not quite ready to hear the answer."

Taya, not considering the hard leather tunic that covered his upper body, playfully punched him in the arm and then shook her hand in pain. "What do you mean I'm not ready?"

Guntharr turned and took both of her hands in his enormous hands. "The reason should become clear tomorrow, if we can talk to Father

Firebane." He tried to put on a smile, knowing that she could see his face clearly. "Then, I will explain to you as much as I can."

"I will yield to your wisdom, Guardian." Taya bowed her head slightly.

"Taya, I asked you . . ." Guntharr paused as she looked back up at him.

"Yes," she inserted.

Guntharr sighed, "Let's get some rest."

Chapter 2

Taya jumped up at the sound of footsteps outside. Drawing her small sword, she took up position opposite of the door.

"Guardian," she called down to Guntharr, "someone is coming."

Guntharr snapped awake and jumped up immediately. Seeing Taya sword in hand, he motioned to her to sheathe her weapon. Taya, with a puzzled look on her face, slowly sheathed her weapon.

As the steps neared the entrance of the barn, Guntharr removed the makeshift lock and threw open the door. Standing before him, a man of some years stood a little startled at the presence of the two standing in the doorway of the barn.

"Good Morning, sir," Guntharr stepped forward with an outstretched hand. "I am Guardian Guntharr Deathhammer from Fairhaven, and this is my ward."

The farmer, still in a state of shock, slowly reached out to take Guntharr's hand. "What on earth are you doing in my barn?"

"I must apologize," Guntharr replied, "we were being overtaken by a band of bandits last evening and managed to find your stables unlocked." Guntharr started pumping the man's hand. "As such, we were able to evade the marauders and spent the night resting. I promise you, your animals have not been harmed and nothing is missing."

Retrieving his hand from the warrior's crushing grip, the farmer responded, "Bandits, you say?"

Taya nodded, not sure what else to do.

Guntharr reached into a small pouch that was hanging from his belt and pulled out a silver coin. He flipped it into the air toward the farmer. "Please accept this as a token of our gratitude."

The farmer fumbled the coin once before clasping it firmly in his hand. Seeing that it was silver, the man's eyes opened wide and a smile spread across his face.

"No harm done, I suppose," the farmer gazed at the coin.

Glancing over at Taya, "We should be going, now. We have far to travel, and I'm sure the farmer has many chores to attend to."

Seeing the opportunity to possibly score some more easy money, the farmer responded, "You needn't hurry off. You're more than welcome to come inside for a warm breakfast."

Taya's eyes lit up. It had been over a week since they'd had tasted real food. They had been living off of rations ever since they'd left Fairhaven.

"Thank you for the offer," Guntharr bowed slightly, "but we really have to be getting on our way."

Taya's face turned from anticipation to disappointment. She fell into step behind Guntharr as they left the premises and headed back out onto the road. "Why couldn't we have stayed?"

"Taya," Guntharr began, "the farmer, while cordial, had more aspirations in his heart. Seeing the silver that I gave him as a means to smooth things over, he saw an opportunity to possibly score a bit more by inviting us to dine."

"But you have plenty of money, would another silver for breakfast have been such a bad thing?" She asked. "It's been forever since we've had any real food."

"Patience," Guntharr patted her softly on the shoulder, "I will promise you a decent meal once we have reached the chapel of the One True God. Father Firebane's hospitality is second to none."

"If you say so," she conceded.

Overhead, the soft beating of wings could be heard. "Hey, wait for me."

Taya looked up to see the hawk gliding lazily overhead. "Good Morning, Raskin. Did you sleep well?"

"Sleep," the bird squawked, "who slept last night? I was too busy watching out for you two."

Guntharr stopped in the road and held out a gloved hand. "Come," he called out.

Raskin spun around in the air once and gracefully came to stop on Guntharr's massive forearm. As he landed the warrior's muscles bulged and tightened under the weight of massive bird. "So, what's the plan?" Raskin asked.

Guntharr tilted his head slightly to look into the hawk's eyes. "How familiar are you with this road?"

The bird blinked his eyes and cocked his head sideways slightly. "I can't say that I've been down this road very far."

"About a day's journey on foot, you will find a small town called 'Brittle'. With your speed, you should be able to fly the extent of this road in about an hour or so," Guntharr explained.

Raskin fluttered slightly, "I can do it faster, if you need me too."

Guntharr shook his head, "That won't be necessary. If you would simply scan the path from here to there, then find a nice resting spot. You can take your rest. We'll find you as we near the town."

Taya reached out and stroked the large bird's side. "What if he spots something?"

"I can take care of it, mistress," Raskin replied.

"No," Guntharr commanded, "return to us immediately with the details of the threat and I will determine what should be done."

Raskin pawed on Guntharr's arm in approval and stretched his enormous wings out. Guntharr responded by holding high his arm so as not to get smacked in the face as Raskin took off. Wings beating steadily, Raskin quickly soared into the sky and on down the road.

"Now, let's hope Raskin is able to make it to Brittle and get some rest," Guntharr smiled at his ward.

* * *

Closing her eyes, Naranda listened as the footsteps nearing the outside of her room. "Come in," she called out to the unexpected guest.

With a click, her door opened and a skinny, dark head peeked around the door. "Were you talking to me, mistress?" he spoke softly.

"Of course," she beckoned with a hand, "you were about to knock and bring me news of the latest mission."

"I was," the creature slowly entered the room.

The lady known as Naranda moved over to a large round table. In the center of the table stood a silver bowl filled with inviting fruit. She motioned to the creature to sit as she crossed over to the far side of the table and grabbed a handful of grapes. The charcoal skinned creature stood only about four feet in height and wore simple, ragged clothes. Its eyes were much larger than those of a human, and its mouth was much wider and filled with vicious teeth.

Lady Naranda knew that the very sight of one of these creatures would frighten the average person into a panic. She merely tolerated them. "Report, Scrag," she commanded.

The creature known as Scrag eyed the bowl of fruit, "May Scrag have one?"

"After your report," Naranda parried, "we'll see if your services warrant a reward."

Scrag nodded and dropped his head slightly, "We attacked the elf princess and her guardian," Scrag paused.

"And?" Naranda inquired.

"We lost several assassins," Scrag reported.

"How many?" Naranda asked with feign concern.

"Twelve are dead, and two have broken bones and are not likely to make it," he explained.

"How many assassins did you take?" she asked patiently.

Scrag smiled, "Twenty, just as the mistress had requested."

She nodded with approval, "Excellent, you have done well."

Naranda reached into the bowl and pulled out a large red fruit. She eyed it approvingly and tossed it to the assassin.

Scrag caught the fruit, but looked puzzled at Naranda. "Mistress is pleased?" He asked.

"Yes, very." She replied.

"Scrag thought you wanted elf princess and guardian dead," he stated.

"Scrag, if I wanted them dead, I would have had you send fifty of your assassins." She stopped at his confused look. "Yes, I want them dead, but not right now." Naranda stood and walked over toward the lone window in the room. "Right now, I need to drive them. I need to find all of the conspirators first before we destroy them in one final strike."

Scrag smiled brightly then sunk his teeth into the blood fruit. Bright reddish juice squirted out and splattered the table and floor.

Naranda looked at him disapprovingly, "Scrag, please try not to make a total mess of my house."

Scrag's eyes opened wide at Naranda's displeasure. He swallowed his bite hard and lowered the half-eaten fruit to the table. "My apologies, mistress," he said cautiously. "Should Scrag go fetch something to clean it up?"

She held up a hand, "There will be no need for that. Now, we must plan our next steps carefully."

"What would you like Scrag to do?" He asked trying to regain her favor.

"First, we must figure out which direction they went after they escaped the inn." She looked over at Scrag.

Scrag began bouncing up and down like a student in school who was just asked the easiest question ever. "Scrag already knows!"

A hint of a smile inched across Naranda's face. "Please, do tell."

"After Scrag's team lost them at the inn, he stationed the remaining assassins at hiding points at each road leaving the city." Scrag settled back into his chair and eyed the blood fruit for a moment. "In the morning, Grog saw the elf's hawk fly off to the south."

The last part of Scrag's report caught Naranda's attention and she took a step toward him. "A hawk, are you sure it was a hawk and not some other bird?"

Scrag's face scrunched as if he was in pain or reliving a painful moment. "No, mistress, it was a large hawk. Scrag got very close to it. Almost too close." He folded his long bony fingers together.

"Hawk nearly killed Scrag last night when it attacked us in the alley behind the inn."

"Is that so?" Naranda asked.

"Yes, hawk tore the heads off Drog and Mog right in front of Scrag." He shivered at the memory.

Naranda turned and walked over to a large bookshelf in the corner and began searching for something. "She must be more powerful than I thought," she spoke to herself, forgetting that Scrag was still waiting for instructions. "She has enlisted the aid of one of the hawk lords. This could be a problem."

"Scrag didn't think hawk lords helped anyone." He said confused. "Hawk lords stay up in the mountains and only come down when hunting for food."

Ignoring his rationale, the woman selected a tome from the bottom shelf and began flipping through the pages. There was silence between the two as she studied various pages of the book. Scrag, not wanting to interrupt her, decided to pick up the blood fruit he had set down and took another bite of it. Again, juice squirted on the floor and table.

Without looking, the woman extended her hand and blue flaming dart shot forward, striking the fruit in Scrag's hand causing it to explode all over him. Shaking his singed hand and blowing desperately on it, he muttered in between breaths, "Sorry, mistress."

"You say they were headed south?" she asked without looking up from the book.

Scrag nodded, not realizing she wasn't looking.

After a moment's silence, Naranda turned to look at the humbled minion, her eyes wide and filled with fire. "I asked you a question," her voice raised for the first time.

Cowering in his seat, he nodded even more feverishly, "Scrag was nodding."

"But I wasn't looking," she responded in a more normal tone. "So, if they're headed south, that means they'll be passing through Brittle. What is in Brittle?"

"Not much, mistress," Scrag began, "Scrag's been to Brittle before. Nothing exciting there."

"Yes, but they must be going there for a reason." She walked over to the table and gently set the book down. Reaching toward the bowl in the center, she grabbed a handful of grapes and began moving toward the cowering assassin. "Tell me about all the places in Brittle."

Trembling as the towering woman neared him, he began to ramble. "Ah, market with very bad prices. Scrag remembers an inn, but he didn't eat or stay there." He looked around for a means of escape as Naranda stood directly over top of him as if to press every last ounce of information from his tiny skull.

"What else?" She ordered.

"Nothing else," he began to cry, "just a church."

Naranda took a step back, "A church."

"Yes," he said, relieved that she was no longer about to squish him. "Scrag saw a small church, just to the west of the main street. Nothing special, just a church to the One True God."

Naranda's hand smacked the table creating a sound that startled the assassin so much that he fell backwards in his chair with a crash.

"That's it, that's where they are headed." Naranda beamed with confidence.

"What do you want Scrag to do?" he asked scrambling back to his feet and picking up the chair.

She turned and moved back to the window, her fists clenched tight. "How many assassins do you have available in Hydesvalley?"

The minion looked at his fingers hoping to find the answer. After several seconds of his eyes rolling back and forth across them, he looked up. "About fifty, mistress."

She spun around and sized up the creature for a minute as if to calculate how many fifty Scrags would be. "That will have to do," she conceded. "Round up your men and head down to the church in Brittle as quickly as you can and lay waste to it. I don't want anyone or anything left standing except for the elf girl and her guardian."

Scrag grinned, showing all of his vicious teeth, "Yes, mistress," he said, his voice almost a hiss. His face changed after considering what she had asked. "But why not kill the elf and her human guardian, too?"

Naranda let out a huge sigh. "Because, you can't. And," she paused, staring right into the assassin's eyes, "I need them alive a while longer."

"As you wish," he bowed his head.

"I will join you at the inn in Brittle shortly, please be prepared with a report on your success." She turned and started to leave the room.

"Of course," Scrag kept his head low.

Opening a door that led into a side chamber, she paused. "And Scrag," Scrag lifted his head to look at her, "don't get killed." With that, Naranda left the room and closed the door behind her.

Scrag turned and scurried over to the door that he had originally come in. Opening it slowly, he looked over at the bowl of fruit back on the table. He thievishly ran back and snagged another blood fruit from the bowl before hurrying out the door.

* * *

The journey had largely been quiet, thought Taya. It wasn't uncommon for the two of them to go hours without uttering a word. It wasn't that Guntharr didn't like her, quite the contrary, he was simply used to only speaking when there was something that needed to be said, and right now there was nothing that needed to be said.

But still, the trip had not been boring. They'd passed through a beautiful valley that was lush with fresh spring wild flowers. Just before entering some hills, they'd stopped for a break at the edge of a stream that was flowing down one of the hills. It was cool and clear. They took some time here and had a snack of wild berries that they had found along the banks of the stream as well as some hard bread that they had left from their journey.

After passing through the hills, they passed through several miles of open range. Taya even spotted a group of wild horses running free across the range, their manes flowing in the wind as they raced around free.

It was upon seeing the horses that Taya had broken the silence. "You know, traveling would be lot faster if we had horses."

Looking straight ahead, Guntharr replied, "Up until now, I didn't think it was necessary. When we originally left Fairhaven, I thought our trip would be routine and the thought of caring for horses seemed a burden."

"But now?" Taya pressed.

"Now . . .," he continued, "I can see where your point of taking a couple of the scouting horses from the Guardians' guild would have been a reasonable idea."

This made her smile on the inside. She always liked it when something she had suggested proved itself true. Not so that she could say "'I told you so," but from the satisfaction of knowing that she was thinking more proactively about situations and planning ahead.

Running several steps ahead of her guardian, she spun around and continued walking at the same pace as before, only backwards. "Any chance Firebane can help us out with this situation?" She smiled.

The guardian looked down at his ward, continuing his march forward. "There is a small possibility that we can solve our transportation issues once we reach the church." The corners of his mouth turned upwards ever-so-slightly, which Taya knew to be his equivalent of a big grin.

"Yes!" She jumped. Spinning around, she fell back in step with the guardian. "I hope they have a mustang or a thoroughbred."

"Young lady," the guardian placed his hand on her shoulder, "when I was your age, I was forced to march for four days straight through bitter cold with only a few hours rest each day carrying full armor."

"Let me guess," she continued, "uphill both ways." Taya giggled.

Guntharr's eyes sparkled at his wards teasing remarks and he let out a devilish growl. "Grrr!"

Taya responded with a squeal when he reached down to begin tickling her side. She leaped forward and began running ahead. Guntharr continued to roar and started running after her. She slowed and turned back to see the guardian closing on her, hands extended out and fingers threatening their most brutal tickle abilities.

With a laugh, she turned and started to run some more, "You won't catch me that easy."

"Oh, just you watch me," he called out charging forward.

That was several hours ago. Taya had easily kept pace with the guardian and kept her distance until she was sure he'd given up. They had traveled a good mile before Guntharr waved her off and slowed his pace acting winded and exhausted. She had slowed in response, and as he approached while she struggled for breath, he sprang forward like a battle cat and got in a good solid tickle causing her to squeal like a pig once again.

"I surrender," she called out, laughing so hard that tears were forming in her eyes.

Guntharr relented and stood back. "Let that be a lesson to you," he waggled a finger at her. "Speed, endurance and even raw strength must always be tempered with wisdom."

"What does that mean?" She gasped for breath.

"It means that you should know your enemy." He began walking again.

Slowly regaining her stride she said with a confused look, "But you are not my enemy."

He nodded. "It works for your friends as well. Study the people around you, and understand what makes them tick. Once you do, you will always know when you are being deceived."

"I will try," she replied.

Chapter 3

At the top of a rise, with the sun setting in the west, the two eyed their destination across a small valley.

"We're almost there," Guntharr commented.

"I judge that we are about an hour away," she looked up at the guardian for confirmation. He nodded.

Guntharr looked around for a moment and scanned the hilltop. The ridge stretched out toward the east with a wall of trees approaching the edge with cliffs and sharp drop-offs jutting out from the side. He studied the tree line with care.

Taya followed his gaze and scanned the area too, although she wasn't sure what she was looking for. She knew that with the daylight fading, his eyes would be struggling soon. "What are you looking for? Maybe I can help?" she asked.

He continued to look over each tree as he responded, "Raskin was supposed to meet us outside of Brittle. This would be the perfect place for him to keep an eye on things and spot us coming."

Now that she knew what to look for, she narrowed her eyes to focus in the layers of trees that lined the ridge. While the growing shadows would make it hard for the human to spot the hawk, even one as large as Raskin, she would have no trouble finding him, so long as he wanted to be found.

Looking down at Taya, the guardian spotted a large rock that had been hewn out of the side of the hill. Behind it, the corner of a large wooden fence came to a stop. He walked over and plopped down onto the rock and stretched out with a small yawn.

"What are you doing?" Taya asked.

"Just stretching," he replied. "You have the super eyes. You'll find him a lot faster than I will."

She continued to scan the forest ridge for some time. "He's got to be camouflaged," she reported with some frustration. "Either that or he's not here."

Taya moved beside the guardian and leaned against the fence. She scanned even harder.

Guntharr looked past his ward in the opposite direction and spotted a lone tree at the edge of what appeared to be a farmer's field. In the tree a large beehive-looking shape began to shift and move. Guntharr let out a slight chuckle.

Taya reached down and flipped his ear. "Don't pick on me, I'm beginning to believe he's not over there after all."

Glancing up at her, he contemplated his next move. Deciding not to add any more flame to the fire, he decided to whistle softly instead. This caused the figure in the distance to instantly stretch out and take flight.

Stamping her foot, she turned away from her observation and looked down at him in frustration. "Why are you whistling?" she asked. "You don't whistle."

"Awwk," Raskin called as he soared closer to the pair.

Taya turned to see the glorious bird descending for a landing. The last remaining rays of sunlight shimmering off of his bright white and gold feathers. "He was over there all the time?"

Guntharr nodded slowly, his face showing no sign of a smile even though she knew he must have been laughing to himself.

"Were you able to get some rest, my friend?" Guntharr asked the hawk as it settled down on the fence beside him.

Raskin twisted his head around so he could take in the pair. "I suppose you could say I did," he reported. "I'm not sure why you've brought us here. This lazy town has very little going on."

The guardian stood to his feet. "Exactly what I was hoping for."

"Where to now?" The bird asked.

"There," Guntharr pointed to a large structure on the far side of the town. "The church of the One True God."

Raskin shook briefly and squawked his approval before taking off.

The three made their way down into the valley and over to the small town. As Raskin had predicted, very little activity was occurring in the town outside of the ordinary. With nightfall near, the little market that dominated the center of town had closed and only a few lights shone out of the windows of various cottages along the street. The only remaining structure besides the church was the inn, unremarkably named "The Brittle Inn". The inviting sounds and smells permeated from the inn, but Guntharr and his ward were not going to be tempted to enter another inn anytime soon.

When they approached the church, Taya noticed it wasn't like any of the other structures. Most of the buildings in the town were poorly built or very old and nearly ready to fall down. The church structure was the largest and by far the best maintained building that they'd seen in some time. Its architecture and condition even rivaled all of the buildings they had seen in Hydesvalley. There were three sections to the building forming a fork shape.

The central and largest section, Guntharr explained, was the worship area. The smaller section stemming off the center to the east, was the residence quarters for those who tended and maintained the church. The western section was reserved for guests of the church and those in need.

"This seems to be a very large church for such a small town," Taya commented. "I suppose that you could house most of the residents of the town in the chapel."

Guntharr nodded sadly at this, "Yes, this hall was at one time one of the central hubs for my faith." For the first time since she had come under the care of the Guardian, Taya thought she saw a tear forming in the corner of his eye.

"What happened?" she inquired.

Guntharr's gaze was distracted as the shadow of Raskin soared overhead and came to land on the pinnacle of the steeple. "There's a lot to it," he began, "but I guess the reality is the world has become more evil. As a result, other religions have sprung up promising riches, power, and a more flexible lifestyle."

"I'm not sure I understand," she replied.

"In time," he turned to her wiping something from his eye, "I will teach you."

He moved toward the center doors that led into the chapel area. Before disappearing under the large canopy that extended out over the doors, Guntharr looked up and called out, "Keep an eye on things. Once I'm sure we're safe here, I'll invite you in."

Not expecting a response, he stepped up to the large oak doors and pushed them open. Casually, he walked inside and waited for his ward to enter before closing the doors securely behind them. The room was large and filled with benches throughout. There were eight supporting columns that ran parallel on either side of the room and several oil lanterns hung around causing a soft yellowish light to radiate seemingly from everywhere. At the far end of the room, a platform stood in front of the rows of benches. The platform held several high back chairs, a couple of banners and large table in the center. On the left side of the platform, a small section was quartered off by a decorative railing. A podium stood inside the section at one end.

Taya's eyes were fixed on the various paintings and murals that were depicted along the outside walls. The detail and splendor captured her attention and she mindlessly moved toward the closest one to study it.

"What amazing artwork!" She exclaimed. "Is there any significance to these or are they just for beauty's sake?"

Guntharr continued toward a door off to the side that would connect them to the east wing. "Each one has significance," he stated, "but now is not the time to go into it. We must find Father Firebane and seek his councel."

Breaking her gaze from the painting, Taya circled around and caught up to her guardian just as he was walking through the door. The door opened up into a large corridor that extended the full length of the structure. On the right side of the corridor, windows were open to the outside to allow light in. On the other side of the corridor, several doors were visible. Each door had a hand carved scene on it depicting various celestial creatures.

They continued down the corridor until they came to a large opening on the side where the doors were. This archway opened up into a large comfortable room. Large cushions were organized neatly around the room and two large tables with chairs were stationed on each side. In the center, a large stone ring extended up out of the floor and the roar of fire could be heard coming from it.

"May I help you?" A steady and commanding voice called from one side of the room.

Guntharr walked up to the man who was wearing simple attire and bowed respectfully. "We are here to seek the councel of Father Firebane," Guntharr announced.

Returning his bow, "Oh, you must be the guardian from Fairhaven that Firebane has spoken of," the man smiled pleasantly. "I am Elder Tronic."

"Indeed, I am Guntharr Deathhammer and this is my ward, Taya." Guntharr replied.

Taya approached and bowed before the elder.

Tronic's face took on a surprised look, "So, this is the one?" he asked Guntharr.

Guntharr only nodded.

"Then it is with utmost humbleness that I make your acquaintance, Taya," Tronic bowed respectfully to her.

Taya wasn't sure how to respond, so she reacted the way Guntharr had always taught her to react when confronted with a stranger who was welcome in their presence. "Your servant is blessed with your presence," she smiled.

The surprised look on his face turned to a smile. He turned to Guntharr, "and she has manners. Please come, sit," he motioned to a couple of large cushions. "I will pour you something to drink. I believe provisions have been made for you to dine with us this evening, and it should be ready shortly."

Taya wanted to shout for joy, but figured given the somber setting she should simply smile with approval.

"Will Firebane be long?" Guntharr asked.

"No, I will notify him of your arrival immediately." Tronic finished pouring them both large goblets of fresh juice. He carried them over and served Taya first before handing Guntharr his. "I hope you like it," he said to Taya, "it's from a fruit that only grows in this valley. The taste is very refreshing."

Taya looked down into the goblet. The liquid was a bright yellow in color and smelled of flowers. She looked over at Guntharr who was already taking a long drink from his goblet. She put the drink to her lips and sipped cautiously. Tronic straightened up with satisfaction and quickly exited down the corridor.

The drink was indeed tasty and refreshing, Taya thought as she took another sizable gulp from the goblet. The flavor was both sweet and sour at the same time. The contrast was interesting but very pleasant.

As she lay relaxing on the cushion, an old and scraggly, blue and gray dog walked around the corner. After closer examination, she decided the animal wasn't exactly a dog. It had all of the characteristics of a typical dog, but this creature's face took on the characteristics of something wild and proud. Then the thought occurred to her. Maybe this was actually a wolf and not a common dog. Its' face had a distinct black mask that encircled its' eyes and flowed down its' muzzle toward its' nose. The nose was the odd part, it wasn't black like a normal dog, but was more gray in color. Its' ears resembled that of a wolf, as did its long tail which showed signs of curling.

Whatever breed of a creature this was, they white whiskers around its muzzle indicated it was clearly old and possibly near the end of its life. It moved slowly and deliberately, and every step seemed to be forced.

Guntharr turned to see the creature enter the room and waved a familiar hand toward the creature. "Rift, it's so good to see you again," he spoke with a serious tone. "Come tell me how life fares for you."

Taya smiled at Guntharr's familiarity with the creature. It stopped and looked over at the two. Taya could see the animal study them for a moment, and then it turned and made its way over toward the guardian.

"Guntharr, old friend. It's so good to see you." Taya nearly jumped off her cushion as the wolf-like creature spoke to her guardian. "Who is this lovely companion of yours? I don't recall meeting her."

Guntharr nodded and motioned Taya over next to him. "Rift, this is my ward, Taya." Guntharr turned to Taya, "Taya, this is an old friend. He and I have seen many battles together."

Taya couldn't help herself and chuckled slightly at the thought of this weak old creature ever being in battle. "Grrr," Rift growled at her disrespect and the bristles on his back rose slightly.

Guntharr held up a hand, "Please forgive her, Rift. She still has much to learn about the world. Your kind is unknown to those back in Fairhaven and the Silverwood." Rift snorted and settled down next to the guardian. Reaching over, Guntharr ran his big hands through the thick blue-gray fur.

"Rift is a battle wolf," he explained. Her eyes indicated that she still did not comprehend. "They have some abilities that might surprise you, besides being able to speak the common tongue. Needless to say, I would take Rift here in a fight over two dozen of those gangly dark creatures we saw in the inn." This description both impressed and stunned Taya.

"Are you saying you ran into some trouble recently?" Rift asked in a low voice.

"Oh, yes," Taya jumped at the chance to talk to him. "We were ambushed in the inn at Hydesvalley by a band of dark bandits." Rift looked up at Guntharr, but Taya continued. "I'm still not sure what kind of creatures they were. But they were no match for the guardian and his warhammer."

"Do not sell yourself short, Taya," Guntharr interrupted. "You managed to put away several of them skillfully with that bow of yours."

"Ah, an archer," Rift spoke, "I don't care much for archers."

Taya, saddened by this statement, walked quietly back to her cushion and began sipping her drink.

Rift lifted his head closer to Guntharr. "Were they really bandits?"

Guntharr shook his head. "No, at least not ordinary bandits. There were too many of them and they were fairly well orchestrated."

"Hmmm," Rift replied.

"If I were to guess, they were a group of assassins, but it's not their occupation that concerns me." Guntharr hesitated.

"Then what is it?" Rift asked.

Guntharr looked over at Taya who was sitting with her back to the two, probably pouting. He leaned in closer to Rift's ear, "I think they were dark goblins."

"From the Midnight Realm?" Rift replied in a low voice of surprise. "But they haven't been seen for over a hundred years. Most believe their kind is extinct."

"Guntharr Deathhammer, at last our paths cross again," a new voice called in from the archway. Guntharr, Taya and Rift all stood together and turned to see the new arrival.

The man that approached them wore similar clothes to that of Tronic. Taya guessed that he was about the same age as the guardian.

He was smaller in height, but even the simple robes couldn't hide the strength that years of battle had hardened into his frame. His hair was mostly dark with streaks of silver scattered around his temples and across his bangs.

"Don't get up, please. Rest," he commanded softly.

Rift reacted appropriately and stretched back out on a nearby cushion. Guntharr instead walked up to meet the man with outstretched arms and the two embraced. "Firebane, my guide and mentor, it is so very good to see you."

"Truly it has been a long time," Firebane smiled back with a stiff pat to Guntharr's back. "Your timing is perfect. I have much to tell you."

Guntharr's face saddened slightly, "I only hope we have time to talk."

"We will, we will," he assured him with a nod. "So, is this your ward that I have heard so much about in recent years?"

Taya bowed her head in respect. "This is Taya of the Silverwood, daughter of Krest," Guntharr said in introduction.

"It is a blessing to finally meet you." He took her hand and patted it gently, as a grandfather would his grandchild.

Lifting her head, she looked somberly into his eyes, "Father Firebane, as a friend of my guardian, I pledge my service to you."

"Thank you, Taya, and I to you. Much more, indeed, I pledge my life to you and your safety," he replied.

Guntharr could see the puzzled look come across her face. He met her eyes to reassure her that everything was going to be fine.

"Father Firebane," a familiar voice came from the hall, "if you and your guests are hungry, there is food prepared in the kitchen."

Taya heard the word food, and like a starving puppy, and looked up at Guntharr anxiously.

"It would seem that your ward is hungry. Which, if she's spent time with you for very long, I can understand perfectly," Firebane joked.

"I feed the girl," Guntharr responded in a hurt tone. "At least once a week," the two laughed loudly.

Taya grabbed Guntharr's hand and proceeded to pull him out into the hall. "Guardian, come on."

"All right, I thought I taught you better manners than to push me around like that," Guntharr threw a wink toward Firebane.

Firebane tried to hold back the chuckle which turned into a funny snort. He ushered them toward the hallway and paused to turn back. "Will you be joining us tonight, Rift?" He asked the now resting form.

The old battle wolf yawned and looked around for the source of the question. "Maybe after I catch a short nap. I just got comfy," he responded and then laid his head back down.

The trio made their way down the hall with Tronic in the lead. Taya stood to the right of the guardian who was looking out through the open windows into the night sky. Firebane was on the guardian's left as they passed several closed.

"As happy as I am to see you, I suspect by the tone of the message I received from Fairhaven, that you are not here simply for a social call," he stated.

Guntharr remained silent for several steps and looked over at Taya. As they neared the end of the hall, the smell of food caused Taya to quicken her steps and pull ever harder on his arm.

"I will explain all once we have eaten," Guntharr said commandingly. "Let us enjoy the feast you have prepared before we burden ourselves with the matter of business and war."

His last word caught Taya off guard. She looked around the room to see if maybe he was talking to someone else, or to see if maybe some else had spoken the word. "War?" she asked.

"Eat," he said.

Chapter 4

The meal was pleasant. It was the best food that Taya had eaten in several weeks. The men focused their conversation on stories of old, mostly old war stories. Guntharr spoke of the time when he and Firebane, along with some others whose names she didn't recognize, had been sent by the captain of the court of Fairhaven to investigate the disappearance of one of the stockpiles of grain that had been held in a border town near the Midnight Realm.

The signs all pointed to bandits that had made their way across the border and broken into the facility. They followed tracks that led out of the facility, and travelled for a week into the Midnight Realm with no sign of the goods or the culprits. Determined not to come back empty handed, Guntharr had pushed them deeper into the barren wasteland. They searched practically every crack or crevasse that could house the stolen goods as they went along. So focused on their task, they lost track of where they had been and eventually made a huge circle. It was at this point that Firebane had to inform Guntharr that they were lost.

Both men had a good chuckle at that part. Several days passed, and they finally ran into a scouting party that had been sent out for them. When they returned, the scouting party had reported that the goods had been located. The shipment of grain that was supposed to have been in the stockpile had in fact not yet been delivered and was still awaiting collection by a caravan to be deposited there.

The group finished their meal and returned to the hall where they had been relaxing previously. As they got comfortable, Firebane brewed some warm tea for them to sip as they talked.

"Guntharr, you have stalled long enough," Firebane said directly. "I know you are here for a reason, and I can only help if you let me in on what is going on."

Guntharr inhaled deeply and his upper body swelled to take in the air. He looked over at Taya as he let out his breath in a very controlled manner. He studied her as she sat looking back up at him.

"Guardian, would it be easier if I left the room? I could go look at the paintings in the large hall, if that would please you?" She offered.
Guntharr shook his head, "No, it's time you learned the truth. I have taken care of you for many years and trained you in the only way I know. I think you are ready."

Firebane slid his cushion closer to Guntharr and Taya followed suit. Rift, after deciding to join them for dinner, had gotten a belly full and lay sound asleep near the fire pit in the center of the room.

Guntharr looked at his audience before beginning. "I've already mentioned that Taya is the daughter of Krest. Krest is the name that I knew him by, but the rest of the realm knows him as the Elven Lord Krestichan of Spire Tree."

This revelation caused Taya and Firebane to react, but each of them in a different way. There was also a sound that came from over by the fire pit, but it was Rift who had rolled over and started to snore.

"Krestichan was thought to have been without a heir," Firebane challenged. "If this is true, then this could change the state of everything."

Guntharr nodded.

"Guardian, what does this mean?" Taya asked.

Without expression, Guntharr laid a hand on her head and stroked her hair, "It means that you are a princess and the heir to the throne of the Silverwood."

"Even more than that," Firebane added. "It means you could be the one to bring peace to the five realms as prophesied long ago." He paused for a moment, then turned to the guardian. "But how can you be sure that she's Kretchichan's? He was killed more than a dozen years ago when the Talicrons overran the Spire Tree and destroyed it."

"Because I was there," he replied with a face that showed no sign of emotion.

This time it was Firebane who was puzzled. "How . . . why?"

"Right after you had made the choice to come out here and take on this position, I was commissioned by the Governor of Fairhave -- Doddleburry, I believe it was at the time -- to go and take a squad of elite guard to the Spire Tree for special training from Krest's best rangers. It was an effort to shore up the defenses on the border. Doddleburry was trying to strengthen relations with Spire Tree, and he felt that one of the best ways to do that was to become a protective fortress at the edge of the Silverwood," he recounted.

"So, you knew my father?" Taya asked.

"Yes," Guntharr answered, "but not as well as I would have liked. You see, in the months that led up to the attack by the Talicrons, my men and I trained with the rangers. We all learned so much. These were some of the best men that the Silverwood could offer. After a few weeks, Lord Krestichan hand-picked two of my team to train exclusively with him."

"And you were one of the two," Firebane finished.

Guntharr nodded in agreement. "Krest worked with us for three weeks. He took us into the sanctuary of the great Spire Tree and shared with us knowledge that was reserved for only a select few in his most inner circle. He taught us how to hone our senses nearly to that of an elf."

"I suppose that's when you found out about Taya," Firebane added.

"Yes. After working and living with Krest during that time, the three of us built up a friendship that was greater than that of brothers. It was then that he shared the secret of Taya's birth." Guntharr stopped.

"But what about my mother?" Taya asked.

"Rayadorn, your mother," Guntharr struggled, "died giving birth to you. I never met her, but Krest spoke often and admiringly of her. From my understanding, she was a woman of great beauty, strength and grace."

Taya tried to smile, but Guntharr could see that the smile was being forced through a wall of pain. "What happened next?" she asked, trying to push forward.

"The time had come for my team and I to return to Fairhaven to secure the border," he paused. "The Talicrons had been sending in small strike teams in the villages surrounding Fairhaven for some time. The Governor had sent word that we should return. It was his theory, and Lord Krestichan's as well, that they were preparing to strike Fairhaven soon. It was for this reason we decided to end our training and return to help."

"So, you just left then?" Firebane asked.

"Not without first being celebrated by Lord Krestichan and the court at Spire Tree. It was truly a magnificent feast. One like I'd never seen before, and refuse to partake in again this side of eternity." Guntharr closed his eyes for just a moment. Taya could see his skin pale and noticed that his hands were trembling in his lap.

"Guardian," she asked concerned, "are you okay?"

His eyes snapped open, pale and hollow. He looked at her, but it was more as if he was looking through her, beyond her to some buried past.

"It was during the celebration, while the men were eating and the ladies were dancing and making music, that the attack came. My team, as well as most of the guards, were far away from our weapons. The Talicrons swept on the Spire Tree like a tidal wave. Because the surrounding elf-folk were allowed to participate in the celebration, the main gates to the great Spire Tree were already open to allow passage in and out."

Firebane held up a hand, "That sounds like they knew about the celebration and the arrangements."

Guntharr didn't respond. He was still lost in the past.

Taya turned to Firebane, "You mean there was someone on the inside that betrayed them."

Firebane put a hand on her shoulder, "It sure sounds like it to me."

"The swarm was upon the grand hall before we knew what was happening," Guntharr continued. "We fought with our bare hands and any makeshift weapon we could find, but they had tainted blades. The slightest scratch caused almost instant paralysis. The men did what they could to protect the King. Several of us formed a perimeter around Krest to keep him safe. We worked our way through the back halls, trying to make our way to the armory to grab some weapons to help even out the odds. By the time we had worked our way there, there was only Krest, myself and Wilstrom."

"I've heard that name before," Firebane said. "Wasn't he the fellow that joined our company just before the break-up? Yes, that's the fellow. He was a bit odd, if I remember correctly, but had quite the hand with a sword."

"Wilstrom stayed on with me after I received the new commission. He was with us during the training at Spire Tree. He was the other man that Krest had taken into his personal confidence and trained along with me." Guntharr took paused and took a sip of tea. His color began to return, but Taya could see sweat on his face.

"After we'd reached the armory and armed ourselves, we were cut off from the rest of the hall. However, with weapons in our hands, we now had a glimmer of hope. Following Krest's orders we worked like a machine, bashing and slicing our way through the sea of Talicrons. Those last few weeks of training kicked in and the creatures fell like dust. Wilstrom was brilliant. His sword, though not his own, rang out like a cymbal. Krest was nothing short of a blur. Never in my life have I seen a living being move as fast as he could. With an iron staff in hand, he was a whirlwind of destruction. We pushed our way up the south hall to try and meet back up with whatever was left of the main group. It took us an hour to push our way back. I have never fought so hard in my life. But with all of our might, we could never seem to get a break in the tide. Bodies lay stacked in some places up to my chest."

"How did you keep going?" Taya asked, totally lost in the story.

"We kept a wedge formation and we would frequently rotate out of the point to allow the other a brief rest." Guntharr switched his tone to sound like he did when he would frequently teach Taya about a given subject. "We entered an anteroom just off of the great hall, but that was a big mistake. Inside the hallway, we had the advantage because they couldn't surround us. However, breaking into the room, we were almost instantly surrounded. Krest called out that we should break for the kitchens to try and narrow the field. But we couldn't manage to hold off all sides. As soon as one side would weaken the other side would strike. That's when Wilstrom made his move. He called out to get ready and then poured it on like I'd never seen before. His motion turned into one continuous dance of death. The singing of his sword turned into a wail that hurt the ears. It was then that I saw the dagger fly in from the side and sink itself into his leg. He let out a roar like a lion, but never slowed his pace, even though the swarm pressed in. It was at this point that Krest and I were able to make it through the passage into the kitchen."

"So, he died?" Taya asked with a tear in her eye.

"Yes, valiantly."Guntharr said sadly. "But what happened next was something that Krest and I couldn't have planned for. The kitchen had been set afire from the battle and smoke filled the room. The stream of minions kept coming but they were harder to keep track of as the smoke was thick. That's when I lost him."

Firebane nodded his head, "Of course, the combination of smoke and exhaustion dulled your senses."

"I called for him, several times. I pushed my way back the way we came but the way was blocked by the stack of bodies that had been destroyed at our hands. I worked my way through the kitchen toward the storeroom. But, I found nothing there. As I continued toward the staff's quarters, the onslaught slowed and the number of dead Talicrons increased. I knew he had come this way. I quickened my pace to hopefully catch up with him. That's when I saw him standing over Krest's fallen body."

"Who, who was it?" Taya commanded.

"His name is Dravious. He is a powerful magic wielder. At the sight of the body of my fallen mentor, the rage within me erupted. I sprinted toward him with the intent of pounding his body straight into the floor. I had almost made it across the room when, with a sneer on his face, he extended his hand toward me and a force not unlike a strike from a war hammer hit me square in the chest, sending me back against the wall. This however did not stop me because by now I felt no pain and this time I knew what I was up against. As I charged, I calculated his next move. As he began to motion with his hand, I dropped to the ground and rolled forward taking his legs out from under him. He came crashing to the ground behind me. I recovered to my feet in time to see him utter a command and instantly vanish."

"Teleportation?" Firebane asked.

"Yes," Guntharr responded. "With Dravious gone, the few minions that were left in the room were not so keen to come up against me in my enraged state and scattered." Guntharr stood up and moved over to the fire pit in the center of the room and looked down at the burning embers.

For the next few moments there was silence. No one moved or said anything. Taya wanted to know more. An unfamiliar emotion began to swell up within her. An emotion that Guntharr had warned her to control as soon as she started to feel it. Anger was powerful and yet frightening at the same time. She began to ask Guntharr to go on when she saw his head jerk to attention. She knew that look and immediately scanned the air for sounds. It was a squawk from Raskin.

"Firebane, we're under attack," Guntharr announced.

Firebane was all too familiar with Guntharr's quirks and tones. He was serious.

"How? Where?" Firebane asked.

"Taya, call Raskin in. He will give us those answers." Guntharr scanned the room for his weapons.

Taya ran to the corridor and called out through one of the open windows for Raskin. Seconds later a shadow covered the full moon and glided to a rest in the window opening. "What did you see?" Taya asked.

"The dark ones have returned." Raskin replied. "They are coming down from the hillside and will be entering the town soon."

"That's bad," Taya replied.

"How many?" Guntharr asked as he handed Taya her bow, small sword and quiver.

Raskin fluffed his feathers. "I didn't count exactly, but there seemed to be at least fifty."

"Hmm," Guntharr looked down at Taya. "It would seem that our last encounter with these creatures inspired them to take us a little more seriously."

"More seriously," Taya started, "I'd say trying to kill us is pretty serious."

"If they knew who they were dealing with the first time, they would have sent 50 assassins then." Guntharr looked past the hawk into the darkness. The glow of the moon cast shadows across the landscape and made it hard to detect movement.

"That's not all," Raskin interrupted. "This time it is worse."

"I agree, fifty is a bit more of a challenge than the dozen or so that we encountered back in Hydesvalley. But, we can handle this." Guntharr reassured them.

"What, I mean is," Raskin shuffled up closer to Guntharr. "They have bowmen this time."

"Ah," Guntharr nodded in agreement, "that would be an additional concern, especially for you."

Firebane approached from behind. He now had a sword at his side and his simple robe had been overlaid with a shimmering shirt of chainmail. "I have notified the elders, we are preparing for a siege."

"I cannot ask you to risk your lives for us," Guntharr placed a hand on his shoulder. "Point us to a way out back, and we'll make a break for the mountains."

"You didn't ask." Firebane looked over at Taya, "It is our honor and duty to stand and defend the princess of the Silverwood."

Taya's eye caught Firebane's, and she bowed her head in appreciation.

"Raskin," Guntharr turned to face the hawk. "Head to safety, you'll not be much help in this fight. Stay out of the range of their bowmen. Once they've all entered the chapel, watch their flank. If any try to escape, bring them down."

"Of course," Raskin replied and he leaped off into the darkness.

Taya stared out into the darkness and scanned the surroundings. "They've nearly reached the edge of the town."

"Quickly, let's make for the chapel so we can establish our positions." Guntharr commanded.

The three turned and started up the corridor. Behind them, five elders including Tronic made their way from one of the side rooms each, carrying a weapon of his preference.

Firebane held up a hand and Guntharr and Taya came skidding to a halt. "Shouldn't we get Rift in on this, he'll be awfully upset if we leave him out."

"You really think you could get away with leaving me out," the battle wolf huffed as he casually trotted up to them.

Guntharr reached down and ruffled the hair around Rift's neck. "Are you sure you're up for this, old friend."

"Watch who you're calling old," Rift playfully snapped at Guntharr's hand. "I'll take these guys on all by myself, if you want me to." He paused for a moment, "How many are there?"

"Fifty or more," Taya replied.

"Oh," Rift stopped. "I probably could use some of your help with that many of them."

Taya knelt down, still feeling overwhelmed by the revelation of her past, and took Rift's aged face into her hands. Rift responded by starting to step back. "Rift, I can see you have a gallant heart and a warrior's spirit, but I cannot ask you to take the risk."

Rift looked at her for a moment then looked up at Guntharr. "Is she serious?"

Guntharr pulled Taya back to her feet and nodded. "Yes, she is, I'm afraid, but she also doesn't know you, so I will just have to ask her to trust us."

Taya's puzzled expression spoke volumes. "You will see," Guntharr said. "Now, places everybody, we have some invaders to crush."

Chapter 5

The seconds passed like hours. Guntharr, Firebane, Tronic and the other elders quickly repositioned benches to form protective barricades to force the incoming enemy into committing to either the center or one side. Taya had been positioned on the platform where she could get the best vantage point. Tronic had also brought with him a handful of arrows to replenish her dwindling supply. They were not the Dagmoor arrows she was accustomed to, but they would kill just the same.

Guntharr had given her strict instructions to target only those entering that looked like they had ranged capabilities. He and the others would take care of the knife wielding creatures.

She was well protected behind the podium, and the platform gave her a good vantage point over the others. She could easily have held the entrance by herself, so long as her arrow supply lasted, but she knew based upon the counts that she would have to be selective about her targets.

Overlooking the scene, she could see that Tronic and the elders were lined up on her left behind one side of the barricade. Firebane and Gunthar were to her right, and poor old Rift stood like a shadow guarding the exposed side of the barricade. She couldn't help but feel concern for the old battle wolf. Knowing in her heart that in his prime he was probably a ferocious ally, but in his current state, he would scarcely be more than an annoyance to these creatures.

What happened next would change Taya's outlook on Rift forever. Sounds came from the doors to the chapel as the creatures pounded against them. Heavier and heavier the blows against the doors came as the monsters pounded away at the solemn wood doors with their weapons. Taya could see Guntharr glance over at Rift who remained motionless. With a final crash, the two large doors gave way under the assault and flew open.

"Now, Rift!" Guntharr cried out.

Taya saw the first wave of creatures file in with their weapons drawn. The light from the numerous lamps temporarily blinded the invaders. And that's when she heard the wolf cry. Rift let loose a cry that made the hair on the back of her neck stand up. It continued far longer than she imagined a wolf cry should. In fact, it didn't seem to die out, but instead grew stronger and louder.

Taya saw the seven creatures that made it in begin to look around for the source of the sound and also at one another. Then, Taya looked down at Rift. What she saw defied all her understanding. Either her eyes were playing tricks on her or Rift had gotten larger, and not by just a little, but he appeared to have more than doubled in size. His scruffy blue-gray coat had been replaced by a dark polished looking fur. Something told her that this fur wasn't soft and fluffy.

Finishing his howl, Rift took off around the end of the barricade and plowed right through the first three creatures sending them flying in different directions. With his new size and speed, he was like a charging bull, tearing his way through the creatures. The four behind him scattered quickly, steering clear of the end they turned and rushed toward the center opening.

Taya watched in awe as Tronic and the elders stepped up and engaged the small force that had found their way behind the barricade.

Rift's massive jaws locked onto the head of one of the fallen creatures, and with a shake of his head, he slung the creature full force into the wall, shattering its back. His giant paws lifted off the floor and he plunged his claws in the two remaining fallen ones before they could scurry away.

"Taya, the door," Guntharr called back.

Taya, realizing that she had been caught up in the excitement of the fight, had forgotten that she too had to play a part. With a thud, a throwing ax sank deep into the railing beside her.

Reaching back in her quiver, she felt for a normal arrow and quickly knocked it. Circling around the podium, she noted that two creatures had stationed themselves just outside the door. She targeted the one on the left, and let fly the arrow. It sailed with precision but struck the frame of the door forcing the attacker back into a covered position.

At this point six, more filed into the room. Two peeled off to the side to distract the battle wolf who was stepping back to assess their strength.

As the four remaining charged down the center, another wave of six entered the room and began pounding on the barricade. This time, Guntharr and Firebane stepped directly in front of the charging assassins. Firebane made an upward arc stroke with his blade, dispatching one of them. Guntharr drove his warhammer forward and it smashed squarely into the assassin's skull. The force of the blow not only killed the creature but sent his body flying backwards into his charging partner knocking him to the ground.

Taya knocked another arrow and waited for another opportunity. This time, an archer on the right side of the door was forced into the main hall by his charging companions. The assassin took aim at the distracted battle wolf, and was about to let fly an arrow but Taya's found its mark first. The assassin spun around sending his final shot wildly at the barricade.

Rift's attention was focused on the two assassins that had pushed him back toward the door to the residence wing. One was holding a small version of a warhammer like Guntharr carried, and the other carried a mace.

With a savage cry, the hammer holding minion charged viciously toward the wolf. This caught Rift off guard, and he instinctively turned his head to avoid getting struck by the hammer. With the full weight of the creature behind it, he missed Rift's head and landed squarely on his shoulder, bouncing off muscle and fur and slamming into the floor with a resounding clang.

"Really, that's all you got," Rift turned to face his attacker. "I must tell Guntharr I was wrong, I could have taken all of you by myself."

With a swipe of his paw, Rift tore a series of gashes across the midsection of the creature sending him backwards and then to the ground. He then charged forward and snapped at the second attacker. More out of fear than skill, the assassin leaped back and brought his mace smashing down on the top of the wolf's head.

"Ow, I felt that one." Rift shook his head. "No more nice wolf." Using his hind legs, Rift launched himself into the air. With a crash, he landed squarely on the mace wielder driving him to the ground, the weight of the wolf crushing him.

Several more assassins came pouring in and continued the assault on the barricade.

"Watch out!" Taya cried out as the volume of creatures finally overtook part of the barricade and sent it crashing down on top of one of the elders.

"Barak!" Tronic tried to respond, but before he could reach the trapped elder, an assassin sprung off one of the benches and drove his sword down into the elder's face. The creature looked up in satisfaction just in time to see Tronic's sword slice him in two.

With part of the barricade down there were now two sides exposed and Guntharr's plan to control the flow of creatures was now void. "Form up!" came the cry from Firebane.

Tronic and the three remaining elders fell back to Firebane and Guntharr in a semi-circle formation.

Two more archers popped into the doorway and launched a volley of arrows. One had targeted Taya and the other had targeted Tronic.

Taya sidestepped the arrow just in time as it shot past her and buried itself into the wall behind her. Tronic was not so lucky. With a cry of pain, Tronic staggered back with an arrow jutting out of his shoulder. Taya responded as quickly as she could as she pulled an arrow from her quiver and sent it hurtling flawlessly toward Tronic's sniper.

This left Taya open and the second archer saw his opportunity. Drawing a bead on his target, the sniper readied his arrow. He saw Taya start to reach back and grab another arrow to the ready. He took a deep breath to steady his aim just as Rift lunged toward him knocking, him off balance and causing him to release the arrow directly into the back of one of his own.

Guntharr had dispatched three more assassins and was sizing up the next, when he turned to yell over his shoulder, "Taya, come help Tronic." A sword bearing assassin thought he would take advantage of Guntharr's distraction and lunged in with a thrust. Guntharr parried the clumsy attack and wrapped his free arm around the creature's neck then twisted.

Taya jumped down from her perch on the platform and ran over to where one of the elders was trying to navigate Tronic through the mess of mangled bodies and benches. She rushed over and helped steady him, as the three of them made their way to the back corner of the room.

At the sight of movement in the corner of her eye, Taya let go of Tronic, causing him lose his balance and tumble to the ground. Grabbing an arrow from her quiver, she quickly knocked, pulled and fired the arrow at the creature that was sneaking up on them. Taya realized the second she released it that it was one of the Dagmoor arrows. It did its job well, and caught the creature right in the throat.

"Sorry," Taya whispered as she turned her attention to the fallen elder who responded with a groan.

Lifting him up again, they managed to get to a corner far enough away from the action for the elder to look at the wound.
"This is going to hurt," the elder said to Tronic.

Tronic just nodded and gritted his teeth for the inevitable. Grasping the shaft at the point where it entered the shoulder, with delicate force the elder pulled the arrow free from Tronic's body. The wound was bad, but Taya was sure, with the arrow out, they could stop the bleeding.

"Up on the platform beside the table of bread, there are towels. Bring me a couple," the elder commanded.

Taya responded by sprinting back out into the center part of the room and toward the steps to the platform. A couple of assassins saw the young elf making for the platform and broke away to attack. Taya knew that she would have to dispatch them quickly so she readied an arrow, but before she could even pull the string back on her bow, a large black shadow came rushing up behind them and smashed them to the ground.

"I hope you weren't planning on shooting me," Rift joked at Taya who was pointing her loaded bow at him.

"No, I wasn't," Taya smiled as she realized she had him in her sites instead, "I've got to help Tronic."

She took off up the stairs to find the towels for Tronic. Rift turned and surveyed the scene. They had mopped up around two dozen of the worthless creatures Rift thought, which meant they were about halfway through.

Guntharr and Firebane had become separated. Firebane had gone over to help the remaining elders stem the tide of assassins over the barricade, while Guntharr held the center of the chapel. The far side, where Rift had been keeping watch, was now unguarded and several of the latest influx of creatures made their way behind Firebane.

Firebane was pulling his sword out of the chest of his latest kill when a bark from Rift caused him to turn and see the approaching assassins coming from their flank. Stretching out his blade, Firebane whispered a prayer softly and the blade began to glow with a bright light. The rays of light streamed forward and blinded the group. They responded by screaming violently and waving their weapons in a futile attempt at defense.

Firebane walked up to the them and casually dispatched them. As he did, a cry came from behind him as one of his elders was surrounded and subsequently run through by an assassin with a pike.

Guntharr turned also at the sound and saw the man go down. The metal tip protruding from his chest was a clear indicator that he was gone. Guntharr spun and swung his hammer in a single motion, catching the next creature under its chin. The impact dislocated its neck and sent it flying to the back of the room with a crash.

Taya returned to Tronic and the attending elder with a handful of towels. Tronic's condition had worsened. His formerly bronze skin was now very pale.

"What's wrong?" Taya asked.

"Poison," the elder answered. "I noticed the black stain on the arrowhead when I pulled it out."

"Can't you do anything?" She replied.

The elder shook his head. "Father Firebane may be able to slow the poison, if we can get him back here in time."

Taya thought for a second, and then an idea came to her. "Hold on, Tronic," she said as she headed back into the fray.

In the center and back of the chapel, things had turned into chaos. Firebane, Gunthar, Rift and the remaining elders stood almost shoulder to shoulder to prevent the assassins from surrounding them.

Taya noticed that three more archers had entered the room and were setting up to take aim. She knew she didn't have time to mount the steps to the platform to get a better angle. They would be firing long before then, and she didn't have time to shoot all three of them. She was fast, but not that fast. That's when she realized that they were standing directly under one of the large chandeliers. Reaching back, she pulled out the next to last Dagmoor arrow. The arrow soared through the air and severed the rope sending the heavy fixture crashing down on the three of them sending their arrows in all directions of which one nearly hit her.

"Nice shot," Firebane called back to her.

The crash caused several of the creatures near the back to look for a means of retreat, and in their panic they managed to trample several of their incoming support.

Taya scurried back onto the platform and returned to her former post. But this time, rather than wait for certain targets, she began taking the intruders out from the back. No sooner had she found her spot than her first arrow went sailing over Gunthar and Firebane's heads, piercing an incoming assassin.

Guntharr turned to Firebane, "Let's end this now." Firebane, covered in sweat and blood, nodded and smiled.

With unified precision, the two slashed, bashed and smashed their way forward, causing the flow of targets into the chapel to slow. Swing after swing the two drove the creatures back either in fear or as corpses.

Taya continued to spot outliers that she could target without the risk of hitting one of her friends.

Rift, sensing the push forward, began swinging first his right paw and then his left, causing the creatures in front of him to either scatter or be slammed into one another.

A scraggly voice from the back called through the door, "Retreat!"

This was more than enough excuse for most of the remaining assassins to turn and run for the door. Guntharr, Firebane and Rift stood and watched the comedic escape. The elder that stayed out to fight beside Firebane staggered and fell, clasping his legs.

Firebane ran to his side and saw the heavy gash across the man's thigh. "It's a good thing they called retreat. I don't know how much longer I was going to be able to stand," the elder said with a painful smile.

Seeing this, Taya grabbed the remaining towel, jumped down from the platform and ran over to the wounded elder. She handed it to Firebane before reporting, "Firebane, Tronic needs your help. The arrow that struck him was poisoned."

FIrebane placed the towel over the gash, then took Taya's hand and pressed it hard against the wound. "Hold this here tightly," he said.

Guntharr knelt down next to Taya and studied the situation. "You held your own out there elder . . ." he cut off his words not knowing the man's name.

"Phandor," he grimaced in reply. "Firebane has been teaching us various fighting techniques.

Rift walked up beside them. "Well, that was fun."

"Rift," Guntharr turned toward the wolf, "follow after the pack and try to capture one of them alive. I want to ask him some questions."

"Now you tell me," Rift spun around and took off into the night.

Guntharr pulled some heavy string out of a pouch and wrapped it several times around the makeshift bandage. "You go see how Tronic is doing. I'm going to get some answers."

The two jumped up together. Taya extended a hand, helped the wounded elder back to his feet and supported him as he limped over to a more comfortable place to rest. Guntharr trotted across the room, carefully avoiding the bodies that lay scattered all around. He noted the four bodies that lay with arrows sticking out of them as he passed through the doors. "Satisfactory," he said to himself as he started to run out into the darkness.

Up ahead, Guntharr could see a large dark shadow closing in on a group of smaller creatures that were lagging behind their faster companions.

"Three . . two . . one," Guntharr counted to himself. Just as he hit one, the large shadow that was still several horse lengths behind them, flashed out of existence and instantly reappeared running directly in front of them.

"Grrrr," Rift skidded to a halt and spun around with a growl.

One of the creatures blindly ran smack into Rift, bouncing off the armor like fur he fell backwards on the ground. The other two screamed and split to one side of the wolf or the other and never slowed down.

Rift placed a heavy paw on the chest of the struggling assassin and pressed down with all of his weight. "Don't move," he growled down into the assassin's face.

He looked up to see Guntharr running toward them. "Don't worry, I'm in no hurry," he called out trying to egg the warrior on.

Another minute passed before Guntharr reached him. "You took long enough," Rift chided. "Good thing he wasn't going anywhere. At least his trembling feels good on the toes."

"Let him up," Guntharr ordered.

"You heard him, on your feet," Rift barked at the assassin.

The creature continued to struggle.

"Rift," Guntharr pointed at his paw, "you'll have to get off of him for him to get up."

"Oh, right," Rift stepped off him and began walking slowly back toward the church.

"Where are you going?" Guntharr called out to Rift, "I need you here."

Rift paused for a second and turned around. "Whatever you need me for, you better hurry. Time's almost up."

Guntharr reached down and picked up the quivering assassin by his tunic. Lifting him off his feet by several inches so he wouldn't have to tilt his head, Guntharr stared hard into the dark hollow eyes.

"We're going to play a game of questions and answers," Guntharr spoke softly but firmly.

The creature just nodded his head.

"I'm going to ask a question, and if you give me an answer I like, nothing happens to you, understand?" Guntharr paused.

His head continued to bob up and down.

"If I don't like the answer or I think you're lying to me, my wolf friend here gets to bite off a part of his choosing." Guntharr looked down at Rift and the assassin followed his gaze.

Rift looked back at Guntharr, "You're not really going to make me put any part of that creature in my mouth are you?"

"Rift likes the taste of dark goblin, don't you Rift." Guntharr threw a commanding glance toward the wolf.

"Oh, all right, if you insist," Rift responded. "Let me at him, let me at him, growl, bark, drool." Rift responded with little sincerity.

Guntharr rolled his eyes and looked back at the creature. "You are a dark goblin, from the Midnight Realm are you not?"

The goblin started the spasm of nodding up and down again.

"Good, I like that answer." Guntharr spoke.

Rift snipped at the goblin for effect, but really didn't get near the creature. The goblin thrashed around in fear, unable to escape while suspended in mid-air.

"Now a harder question, who sent you to kill us?" Guntharr asked.

The creature started to utter something that sounded like a cough. His eyes grew very large and his head slumped forward. Guntharr noticed an arrow tip protruding out of the goblin's chest. "That's just great," he said in a hushed tone.

Looking out past the dead goblin, Guntharr tried scanning the edge of the town and the surrounding landscape to see where the arrow came from.

"Over there," Rift directed toward the edge of a small clump of trees. A dark body disappeared into the dark covering provided by the tree line. "Shall I go after him?"

"No," Guntharr tossed the dead goblin aside.

"Good, because time's almost up and I need to get back inside." Rift turned and began walking back toward the church.

Guntharr stood in the darkness, looking around for any signs of stray goblins. After scanning the area around them, he took several steps backward, and finally turned and trotted to catch up with Rift.

"You know, I can't believe you were actually going to make me take a bite out of that nasty thing. Do you know how long it takes to get that taste out of your mouth?" Rift rambled as they made their way back inside the church.

Chapter 6

Guntharr and Rift entered the chapel area and saw Firebane and Phandor searching the bodies and then loading them into a cart.

Firebane looked up as he entered, "Ah, were you able to gather any information from them?"

"Just that they are dark goblins," Guntharr began. "Apparently, the last group or two hung around and decided to assassinate their comrade once they saw he'd been captured."

"Well, that's more than we had," Firebane went back to work. "Regrettably, it was very expensive information."

Guntharr looked around the floor and spotted three human sized bodies covered with blankets. "Who were they?"

"Barak and Tronic," Phandor replied as he limped over to the next goblin body.

Guntharr bowed his head for a moment and uttered a soft prayer. When he had finished, he looked around for Taya. "Where's Taya?"

The Silverwood Chronicles

"Duskin took her back to the common area to rest." Phandor reported.

Rift was making his way in the direction Phandor had indicated when he let out a painful whimper. He stopped in mid stride and laid quickly to the ground. Even though Guntharr had seen this happen many times, this process always saddened him. As fierce and powerful that the wolf had become, the transformation back to his normal form could be excruciating.

He walked over and bent down to pick up the normal-sized wolf. Gently laying him over his shoulder, Guntharr carried him back into the common area where they had been relaxing before the attack.

As he rounded the corner, he saw Taya curled up on one of the large pillows, shivering. He recognized the shock that had overcome her from all of the action. It took even mature humans, as well as elves, years to get used to the trauma of combat. Taya was strong in spirit, but she had not seen this kind of action and death before.

Guntharr crossed over to the firepit in the center, and carefully laid the wolf on a pillow.

"Thank you, my friend." Rift spoke in a very weak voice.

Seeing Rift in his smaller state, Taya immediately jumped up and ran over to them. "Is he okay? Did he get hurt?"

Guntharr took her by the arm and led her back to her cushion and sat down with her. "He'll be fine." He replied.

"What happened?" she asked.

"Battle wolves have the ability to change form for a period of time, when the situation warrants it." Guntharr began. "The howl that you heard just as the goblins entered the chapel, is a sacred prayer that battle wolves cry to the One True God to give them this power. The transformation is usually only good for an hour or so, depending on the strength and age of the wolf. Once they've exhausted themselves, the power leaves them and they return to their normal size and strength. However, they are typically completely drained and have to rest for a period before they can go about."

"How long will he need to rest?" She looked over at the sleeping wolf.

Guntharr lifted his shoulders slightly and let them down. "It's hard to tell. Rift isn't getting any younger, and he fought pretty hard. He even expended a lightning jump which . . ." Taya interrupted him.

"What's a lightning jump?" She asked with fascination.

Gunthar stretched out on the floor beside her and yawned slightly. "Every battle wolf is blessed with a special gift that he can use during his altered state. Each battle wolf I've ever met had a different gift. " Guntharr turned and looked over at Rift. "I call Rift's gift a lightning jump. It's like teleportation, but he can only go in the direction that he's currently heading, and he can only go so far."

"Wow, I wish I could have seen it," Taya's eyes were wide open with wonder, "It must have been amazing."

"It's quite an impressive gift. But, like the transformation itself, it takes a lot of energy." Guntharr turned back over to face Taya. "I'd say he'll be out till morning, maybe even most of the day."

"Are you kidding?" A groggy voice called from the fire pit, "I'm ready to go again now."

"Go to sleep, Rift," Guntharr ordered.

Taya let go of a slight chuckle at the exchange, and turned to look Guntharr directly in his deep dark eyes. "What's going to happen to me, Guntharr?"

Guntharr could tell by the tone of her voice that she was scared. "I'm going to keep you safe, don't you worry about that. It's going to take a lot more than a couple dozen dark goblins to get to you. Today was barely a workout."

"It wasn't a workout for Barak, Tronic or Henlick," she responded, her eyes falling to the ground.

He nodded. "You are correct."

"I don't want anything to happen to you, you're the only family I've really ever known," she pleaded.

"And you, me," he echoed.

Her eyes lit up for a second and she jumped up with an idea. "You said I'm a princess of some kind, right?"

He nodded slowly.

"So, why can't I order an army to go out and find out who is trying to hurt us and bring them to justice?" She asked.

Guntharr reached up, took her hand and pulled her back down to his level. "Well, there's a slight problem with that."

"Oh," she sighed. "What's that?"

"The first problem is the kingdom of Silverwood has fallen into disarray since Spire Tree fell." He paused for a moment thinking to himself. How much detail should he go into with her at this point?

Finally, sensing her eagerness for him to continue he added, "In order for us to bring back unity, I will need to have proof of who you are besides my word."

She shook her head, "How are we going to do that?"

The 'we' caught him a little off guard. She was really ready to accept the fact that she was more than just an estranged orphaned elf, that had been under the care of a wandering warrior for the last fourteen years.

"I don't know, yet." This time it was Guntharr that had to lower his eyes. "That's one of the things I've been doing the last several years is trying to come up with some good evidence that substantiates who you are."

"You're going to have to find the talisman," the voice of Firebane came in from the hallway.

"Come sit with us," Guntharr directed.

"Where's Phandor?" Taya asked.

"He and Duskin went back to rest before establishing a watch," Firebane replied.

"That won't be necessary," Guntharr held up a hand.

Firebane turned his head slightly, "And why is that?"

"Two reasons," Guntharr replied. "First, it will take them a while to regroup and gather the courage to strike again."

"And the second reason, assuming that they have a harsh task master that sends them back to finish us or die?" Firebane countered.

Guntharr held up a hand to add emphasis to his point, "The second, is we already have a night watchman hovering overhead who likes nothing more than to fly around and keep an eye on things, particularly at night."

"Raskin!" Taya shouted, having completely forgetting about her feathered friend. She jumped up and ran back out to the hall and peered through a window.

Firebane smiled after Taya as she bounded away and then looked at Guntharr, "Who is Raskin?"

Firebane and Guntharr turned to look out into the hall as the musical call went out from Taya into the night sky.

"You can certainly tell she's a royal elf," Firebane smiled, "that melodic voice of hers has healing properties in it."

Guntharr stood and began to make his way over to Taya. "Unfortunately, teaching her how to use those gifts has been outside of my realm of expertise. I know that you have training in such gifts, and I was hoping that maybe you could help her."

From outside a squawk and the beating of wings could be heard approaching the window where Taya stood looking outside.

A looming shadow that circled through the night sky slowly descended toward them, and more and more of the stars disappeared as the great wing span of the hawk lord neared, until finally he landed on the stone ledge of the window.

"That was some group of dark creatures that I saw come and go," Raskin spoke. "I take it they were not well received?"

"We dispatched them successfully, but at a sizable cost," Firebane responded to the hawk lord.

Raskin jerked his head sideways so that he could get a good look at the new voice. "Is this a friend?" he asked.

"Yes, Raskin," Taya replied, "this is Father Firebane."

"Raskin," Guntharr cut in, "how are you feeling right now? Are you up for another watch till morning?"

Raskin stretched out his wings slightly and shook. "Are you kidding," he responded as he settled back into his well poised stance, "that would be a treat. Are you thinking the dark ones might be returning for another go?"

"Not likely, but there is an outside possibility." He acknowledged.

"Then I will tend to the skies," he turned and soared out of the window.

"You've enlisted the aid of a hawk lord?" Firebane was impressed.

"Not exactly," Guntharr replied.

"About a year ago, during one of our trips," Taya spoke excitedly, "we found Raskin lying wounded in an open meadow."

"He had been badly wounded in a fight against a competing hawk faction, and left to die at the hands of some ground predators." Guntharr added.

"But we happened along," Taya smiled, "and rescued him, then helped repair his wings."

"Indeed," Firebane marvelled.

"Lots of singing was involved," Guntharr prodded.

Taya blushed slightly, "Yeah, that seemed to help more than anything." She stopped and then realized that what she'd just said sounded very boastful. "But, Guntharr is very skilled with healing medicine."

"I am aware of your guardian's abilities, for I was the one that helped teach him those skills," Firebane smiled and jabbed an elbow into Guntharr's side.

"And a fine teacher you were," he added.

"Am," Firebane corrected, "I still have plenty to contribute to anyone who will listen and devote themselves."

"Do you think Firebane can teach me?" Taya asked.

"I'm quite counting on it," Guntharr replied. "But before we go into that any further, you mentioned something about a talisman. What talisman would that be and how could it help us?"

"Let us return to the resting chambers and we will discuss it." Firebane turned and headed back to the comfortable room where they had been resting before the attack. He pulled up a small stool that was against a wall, and sat next to the fire pit. He stared down into the shimmering coals as the two got themselves situated.

"The Talisman of Alterian was a gift fashioned long ago by the leaders of the five realms for the ruling house of the Silverwood. It's very purpose was to seal the royal line so that no one could infiltrate and take over. The wearer of the talisman, if he or she is of the line of Silverwood, is granted certain magical gifts." He closed his eyes searching his memory.

Taya was very curious about this and had to ask a question, "What happened if you weren't of the royal line and you wore it?"

Firebane's eyes opened and looked curiously at the girl, "I don't know. I've never heard of anyone other than a royal putting it on." He paused. "It could do anything from nothing at all, to killing them instantly, I suppose. There's nothing in lore that talks about the consequences of putting it on and not being an heir of Silverwood."

"Then all that we need to do is get this talisman and put it around my neck and hope it doesn't kill me," she stopped for a moment thinking about what she'd just said.

Firebane pursed his lips together and nodded his head slightly, "I suppose that would do it."

"Great, so where is it?" Taya asked ready to give it a go.

Firebane let out a great laugh. The sound of the outburst startled Taya and she slid closer to Guntharr.

"Forgive me young one," he apologized, "I do not laugh at you, I merely revel in your spirit. Surely you are of the line of Silverwood to have such courage. Alas, I have no idea where the talisman may be. The last time anyone knew of its whereabouts was before your father, Lord Krestichan, was killed. He was the last to wear the talisman."

Taya looked at the guardian, "You were with my father before he died, did you see it then?"

Guntharr turned away from the girl and stood up slowly. He began to pace the floor, his eyes searching the room for clues, clues to memories long forgotten, yet etched in the stone memory of that tragic day. "What did it look like?" he directed his question at Firebane.

Firebane grabbed a poker that was lying beside the pit and pushed some coals around in the fire. "Well, it's round," he stretched out his hand and looked at it closely, "about the size of my open hand. It would have been made out of silve,r with five stones representing the five realms."

Guntharr had reached a small table and brought down his fist in a fit of anger. The sound echoed through the large room like a clap of thunder. Even Rift was groggily awakened by the sound. After a cursory glance, he gave a snort and rolled over.

"Yes, I remember seeing it," he said. "Many times over the course of our stay there at Silverwood, I would see Krest in his formal attire wearing it. I had no idea of its significance at the time."

"What about that night?" Taya asked softly with an emphasis on 'that'.

Guntharr shook his head. "The celebration is a blur compared to the battle that ensued. During our haste to try to find weapons and shore up a strategic position, I had little time to worry about what he was wearing."

"What about afterward, after you'd chased off Dravious?" Firebane tried to redirect his focus. "What happened then? You were standing over him at that point. He was dead, correct."

"No," Guntharr shouted as he turned around. "he wasn't dead, but he was dying, and there was nothing I could do to save him." He marched back toward the two and after just a couple of steps he fell to his knees, his shoulders sagging with grief. "I tried, Firebane. I did everything I knew to do to save him. Everything you'd taught me. Everything I ever knew about healing, but nothing worked. I knelt there and knew that the wounds were not natural, but supernatural. I prayed, and called on God to heal him to pour His power through me to heal one of the closest friends I had ever known. And nothing." Guntharr's voice weakened.

Taya got up and walked over to him and knelt down beside him, her small hand reaching to touch his. Guntharr's fingers responded to her gentle touch and he slowly wrapped his hand tightly around hers.

He looked up, "That's when he told me where to find you." He stopped for a moment and that's when Taya noticed tears forming in his eyes. "His last words to me were to take care of you and to protect you. I pledged to him that I would."

"Guntharr," Firebane commanded, "did you see the talisman then?"

He shook his head. "No, I would have remembered it, because I had my hands over his heart as I prayed."

"Then it's been taken, and we must find it." Firebane said matter-of-factly.

Taya turned to look at Firebane, "If he wasn't wearing it, then somebody must have stolen it. How will we ever find it?"

"It may not have been stolen," Guntharr reacted, "it's possible it was hidden or stowed away in Spire Tree."

Firebane snorted, "Not likely. Spire Tree was razed by that attack, it's not very likely that the talisman went unnoticed."

"Then that means that either Dravious or the Talicrons have it." Taya commented.

Guntharr stood up and moved over to the fire pit. He stood opposite Firebane and looked down into the glowing embers. "Possibly, but I want to cover all of my bases, and we'll start with the easiest one first."

"Easy," Firebane rolled to his side, "you call marching into the heart of the Silverwood, crawling with Talicrons, easy?"

"Firebane, it's going to require a process of elimination. The easiest things to eliminate are the knowns." Guntharr stated.

Taya approached him and looked up at him, "And what do we know about Spire Tree?"

"Mostly, where it is," he replied. "If your theory is true, Firebane, we're going to have to find some clues as to who took it. And what better place to look, than the place that it was last seen."

"But that was years ago," Firebane argued.

"True, but it's all we have at this point." Guntharr turned a hand over.

"Okay," he conceded, "when do we get started?"

"We?" Guntharr asked, surprised.

"We!" Taya clapped her hands.

Guntharr reached over and held the girl's hands together, then turned to his friend. "Who mentioned anything about 'we'?"

"I did," Firebane stood up. "We have standing here with us one of the most important elves in existence and a lot is riding on finding that talisman. You need all the help you can get, and besides, I happen to like Taya." Firebane winked at the girl.

"No, if you like her so much, she can stay here with you and that way, she'll be protected." Guntharr replied.

Taya stepped back and held up her hands, "Hold on just a minute. You are not going to leave me here while you go back to the place of my birth and try to find clues to my life, without me."

Guntharr turned and knelt before his ward, "Taya, I promised your father that I would care for you and protect you. The safest place in the whole world, right now, is here in this church with Firebane. If I take you into the Silverwood, to Spire Tree, I can't promise any of us will make it out alive."

"Guntharr, my friend, she has a right." He looked over at the young elf. "Taya is growing up, and she needs to know what's at stake here. You have done an admirable job protecting her over the years. I don't think she is safer anywhere in the whole world than beside you."

"No," he said emphatically, "she'll be safer here."

Firebane walked around the fire pit to him. "You really think she'll be safe here?" He asked. "Take a look in the chapel and tell me how safe you think she is here. They know where she is. They'll be back, and it's just a matter of time before they bring enough dark goblins or worse. They could decide to bring something more terrible than goblins. Something that Rift, the elders and I can't handle."

Taya reached over and pulled on his arm, "Don't forget I took out a good share of them."

Firebane nodded, "Yes, you did. But my point is still valid. Three elders died tonight. If they return and find her still here, they will continue to send wave after wave until we're eventually crushed." He paused to let those last few words soak in. "Taya will be safest on the move, surrounded by the people that care about her the most. Whoever is after her must know who she is and is trying to stop her from reclaiming the throne."

Guntharr turned and walked away from the two. "You can't possibly know that."

Firebane followed. "My friend, we have both made our share of enemies over the years. But the last few days have been carefully executed. No one that holds ill toward us would be that contriving. They have to be after the girl."

"If you're right," he started.

"You know I'm right . . .," Firebane responded.

"Then there is no choice, she will have to stay with me," he conceded.

Taya smiled at Firebane, but snapped to attention when Guntharr caught her eye.

"Firebane can teach me about healing as we go along," Taya mouthed quietly.

"Yes, that is an excellent idea," Firebane replied trying to lighten the mood.

"Who will look after the church?" Taya asked, suddenly realizing what he was doing.

"Phandor and Duskin can manage without me for a time," he patted her shoulder.

"Then it's settled," Taya moved over to a cushion and sat down.

Firebane turned to Guntharr, "So, what's your plan?"

"We rest tonight, for it will probably be the last good night's rest we get for a while. We stock up on provisions tomorrow, and head out by mid-day," he said.

Firebane turned to leave. "Very good, I best be getting some sleep then. It sounds like tomorrow is going to be the first exciting day I've had in a long time."

The two watched Firebane leave, and Taya settled down on her cushion. Guntharr walked to the corner where more wood was stacked. He grabbed an armful of logs, and brought it over to the fire pit. After tossing a few into the fire and setting the rest aside, the guardian gathered a couple of cushions near his ward and stretched out.

"Guardian, what does he mean by his first exciting day in a long time? What was today, if not exciting?" she asked.

The corner of Guntharr's mouth inched upwards, "Taya, with Firebane, today was a simple exercise. When Firebane talks about excitement, he's referring to things your young heart can't imagine." He stopped for a moment before continuing, "I just hope, for your sake, things don't get too exciting."

Chapter 7

The room was dark. Only the light from a single candle illuminated the outline of a figure sitting at table. The candle rested on the edge of a small stand adjacent to a large ornate chair. The figure was clothed in a simple robe and wore a chain with medallion attached.

A knock came from an unseen door, and the figure extended a slender hand in the pale light and twisted symbolically in the air. As if in response to the figure's will, the knob on the door turned and the door swung open revealing in the dull light, the figure of a woman.

"Enter, Naranda," a gruff masculine voice whispered. "What do you want to see me about?"

Naranda scanned the room, but due to the darkness she was unable to see anything but the figure in the chair. "May I come in," she asked formally.

"Are you alone?" the figure asked.

"For the time being," she replied. "I am expecting a visitor shortly, but he is of no concern to you."

The candle light flickered slightly as if disturbed by some tiny breeze. The light danced across the features of the figure and Naranda could not tell if the stranger nodded or not.

Rather than risk getting the stranger riled she decided to verify the invitation. "I see you like it dark, as do I, but I'm afraid I'm not as nimble as I once was and I require a little more light to navigate the room."

The stranger slowly lifted the same hand that had just opened the door an inch. As he lifted it several other candles ignited and began to glow softly casting beams of light throughout the room.

Naranda, now able to make out the furnishings of the room, slowly entered and made her way through the array of furniture that littered the room. She came nearer to the stranger, but even with the light from the additional candles, the stranger's face seemed to be lost in shadow. After a couple more steps, the stranger held his hand up and Naranda could feel a magic force cause her to move no closer.

"That's close enough," the voice commanded.

"You don't trust me," she asked.

"I trust no one," he replied. "I have suffered your presence only because you indicated that you have some news that may interest me."

She bowed her head in a single nod. "I believe I do." While she could not see any clearer his facial features, the medallion that he wore sparkled in the candlelight. The sparkle came from the white gem lodged in its center complemented by the burnished silver setting that the medallion was made of. "That is a rather striking medallion you possess."

The stranger instinctively reached up and touched it. "This," he directed, "It is merely a bauble, a trinket. Pay it no mind."

"Then you would not mind if I take a closer look at it," Naranda started to reach out and she felt the force that had kept her from moving forward suddenly push her back.

The stranger chuckled softly, "You begin to try my patience. Get to the reason you are here before I expel you from this room."

Naranda could feel the magic force increase around her. She resisted the urge to lash out with a counter force knowing that would only provoke the sorcerer and induce his rage.

"As you wish," she focused her eyes as closely as she could on the face of the stranger to watch for any reaction to her next words. "I have found the heir to the throne of Silverwood."

Laughter this time, not just a chuckle, echoed from the stranger. "You have come to taunt me with folly?" his voice now a growl. "I could crush you where you stand."

The pressure that was previously only directed at Naranda's front was now completely surrounding her, enveloping her in a tight cocoon of energy. She was nearly at the stranger's mercy and if she didn't convince him they were on the same side she would soon be suffocated.

"The night that Spire Tree fell," Naranda spoke. "You were there."

"I was," he replied.

"There was a warrior, a guardian of Fairhaven," she could feel the cocoon tighten.

"I remember," was all that he said.

"He has been spotted, leading around a young elf maiden," she gasped for breath. A beat of silence indicated to her that she'd struck a chord. A since of unseen prying eyes searching for any hint of deception drove her to add, "I speak the truth."

"Go on, I'm listening." In his mind, he felt Naranda struggling against the force of his will.

Naranda took in a deep breath. The pressure was great, but at least it had stopped increasing. "I've been tracking their movements throughout the land. They are currently in Brittle seeking help. I suspect that the guardian is recruiting help to try and make a run against Spire Tree."

"To what end?" he asked.

"To re-establish elvish rule. To reunite the realms." Naranda was starting to grow weak. Maybe she had mistaken this sorcerer's hatred for the old ways. Maybe time had made him apathetic. Would this be a mistake she would pay for with her life?

A rapping sound at the door caused the stranger to relax his grip on Naranda. She quickly took in much needed air as the stranger waited for the unexpected visitor to leave.

Silence filled the room for several moments and then the persistent occupant on the other side of the door began knocking some more. "Mistress, are you in there?" Naranda recognized the familiar voice.

Not waiting for permission, Naranda decided to risk both of their necks and invited him in. "Scrag, please do come in."

The door opened naturally and Scrag had barely had time to take in the scene around him, when the stranger brought up his second hand and symbolically reached out and grabbed the assassin and slammed the door.

Scrag, completely caught off guard, struggled violently but was unable to break free of the magical grasp. "Mistress, why do you hold me?" he cried. "Scrag did as you ask."

"Enough," the stranger in the back called out. "Who is this and why is he here?"

"Calm yourself, Scrag. I'm afraid our host is responsible for holding us both." Naranda tried to speak in a natural tone as to not panic the neurotic creature. "Scrag is the leader of an assassin clan of Dark Goblins."

"Impossible," the stranger spat, "Dark Goblins haven't been seen in years. They were wiped out at the dawn of the last unification."

Naranda felt her confidence return, Scrag's arrival was both opportune and timely. She would be able to use that to her advantage. "Not entirely," she began, "I encountered Scrag and his clan on a journey through the Midnight Realm. Let's just say that we have come up with an arrangement that suits both of us."

"Interesting," the stranger released both Naranda and Scrag. Naranda slumped slightly, weakened from the time in the magical grip and Scrag immediately ran for the door.

"Wait," Naranda commanded. "Report on your mission."

Scrag stopped in his tracks and turned to look at the one whom he had sworn allegiance to. He hesitated as he looked and saw the flickering shadows dance over the robed stranger in the chair.

"It's alright," she tried to reassure him, "anything you want to tell me, he can hear."

Scrag turned slowly and walked over toward Naranda as if looking for protection from the mean dark figure that had somehow grabbed him earlier and held him against his will.

"Scrag took fifty assassins, just as Mistress commanded," he began.

"What did you find when you got to the church?" she asked.

Scrag's eyes stayed focus on the stranger even though his report was directed at the woman next to him. "They were ready for us. Not surprised at all," Scrag began. "We broke into the church, the chapel was arranged with a barricade in it. Scrag's men had to fight to knock it down."

"Were the guardian and the elf girl there?" she asked.

"Yes, as well as several robed ones. They fought well, but Scrag's men killed three of them," at this he turned and beamed a flashing smile at Naranda.

"Oh, Scrag almost forgot, there was a big wolf too. Mean, nasty wolf." Scrag shuddered.

Naranda glanced briefly over at the stranger for a moment to catch his reaction and then looked back at Scrag. "How big was this wolf, Scrag?"

Scrag held out a hand that reached just below his chin. "About this high, and its fur was tough like chainmail."

The stranger chuckled from his seclusion. "They have a battle wolf."

"When Scrag ordered the retreat, the wolf chased Vatog and caught him. The guardian then tried to talk to him, but Scrag sent an archer back to kill Vatog before he could talk." Scrag lowered his head.

"And you're sure that he didn't talk?" the question came from the chair.

Scrag looked over at the stranger and then back at Naranda, but didn't know whether or not to answer. "Answer the question," Narada ordered.

"Yes," Scrag nodded, "As soon as I saw that the wolf didn't eat him, I had him shot."

"This means nothing," the stranger called out. Naranda and Scrag turned their attention toward him. "You tell me there's an heir, but all I hear about is the guardian, some priests and a battle wolf. Nothing I hear gives indication that your story is true."

Naranda looked down at Scrag, "You saw the elf girl in the battle, yes?"

Scrag nodded.

"Did she fight?" she asked.

Scrag nodded some more, "with amazing skill. Her bow was quick and sure. Scrag almost got hit by one of her arrows."

"Any elf with reasonable training is a viable threat," the stranger mocked. "This means nothing."

"No," Scrag countered, "Scrag has encountered many elf clans. This one is different." He paused and looked back at Nararnda, "she took out three Ug, Rog and Cag by shooting down a chandelier with a single shot."

Naranda patted Scrag on the head. "You can always count on Scrag to have a very detailed report," she remarked. "An elf of her age with that level of skill can only mean one thing . . ."

The stranger snorted, "Yes, the guardian is an excellent teacher."

"So you're not convinced," Naranda scoffed.

"Not in the least," the stranger flicked a hand and the door behind them opened and the surrounding lights began to dim. "Now, I've heard your fairytale. Be gone with you."

Without a word, Naranda bowed and turned and left. Scrag stood there for a minute and looked over in the corner and stared for a moment in the darkness.

"I said, be gone," and the stranger made a fist which caused Scrag to be flung out through the door, almost knocking Naranda down. The door slammed shut behind him.

"Well done," came a whisper from the corner.

"Do you think he saw you?" the stranger in the chair asked.

"No matter, the point is the guardian is on the move and appears to be looking to rally support," the whisper replied.

"But do you think her tale is real? Could this elf girl really be Krestichan's daughter?"

A shadow stirred from the corner and grew closer to the chair. "You had better hope for your sake, that she is, as she will be the key to finding the missing gems." The chair's occupant reached down and felt the four recesses that once held gems. "That medallion carries quite the power with it, doesn't it? If only it had all of the gems. As it is, it's more of a curse than anything else."

"I ought to suffocate you," the stranger spat.

Once again the shadow shifted, and the lone candle flickered on the table beside the stranger. "You could, but you won't as I am the only one who can free you from your prison."

"My patience is wearing thin," he remarked.

"Indeed, fourteen years is a long time to wait," the shadow replied, "but with the finding of the girl, your wait is near its end and we shall soon be ruling from the throne of Spire Tree over the Silverwood and the five realms."

The shadow shifted away from the corner and inched its way to the door. "So what's next?" the stranger asked.

"I must see to some details," the whisper returned. "I will return for you when the time is right."

The door opened and the shadow exited the room, leaving the candle and the stranger in the chair.

Outside in the cool, starless evening, the shadow carefully scanned the surrounding area to make sure that Naranda and her crony were not waiting in ambush. The streets were deserted and no living thing seemed to be stirring. He turned and left the concealment of the small house and headed off into the night. It would take him two weeks to journey back to Fairhaven, but he had to hurry to make sure he had ample time to prepare for the guardian's arrival. With Naranda's ambitions in play, time would be critical. Her actions had yielded some positive results. It would keep the guardian off of his scent and out of his plans until it was too late. But, it also caused some problems. If her assassination attempts drove him back to Fairhaven too quickly or caused him to disappear, it could result in another long search; and he had waited fourteen long years for this day. He could not risk his goal of power to the likes of Naranda and the useless vermin she employed. He decided he would have to make a detour on his way, and arrange some insurance that she wouldn't overplay her hand.

Walking through the night toward the small house she had secured for the night, Naranda considered the reaction she had gotten from the sorcerer.

"Mistress," Scrag broke the silence.

"Yes," she replied without looking at him.

"Scrag saw someone else back in that house," he touted.

"Are you sure?" she asked.

He nodded at her, even though she wasn't looking in his direction. "Yes, Scrag's eyes very good at night. Almost as good as elf eyes."

"So, you've said," she replied. "Do you know what it was in the shadows?"

"What, mistress?" he didn't understand the question.

"What kind of creature was it?" she said in her normal emotionless tone. "Human, elf, goblin, troll, dwarf?"

"Too tall to be goblin or dwarf," he replied. "To large to be elf, maybe human or troll."

"Probably human," she answered. "A troll we would have smelled and most likely it wouldn't have remained hidden for as long as we were there without us noticing."

"Scrag didn't notice until the sorcerer dimmed the lights." Scrag explained. "Too much light for Scrag's night eyes to work before then."

"I wonder what he's up to," she whispered to herself.

The two rounded another corner and came to an unremarkable small cottage located by itself at the end of the street. She paused at the door and turned to the assassin.

"It's almost morning, they will probably be making a move soon. Send scouts out to follow them. Have them keep their distance. I don't want them to be spotted. They will travel by day, so you will either have follow off the main road, or wear disguises." She instructed.

Scrag smiled, "Scrag have good scouts. Scrag keep close tabs on the guardian and elf maiden."

Naranda reached into a pouch that was on her belt and pulled out a small figurine of an owl. She held it out with one hand and covered it with the other and whispered some magic words. A red glow enveloped the figurine for a moment, then died away. She handed the figurine to Scrag before continuing. "You will be on the move, and I expect constant reports. Find a quiet place, and place your hand over the owl. Clear your mind as best as you can, and I will be able to speak and hear you, so long as you have your hand on the owl."

Scrag stared with amazement at the figurine. He gently took it from her and admired the details with which the wooden figure had been carved. Wanting to see how it worked, he immediately started to place his free hand over the owl like he'd seen Naranda do.

"Not now," she chided him. "When you have news for me. Whenever they make a change in direction, whenever they talk to a stranger; those types of things, I need to know."

"Scrag understands," he bowed holding the owl figure high.

"Now leave me, and don't lose them," she barked then turned and opened the door and went inside, leaving Scrag outside admiring the carving.

Chapter 8

Taya still wasn't sure where they were going. Looking back at the morning, the day's activities all seemed to blend together. To start with, she slept longer than anybody. Apparently, the previous night's "exercise" as Firebane would have called it, had really tired her out. By the time she had awakened, Firebane, Rift and Guntharr were nowhere to be found. Over on the edge of the fire pit, which was now just a large pile of burnt ash, lay a plate with a chunk of fresh bread and several pieces of fruit nicely arranged.

After demolishing her breakfast, she got up and rushed out to the chapel area. She was amazed at the sight. Had there really been a battle there the night before, or was it all a dream? The benches were all back in place, the floor seemed to be nicely polished and there was no sign of blood anywhere. Then two things caught her eye that made her realize that it had happened. The first was the missing chandelier that she had shot down. The second were the front doors which had been expertly repaired, but still the damage could be seen.

"Good afternoon, Taya," a familiar voice called from behind her.

Taya spun around and saw Phandor standing in a doorway that led out behind the church. "Oh, hello. Is it really afternoon?" she asked embarrassed.

He nodded, then moved in and pretended to readjust one of the benches. "Just slightly," he smiled back at her. "Guntharr felt that you needed your rest today, since you will be leaving shortly on a long journey."

"Where are the others?" she asked.

Phandor pointed twoards the back door that he had just came through. "Out in the stables."

"Horses, you have horses!" she shouted and ran toward the door.

"Stay away from the . . ." Phandor's voice was cut off by the slamming of the door as Taya had run outside to find the stables.

Outside, Taya had stopped and was immediately taken aback by the large cloud of black smoke that was rising from a large heap of garbage off to one side of the courtyard. She looked around, and the arms of the church extended in both directions forming a protective wall around the courtyard that butted up to the back of a steep cliff.

In the back, she saw a small white barn nestled among some trees. She headed toward it, but her eyes couldn't stop looking at the burning heap. Curiosity getting the best of her, she detoured and walked closer toward the burning mound. Whatever it was, the smoke that came from it was tremendous. As she got nearer, she was able to make out distinct items in the fire and then she realized what was burning. Her stomach turned over and she held back a gag.

The burning heap was in fact the stack of dark goblins that they had killed last night, and they were disposing of the corpses. A whiff of the smoke floated near her and the smell nearly caused her to pass out.

Quickly, she turned and made a straight line for the barn in the back. The courtyard was bigger than it seemed from the back of the church, and the small, white barn turned out to be a large barn that was capable of holding a dozen horses or more. On the one side, she found a door that stood open, and she didn't pause to knock, but instead ran straight in nearly tripping over a saddle that had been laid on the ground.

"Ah, Taya, you found us," Firebane spoke.

"Did you find the food that we left for you?" Guntharr asked as he studied the bridle of a dark brown horse.

"Yes, thank you Guardian," she replied, then carefully wove her way through a maze of saddle bags toward the mare.

Stroking her dark black mane, Firebane introduced the two. "Taya, this is Silverfoot."

Taya quickly studied the horse's features and immediately noticed that her front right hoof had a silver streak leading from halfway down the leg to the hoof itself. "I've never seen a horse with a marking such as this!" She exclaimed.

Taya reached out and slowly stroked the neck of the horse. Silverfoot snorted and trembled briefly at the new touch, but Taya whispered softly to the horse, and it settled down immediately.

"It would seem we found a good match for her, Firebane," Guntharr commented as he moved away from the horse and over to the next stall.

Taya's eyes nearly popped out of her head, "You mean I get to ride her?"

Firebane chuckled, "More than that, you get to take care of her, she's yours now."

Taya squealed with glee, so much so, that Silverfoot turned and looked at her with a questioning stare.

"Oh thank you, Firebane," and she ran over and threw her arms around him, giving him a big hug.

He patted her on the back for a moment then gently pulled her away. "Don't thank me. Guntharr donated a sizable chunk to the church to cover the cost."

Taya looked over at the guardian for a moment, speechless.

"You said you wanted a horse," he responded.

"I know, but I didn't think you'd have to . . ." her words trailed off.

Guntharr held up a hand to indicate she need not say more, and then opened the stall door to release a tall dark stallion. He guided the glossy black creature over beside Taya.

Taya's eyes searched the horse for a single hair that wasn't pitch black, and she couldn't find one.

"This is Nightfury," Guntharr said.

Meanwhile, Firebane had walked across the barn to a stall that appeared to have been beaten up. As he neared the stall the horse whinnied with passion. Taya stroked Nightfury as she looked under his head to see what type of horse Firebane would pull out.

"Yes, yes, we're going out, just settle down now," Firebane spoke softly to the creature inside.

Seconds later, Taya saw a beautiful bluish-gray mare stride meekly out of the stall with Firebane in tow. From her angle, Taya marveled at the colors that this horse's coat displayed. In one light, the aspects of gray and an almost silver hue would show through, and in the shadows, the coat took on a bluish sheen. The mane was pure white; there was no mistaking that.

Taya had to blink her elf eyes twice when Firebane brought her up next to Nightfury. As the mare turned sideways, Taya saw a definition of a wing slope over the side of the horse, that wasn't apparent from the other side. Taya moved around Nightfury and got a closer look at the specimen that Firebane had brought over.

A snort and pawing at the ground seemed to indicate that the newcomer was as much interested in getting acquainted with Taya as she was to it.

"Is that really a . . ."

"Wing?" Firebane interrupted, "yes."

"Does that mean she's a . . ."

"Pegasus?" Firebane again interrupted, "I'm not exactly sure. Angel Dance came to us a few years ago as a young foal. A farmer had come by her trying to acquire several steeds to help out on his farm. One sight of the wing indicated that a yoke and harness would not be very fitting for this creature, so he brought it by here to see if we could find it a home."

Taya half listened to the story as she stroked this strange creature.

"I fell in love with her the minute I laid eyes on her, and couldn't bare to give her away, knowing she'd either be destroyed or paraded around as a freak of nature." He paused and stroked the bluish-gray neck. "I managed to break her just recently, so she's a bit on the wild side, but she sure is a kick to ride."

"Can she fly at all?" Taya had to ask the obvious question.

Firebane shook his head, "No, at least not that I've seen. She can jump better than a typical horse. She will extend that wing and push off with it. It seems to give her a little bit of lift, but I've never been on her when she did it." He reached up and scratched her big nose and then bent down to pick up the special saddle he'd made and began to put it on her.

Angel Dance threw her head back and complained lightly.

"This is the part she doesn't like," Firebane said. "Once we get the saddle on her, she seems to settle down."

Guntharr came up behind Taya and put his hand on her shoulder. "We need to get loaded up and get on the road as soon as we can."

"Have you decided on our next move?" Firebane asked.

"I believe so, but we're going to need a few more things," he replied.

Taya turned and looked at him puzzled. "Like what? We have food and horses now, what else do we need?"

"Information, mostly." Guntharr scanned the elf's body and tried to size her up. "And some kind of armor for you. I was content with the gear you have as long as I knew we weren't intending to go into battle, but given the situation as it is now, I know you're going to need all of the protection we can get for you."

"But, I've never worn real armor before. How will I be able to move if I have that heavy stuff on?" She asked concerned.

"That is something to consider, Guntharr," Firebane added.

He nodded, "I have. I know just the armor-smith to help us out. Unfortunately, it's going to take us a couple of days journey off our direction, but I think it will be well worth it." He reached down and grabbed a pair of stuffed saddlebags and slung them over Nightfury. "Taya, your bags are over by the door, please load them up on Silverfoot. The sooner we can get out of here the better I'll feel."

Taya responded, went over to the door and picked up the bags that she had nearly fallen over after dodging the saddle that Firebane used on Angel Dance. They were full of stuff and it was all she could do to lift the bags onto the horse. Silverfoot didn't seem to mind, and just looked back at her as if to make sure she hadn't hurt herself when throwing them over her back.

"This is your last chance," Guntharr called out to Firebane as he placed one foot in the stirrup and threw his other leg over the saddle.

Following suit, Firebane mounted Angel Dance who shook her head and pawed again at the ground, ready to go. "It is the right thing to do. Any help that I can provide to you and her, I gladly give it."

Guntharr guided Nightfury up to the door. He paused to watch his ward mount the horse. "Is everything secure?" He asked.

"Yes, Guardian," came her automatic response.

"Satisfactory, let's be off then," he commanded.

The trio guided their mounts across the pasture and through the narrow gate at the end of the church wall. Standing in a line, the elders stood somberly at the front of the church in a silent send-off to the adventurers.

Taya waved at them frantically as they plodded by.

That was nearly four hours ago. Taya hadn't said much as Guntharr and Firebane led the way and she and Rift followed behind.

Rift was trotting alongside Silverfoot in his rugged old dog form, but he managed to keep up. However, Taya couldn't help but notice that the wolf's tongue was hanging out to one side.

"I'm really glad you decided to come along, Rift," she called down to him.

"Are you kidding?" he spoke in huffs. "And miss all of this excitement and the chance to run for miles and miles without knowing where in the world we're headed. I dream of days like this."

Taya had to think about that last part to be sure he was joking.

"Everyone ready for a break?" Firebane called back to the two.

Taya looked up ahead, and she saw a small friendly stream running across the path. The source of the stream seemed to wind upwards up the mountain that they had been circling. "You bet!" she shouted ahead.

"If we must," Rift wheezed.

Firebane and Guntharr guided their mounts off the path and over to a flat grassy area adjacent to the stream. After dismounting Silverfoot, Nightfury and Angel Dance they walked over to the edge of the stream to drink, where Rift was already stomach deep in the stream cooling off.

Guntharr walked over to the stream and splashed some cool, refreshing water onto his face. He scanned the area intently before walking over to Nightfury to grab something out of one of the pouches.

"At this rate, we should reach the border of the Iron Realm by midday tomorrow, I think," he reported.

Taya stretched by reaching her hands up to touch the clouds and then again by touching the ground between her leather-booted feet. "Where are we going, guardian?"

"Well, the plan is to make our way back to the Silverwood."

"But, isn't that near Fairhaven?" she asked.

"Yes," he replied.

"I don't remember coming this way."

Guntharr nodded, "Your memory is as excellent as ever. We didn't come this way."

Taya stood with a confused look on her face.

"Call in Raskin, I need to know how many assassins are following us." Guntharr eyed the strip of dried meat that he'd just pulled out of the bag that Firebane had prepared back at the church. He sniffed the dark meat and studied the aroma for several seconds.

Taya turned and walked over to Silverfoot to see how the horse was doing before she started her call.

"Bruburn?" he asked Firebane.

"Quite correct," Firebane smiled back. "I see you still have your keen nose for meat. Now, what seasoning did I use before I dried it?"

Guntharr closed his eyes and imagined the slices of thick Bruburn slowly roasting in an oven. "I smell Fangberry leaf and just a touch of casper salt?"

Firebane stood back for a moment, his eyes wide open and mouth half hanging down. "The Fangberry leaf was easy, but how did you know about the casper salt."

Guntharr wiggled a finger at Firebane, "You forgot, friend Firebane, I spent a summer as a boy with my grandfather who lived downwind of the casper salt marshes. Once you spend time around the marshes, the smell of that incredible salt is hard to forget."

Taya walked away from the crew and searched through the trees and sky to see if there were any signs of her airborne friend. After no immediate sign of Raskin showed itself, she began calling out in her musical voice. The sound caused the normal sounds of the world to fade into the background for just a moment, and her voice was the only thing that could be heard.

After several seconds, she again scanned her surroundings, but saw and heard nothing that indicated that Raskin was on his way. She took in a deep breath in order to start another call, but a large familiar hand on her shoulder made her catch her breath.

"If he's anywhere near us, he heard you. Best not to make our position any more apparent than it already is," Guntharr reassured.

"I'm worried, he normally shows up before I finish or immediately after," she said, with a hint of worry crossing her face.

He patted her shoulder, "Come on," he said. "Firebane found some wild dewberries over by the stream that are ripe. They're absolutely perfect."

Taya loved all kinds of berries, although she didn't remember ever trying dewberries, but if Guntharr liked them, then they must be something she had to try.

They walked over to the horses who were busy swatting insects out of each other eyes with their respective tails, and Firebane stood there with a hand full of long slender orange objects. They were about as long as one of Taya's fingers and the color was that of the sun.

"Do you like dewberries?" Firebane asked.

"I like all kinds of berries," Taya replied reaching out to take one of the orange berries.

"Have you ever had a dewberry before?" Firebane asked as she took the berry and placed it into her mouth.

"No," as she bit down.

Firebane's eyes opened as he smiled and Guntharr turned away from Taya, holding his hand over his mouth surpressing a laugh.

"You two are so cruel," Rift said, standing between Guntharr and Firebane.

Taya's eyes opened wide as the burning sensation started from her lips, and her whole mouth exploded with a burning feeling. As she instinctively swallowed, the burning then coursed its way down her throat and into her stomach. Turning and diving for the stream, she sunk her face into the cool water and began swallowing large gulps of water.

Firebane leaned over to Guntharr, "You didn't tell her about them?"

"No," Guntharr coughed, trying not to laugh, "I didn't think she would just go and take a whole mouthful like that."

Taya raised up out of the water; her face, hair and upper tunic soaking wet. Her eyes narrowed at the sight of Firebane and Guntharr sharing a laugh and she began marching over.

"That's my cue to go look for a bone somewhere," Rift spoke as he turned and moved away.

Guntharr, seeing his ward charging up to them, held up his hand with a stern serious expression. "Wait for it."

Taya's glare turned to a puzzled look and then a pleasant smile took the place of the frown that had been there just moments ago.

"If you hadn't rushed the bite, I would have told you that you should take a small taste and hold it on the front of your tongue till the berry had passed the hot phase and became sweet." Guntharr reached out and took the remaining half of the berry from her and bit off a small portion and held it in the front of his mouth.

Taya could see the color in his cheeks rise as she knew the initial heat phase of the berry was exploding in his mouth. As quickly as it had come it was gone and Guntharr was expressing what Taya had seldom seen, and that was a real smile.

He handed the remaining morsel over to her and she stared down at it for a moment.

"Go ahead and try it again," Firebane said.

Taya placed the bite in her mouth and closed her eyes, dreading the fiery explosion in her mouth which lasted for just a few seconds and then was quickly replaced by a tremendously sweet flavor.

"That was just plan mean," Taya finally said after enjoying the last seconds of the sweet dewberry.

"Come," Guntharr waved her over to the edge of the stream where the dewberry bush was, "let's stock up and then get back on the road."

The two loaded up a spare sack with the hot, sweet berries and started to mount their rides.

"Guardian," Taya called out, "I just remembered, Raskin hasn't shown up."

Guntharr paused mounting Nightfury and scanned the area for signs of the hawk. Listening carefully, he determined there was nothing worth waiting around for, so he stepped into the stirrup and pulled himself over the saddle.

"We need to push on," he commanded. "Raskin will find us."

Taya reluctantly climbed up on Silverfoot and whispered to herself a prayer to Guntharr's God for Raskin's protection.

Angel Dance and Rift took off across the stream and headed on up the path. Guntharr pranced around on Nightfury, and waited for Taya to get settled into her seat and then guide Silverfoot across the stream. Once across, the two urged their steeds into a gallop to catch up.

The four traveled on for several more hours and the daylight began to fade. The terrain had grown more dense as the trees grew closer and larger. The horses had since slowed to a walk, and Rift had disappeared on up ahead after having a conversation with Firebane.

Taya's ears perked up when the sound of a wolf howling caught her attention. "Guardian, that's Rift. Is he okay?" She asked, very worried.

He shook his head. "Yes, he's just found us a clearing off of the path where we can rest for the night."

The three steered themselves off of the main path and into the thick growth. The light that had been getting dimmer was now almost gone in the dense covering of trees.

Several hundred feet they traveled away from the path and finally worked their way into a clearing where the tree canopy opened up to the sky and allowed the remaining light to shine down.

"Excellent spot," Firebane called out to Rift.

Taya looked around and spotted the battle wolf sniffing around the area. To her surprise, he had not changed into the large powerful version of himself, like the last time she heard him howl.

"Why didn't he change?" She asked Guntharr.

"Because he didn't need to," he replied. "You'll learn that the One True God doesn't extend his power to be used carelessly or haphazardly. He expects us to use it only when we need it. He wants us to rely on him always, but sometimes miracles come in the form of everyday things."

Taya nodded in understanding.

"I've smelled around," Rift began, "and I haven't noticed the scent of anything foul."

"Good," Firebane replied.

"Although, if you are hungry for some yummy boar, there was a wild one that crossed through here just as I got here." He tilted his head in the direction that led away from the direction they rode in.

"Taya, want to hunt a boar?" Guntharr asked knowing what she would say.

Taya, still atop Silverfoot, scanned the tree line in the direction that Rift had nodded.

"He's just inside the trees," she said as she carefully pulled her bow off of her back.

"She can't make a shot from there," Rift called up to Guntharr.

"A silver says she can," Guntharr wagered.

"You're on," Rift agreed. "You want in on the action?" He asked Firebane.

He shook his head, "I better not, it wouldn't look good for a person of my stature to be caught gambling."

Rift snorted and Guntharr closed his eyes in disbelief. Taya had pulled out an arrow and knocked it onto the string. She leaned over and whispered something into the horses ear and it nodded in agreement.

With one hand on the bow and arrow, Taya took her free hand and balanced herself on the saddle as she pulled her feet up and slowly stood up on Silverfoot's back. Silverfoot stood perfectly still and Taya focused her eyes into the edge of the woods. The boar was munching away at some berries, oblivious to any threat.

Drawing back on the string, she stood with perfect balance staring down the end of her arrow onto her target.

"Anytime now," Rift barked.

Taya looked down for a moment at the scraggly old wolf and gave him a brief wink before releasing the arrow.

A loud squeal could be heard coming from the edge of the woods.

"Sounds like meat's on the menu for tonight," Firebane said.

Rift strolled over to Firebane and leaned up next to him. "I don't suppose you could spot me a silver?"

Firebane responded with a smile and a nod.

Rift turned and faced Guntharr, "You probably want me to run into the woods and drag the carcass back here, don't you?"

"You and Firebane get the fire started and I'll go track down our dinner," Guntharr ran off in the direction of the boar.

Rather than climb down off of Silverfoot, Taya waved Rift aside and dove head first straight at the ground, performing a forward flip in mid fall and landing squarely on her feet looking right into Rift's dark eyes.

"Show off," Rift whispered as he turned to go find some sticks.

Guntharr jogged across the clearing till he reached the edge where the woods resumed control of the landscape. He slowed his pace as he crossed through the brush and spotted a blood spatter that must have been where the boar was standing when the arrow struck. He knelt down and studied the pattern in the dim light, and noted the direction that the creature had run after being struck.

Judging from the amount of blood on the ground, Guntharr figured that the boar couldn't have gotten more than a couple of hundred feet away. It depended on the actual size of the animal. Since he hadn't seen it, he could only guess. Standing up, he began to pick his way through the woods taking care to keep a keen eye on the fresh trail.

Two hundred feet had passed, and Guntharr could no longer see the clearing where the rest of his group had set up camp, and there was no sign of the boar. The trail continued on down into a ravine. Based upon some of the smashed foliage, it looked as if the boar may have tripped and rolled down the slope. By the width of the crushed grass, this was a fairly mature animal of good size.

Guntharr navigated his way down the sloping trail, half sliding and half hopping from foothold to foothold. The ravine wasn't straight down, but it was rather steep and the ground was slick in spots.

As he neared the base of the of the ravine, he could see the mangled boar lying on its side with a broken arrow shaft sticking out of his midsection. Two more hops and he was at the bottom looking over a fine kill. He bent down to make sure that the boar was dead so as not to prolong the creature's misery, and he noticed that it no longer tried to breathe. The long tumble down must have finished it off.

"I guess we won't be reusing that arrow," Guntharr said to himself as he examined the broken shaft.

For a moment, he reflected on how proud he was of Taya and her abilities. She had been a great student and tried to absorb as much as Guntharr could give her. She was everything that he could ask for in a ward, and it made him think of the daughter he would never have. But she was it. She had been brought into his life to fill that desire. This he was sure of.

As he wrapped his hands around the boar's large shoulder, a snapping sound came from somewhere behind him and caused him to pause for just a moment. As he turned to see what it was, the last thing he remembered was seeing a large rock coming at his face.

Chapter 9

Firebane and Rift gathered up a nice stack of dead wood and brush, then started a nice fire. Taya, at Rift's request, put out a bowl with some water in it since there weren't any pools or streams nearby for him to drink from.

"So where did you learn to shoot like that," Rift asked her in between drinks.

She shrugged and sat down cross legged beside the wolf. "Guntharr has taught me almost everything I know," she said as she stroked his wirey fur.

Rift sat on his haunches which made him almost eye level with her. "You mean he told you how to stand up on the saddle and take a shot like that?"

She laughed and smiled, "No, not exactly. I was just showing off. Balance seems to come naturally to me."

"As it should," Firebane said as he came near and joined them. "You come from a very special line of elves. If a normal elf has the agility of a fox, you have ten times that much ability."

"Please, Firebane," Rift groaned, "don't encourage her, she's liable to do something dangerous."

"Thank you," she said as her pale checks turned red.

"Guntharr should be back by now," Firebane looked around. "Even stopping to field dress the boar first, he should have been back by now. You're sure you hit the boar and didn't just scare it."

Taya looked up at him, "Oh I'm sure," she replied with confidence. "Do you think something's happened?"

"I'm not sure, but we probably should go find out." Firebane stood up and looked down at Rift. "I'm probably going to need your help, Rift."

Rift laid down, "I'm a wolf not a blood hound."

"Come on," Firebane ordered. "You stay with the horses," Firebane said to Taya.

Rift stood up and looked over at the elf girl. "I don't think that's a good idea, if there's something out there, she's going to be safer with us."

Firebane considered it for a second and nodded in agreement. He picked up his staff and then the three of them headed off in the direction that they had seen Guntharr run off to over an hour earlier.

At full speed, it took them less than a minute to cross the darkening clearing. At the edge of the wood, the light was almost completely gone.

"Sorry guys," Firebane said, "but unlike you, I need light in order to poke around in the dark."

Reaching back into the pouch he had strapped to his belt, he grabbed a headpiece that slipped tightly onto the top of his staff. The jewel that was mounted in the head piece glowed like a small torch. Rays of bright light illuminated the previously dark area.

"Well, it looks like she was right," Rift looked up from a dark spot on the ground. "Here's where the boar took the hit."

Firebane knelt down and studied the blood and noticed some familiar boot prints in the soft ground beside it.

"Which direction did he go from here?" Firebane asked.

"That way," Taya and Rift said in unison pointing in the same general direction.

Firebane studied the two for a moment, then he just shook his head and moved forward into the direction that they had pointed.

Careful to hold his staff out in such a way that the brightest light shown down on the ground, the three followed the trail of blood several hundred feet to the edge of a ravine. Skid marks in the soft ground indicated a clear trail that Guntharr had used to descend into the ravine.

"Be careful. It's a long way down," Firebane instructed.

Rift looked both directions to see if there was a less steep route to the bottom, but he was unable to find such a route. "You two go first," he peered over the edge.

Firebane, his staff in hand, began guiding his way along the slope into the ravine. He used the staff, in its more traditional role as a walking stick, to help keep his footing. Fortunately, the ground was soft enough that he could stab it deep into the ground which gave him a steady support.

Taya's agility made descending the slope into the ravine almost as easy as walking across the flat ground. There was one spot in which a cluster of briars reached out and grabbed the corner of her boot and tore into her skin slightly. This disrupted her concentration and she almost went tumbling forward, but she recovered by grabbing hold of a young sapling. Reviewing her progress, she decided to glance back up the slope to see how Rift was doing. Being lower to the ground and on four legs, made the going even more tricky.

He started out trying to skid his way down similar to what Firebane was doing, but this almost caused him to tumble and go into a roll. He immediately dropped to his belly to keep himself from moving any further.

"You can do it!" Taya called up to Rift trying to encourage him.

I'm not a mountain sheep, he thought to himself. He decided to take a different approach. He stood up in a semi-crouching position still keeping low to the ground. He started out by taking small steps forward. The problem with this was his backend wanted to go past his frontend so he had to pick up the pace. Before long, Rift caught himself running uncontrollably down the hill.

"Help!" he called out as he flew past Taya.

She watched as the wolf picked up speed and then tried with all his might to dig his paws into the ground. He slid for several feet and then the inevitable happened. He flipped end over end and descended the remaining several feet rolling like a log. He bounced off a few small saplings and managed to recoche off Firebane's leg.

Trying desperately to regain his footing, he went crashing through a patch of briars similar to what had almost tripped Taya.

With a final thud, Rift finally hit bottom. Several seconds passed before he tried to lift his head. Slowly, he looked around trying figure out which way was up. Firebane reached the bottom and looked down at the dizzy wolf. He then bent down to rub the spot where Rift had slammed into the side of his leg.

"Well, that's one way of getting down," Firebane chuckled.

Taya, having skidded the last few feet down, stood silent for a few seconds. As Rift was struggling to get to his feet she asked, "Are you okay?"

"Sure, kid," he replied, taking a few wobbly steps to try and convince them.

"Over here," Firebane pointed with his staff at a patch of blood.

Taya followed him over and bent down to look closely at the scene. "He was here," she replied and held up a fragment of the arrow shaft that still lay on the ground. "The grass is flattened out here. Do you think he fell down like Rift?"

"I heard that," Rift staggered up to them. "I did not fall."

Firebane looked over at Rift with a questioning look. "You don't call what you did back there falling?"

Rift shook his head in part to say no and in part to try and get the world to settle down just a little bit more. "No, that was a controlled roll," he responded.

Rift stepped around to survey the area where the boar and possibly Guntharr had been. "He was definitely here, but you're not going to like what I think I just found." He put a paw just outside the circle of light shining from Firebane's staff.

"What is it?" Taya was getting worried.

"More blood, and this time it's not the boars," Rift reported.

"Guntharr's?" Firebane asked.

"I think so," Rift nodded. "I'm not a blood hound, but I can tell the difference between boar blood and human blood, and that's definitely not the same as that," he shifted his head in the direction of the boar's blood.

"He must have been attacked while he was checking out the kill," Firebane looked around.

"We've got to find him," Taya said frantically.

Firebane put a hand on her shoulder, "we will." He held his staff high and scanned the surrounding ground for any signs of direction which they may have taken him.

There appeared to be impressions heading out from this point in all directions except for up the slope. "I wish our roles were reversed," Firebane sighed.

"Why?" Taya asked.

"I'm not the tracker," Firebane began, "Guntharr is a much better tracker than I."

Taya's eyes grew wide, "the guardian has taught me a lot about tracking."

"Indeed," Firebane smiled. "Maybe you can figure out which one of these tracks is the real deal. Otherwise, we could waste a lot of time following tracks that lead to dead ends."

Taya got busy and closely examined the different tracks. Rift followed her around and sniffed at the various imprints in the ground but wasn't coming up with anything conclusive. Firebane stood back and tried to keep the light high enough so that she could see the ground clearly.

After she bounced between two sets of tracks, she stood and pointed in a direction that ran along the base of the ravine. "He went that way."

"How can you be sure?" Rift asked.

"The tracks are deeper." She responded.

"And if they were carrying him, the extra weight would have caused the impressions to be deeper in the ground," Firebane reasoned, "good work!"

The three carefully headed out to try and track down where their friend had been taken. Rift sniffed the impressions and picked up enough of a scent that he felt he could help keep them on track.

* * *

Guntharr slowly opened his eyes. He was greeted with the soft yellow glow of torches and the smell of fire floating down a rocky cavern wall. A sharp pain shot through his head as he struggled to recall where he was and what had just happened. The sound of laughter and discussion echoed down the corridor, but he struggled to discern what was being said as his thoughts still swirled around in a dense fog.

Attempting to move, he realized that his arms where lofted above and behind his head and were somehow fastened to something. The fog in his mind slowly began to clear and he remembered getting struck very hard in the head, but what had he been doing? Oh, yes, he was fetching dinner. The realization that he was missing Taya, Firebane and Rift now caused him to strain against the rope that had his hands fastened tightly overhead to the wall.

"So you are alive," a soft, weak voice drifted from a dark corner of the cavern.

"Who said that?" Guntharr called out softly.

The rattling of chains and a slender shadow appeared in one corner of the room. As the shadow and the chains drew closer it began to take shape, and the outline of a woman appeared. She was wearing a tattered studded leather tunic and black knee-high pants. Her hair was long, dark and matted from weeks of no attention.

"My name is Arnethia," the woman replied. A snapping of chains caused her to jerk to a stop.

At the same moment, a searing pain shot across Guntharr's head causing him to wince. "Ahhh," he groaned.

Arnethia turned to look down the tunnel to see that no one was coming this way. "They hit you pretty hard," she reported.

"Yeah, I figured that," he replied as he took in several deep breaths to try and control the pain.

"Manni thought they had killed you," she added.

"Judging from the throbbing in the side of my head and the taste of dried blood on my lips, I'd say they came pretty close." Guntharr tried pulling against the rope, but he gave up as the strain caused his head to ache.

"Why are you here?" She asked as she leaned against a rock.

"I was hoping you could tell me," he replied. "I was out chasing down my dinner when the next thing I know I'm waking up here in this dungeon.."

"It's a cave," Arnethia corrected him.

"Very well, this cave," Guntharr said correcting himself.

"So, you are not from Falcon Roost?" she asked.

"No, not even close," he replied. "I'm a guardian from Fairhaven."

Even in the darkness Guntharr could see Arnethia's expression change at this revelation. She looked again down the tunnel to make sure there was no reaction coming from the group that was at the other end.

"You're a guardian?" she asked.

"I am," he replied.

"Whatever you do, if you want to stay alive, don't tell them that. They'll kill you without a second thought," she warned.

"Understood," he tried to nod but the throbbing increased when he tried to move his head. "Who are they?"

"You really not from around here, are you?" She chided. "They are the Kimmels. A family of cut throats and thieves that have made their name terrorizing the people of Falcon Roost and . . ."

Arnethia stopped suddenly. She took in a deep breath and slowly lowered her head. Guntharr studied the sudden pause. He guessed that she was doing her best to hold back a sob. One of her hands reached up and wiped away something off of the side of her face.

"And they took you from your family," Guntharr added.

"No. They murdered my family," she responded in a whisper.

"I am very sorry," he replied. "That is a difficult burden to carry."

She looked up from her hands, "How would you know?" She asked with indignity.

"I know," he said softly trying to reassure her. "I too carry burdens such as yours."

The noise from the end of the tunnel began growing louder and the light grew brighter. As it did, the form that was Arnethia grew more defined. She was understandably quite disheveled being imprisoned in this cave for who knows how long, but yet she radiated a beauty that Guntharr hadn't observed in some time. He only hoped that they would be able make it out of there alive.

On the other side of the tiny cavern Guntharr could now see his war hammer and other gear including his dagger and the pouch that he carried around. It had been turned upside down and the few silver coins that Guntharr kept in there were obviously missing.

"So, you did live," a smooth voice called out.

Guntharr turned to look at the new arrivals. The brilliant glow of the torch caused him to squint his eyes, and the pounding in his head increased.

Three sturdy looking men entered the cavern prison and sized up Guntharr. The one that had spoken to Guntharr was also the tallest. He appeared to be middle aged with sandy brown hair with just a touch of gray highlighting his temples. He was not fat, but he was clearly not as toned as his two associates. The man standing next to him who was only just slightly shorter, was much leaner and stronger than either of the two beside him. He was clearly younger, too as his brown hair nearly matched in hue that of the taller man, but without the gray highlights. Guntharr judged that he was probably half his own age and probably as strong. The last of the group was shorter than either of the others. He had dark black hair and a sizable scar on the left side of his face that extended from just below his eye down to his jaw. He was thin and scrawny, but Guntharr detected a hidden agility that he should be concerned about.

"It looks like you're right, Vandor," the sandy haired man said to the younger man next to him.

Vandor nodded his head, "I told you, Manni, I didn't think I hit him hard enough to kill him."

So now Guntharr knew who tried to take his head off with a rock. He'd have to make sure that if the opportunity arose, that he would repay in kind.

"Has he said anything?" The man with the scar directed his question to Arnethia.

Realizing that her proximity to him clearly indicated that she had been engaged in some way with Guntharr, she decided to downplay the situation. "He's muttered something about chasing down his dinner."

"Ah, yes, that fine kill that we're just now getting ready to enjoy. You should smell that succulent meat roasting," Manni chided.

Guntharr's eyes had finally started to get use to the new level of light in the cavern and just glared at his captors.

The man with the scar walked over to stand right next to Guntharr and looked up into his face. "Strong, silent type, huh?" He then proceeded to punch Guntharr in the stomach. Guntharr saw the punch coming and tightened his muscles as the blow landed. The man's fist nearly shattered on the impact and he withdrew his hand with a yelp.

Vandor chuckled at his companion's surprise and pain.

"Really, Klaffin?" Manni scolded his associate. "Is that any way to treat our guest? I must apologize for my Klaffin. He sometimes gets a little carried away when he runs into somebody that has the potential to be a valuable asset to our . . ." Manni pondered his next word for a second, "mission."

"I see," Guntharr replied. "I hope your hand isn't too badly damaged."

Vandor roared out load at the platitude Guntharr made to his companion.

"Very funny," Klaffin responded still shaking his hand.

Manni walked around and picked up the war hammer expertly and continued on over to Guntharr smacking the head of the hammer into the palm of his free hand. He stood evenly with Guntharr and looked deep into his eyes.

"It would seem you're pretty tough," Manni said without blinking. "That's nice to know, because I won't feel quite as bad when I do this," and he drove the head of the warhammer into the spot that Klaffin had hit but with more effect.

Guntharr immediately coughed in response and his upper body suspended by the ropes around his hands slumped forward for a second while he regained his breath. Arnethia winced in reaction from the sight of the impact.

"See," Manni looked over at Klaffin, "we now know that he is susceptible to certain arguments."

Guntharr now tried to determine which hurt worse, his head or his stomach. Deciding that they would both have to fight it out amongst themselves, he took in a deep breath. "What is it you hope to do with me?"

"Oh, so now you're ready to have a conversation?" Manni turned and heaved the war hammer over to Vandor. He stepped away from Guntharr and over toward Arnethia. She instinctively slunk away from him but was unable to move farther when he reached out and grabbed her arm. He reached up and began to stroke Arnethia's unkempt hair in fain tenderness.

Guntharr felt a swell of anger build up in his soul, unexpectedly, which both shocked and concerned him.

Manni turned to face Guntharr and Vandor had taken up position next to Guntharr ready to use the war hammer again at Manni's signal.

"You see, I like to find out as much about you as I can. Things that I can turn into either money or influence." Manni flashed a smile.

"You see, I've found that money can procure influence, and influence produces money. So, they work together to perpetually keep me happy."

"What makes you think your tactics will yield anything?" Guntharr said.

"Oh trust me, I can already tell by your size, and equipment that you're a skilled soldier or mercenary. So, I suppose I could let Vandor beat you to the point of death and I wouldn't so much as get an interesting conversation out of you, let alone anything useful." He walked over to Guntharr again and studied him up and down.

"I see you skewered the boar with a well placed bow shot," Manni looked over at the dagger and pouch that lay against the cave wall. He walked over to the objects and kicked them about with his foot. "I don't see any bow. What did you do with it?"

"It's in my camp," Guntharr replied not wanting to give away the rest of his companions existence.

Manni picked up the dagger and flipped it about in his hand. He nodded approvingly. "Well balanced." He strode back to Guntharr and flashed the blade near Guntharr's face and throat in a threatening fashion, but Guntharr was unimpressed. "I can see why you would carry the dagger to track down the boar, of course, to field dress the animal, but why the hammer?"

"To put the creature out of its misery should my shot not have proven lethal," Guntharr replied matter of factly.

Manni looked over at Vandor who was studying the hammer and enjoying the feel of it in his hands. "Maybe," he added, "but the dagger should have sufficed for that, would it have not?"

Guntharr studied the man's face. He knew no argument would convince him otherwise, so he simply remained silent.

"You know, it's fortunate that I don't have to rely on typical tactics to get the truth from you," he smiled.

"That's too bad," Guntharr smiled back, "I was starting to look forward to it, because this conversation is much more painful."

Manni's smile turned to a glare. "Vandor, hit his leg."

Vandor wasted no time and swung around with Guntharr's warhammer and slammed it hard into his shin, smashing it against the rock wall. The bone in Guntharr's leg shattered and the pain ravaged his body. Crying out for a moment he struggled to regain control

"I said I didn't have to rely on those tactics, I didn't say I wouldn't use them for my own purposes." He turned and walked over to Arnethia with the dagger extended from his hand.

"What are you going to do to her?" Guntharr spat his words out through clinched teeth. His right leg was now crippled, he did his best to balance his weight on his left and steady himself by using his arms and the ropes overhead.

He turned back amazed that Guntharr was able to control the pain enough to get any words out. "Don't worry, I won't hurt my precious Arnethia. Her skills are too valuable to me."

"I won't," she barked at him and stepped back from the dagger.

"Really?" Manni looked shocked. He saw the compassion in her eyes for Guntharr's plight. "My dear, either you take this dagger or I have Vandor take a crack at his other leg."

Arnethia's face filled with fear. She couldn't bear to see this courageous soldier tortured any more, so she reached out and took the dagger from Manni.

"Now tell me, is he alone?" he commanded.

She bowed her head and closed her eyes. The dagger sandwiched between the palms of her hands. Several seconds past and she began to twitch and shake, then she opened her eyes. "He is not alone," she replied.

"How many are with him?" Manni prodded.

She looked over at Guntharr who was struggling to keep himself upright. Sweat was pouring down his face and pain filled his eyes.

"There are three others," she confessed.

Manni turned to face Guntharr, "You see, my tactics prove to be very effective indeed."

"What's our next move?" Klaffin called out.

Manni looked from Vandor to Klaffin, "Round up the others, let's go find them and see what other treasures await."

Even in his pain, Guntharr felt anger and power surged through his body. In a vain attempt, he pulled with all of his might against the ropes that held his hands above his head. The muscles in his arms strained and convulsed, the ropes dug into his wrists adding to the already immense pain he was in. Manni, Klaffin and Vandor watch in awe as the wounded captive exherted such heroic force against the immovable rock that he was fastened too. With a cry laced with frustration more than pain, he yielded to the ropes. Taking in a deep breath, he lowered his head and tried to quiet the fury that was raging inside him. Then, in the distance, he heard the welcome sound of a familiar wolf howl.

Chapter 10

When Rift finished his transformation he stood nearly as tall as Taya's horse, Silverfoot, except with claws like daggers and a fur coat as strong as chainmail.

Taya was positioned high up in a tree behind Rift and Firebane. They were standing opposite each other behind a large pile of dead trees staring toward the entrance to a cave in the side of the valley wall. They had been searching for Guntharr for over two hours when they traced his scent to this well hidden corner of the valley.

The trail had been easy to follow for both Rift and Taya until they came upon a small stream that ran through the center of the valley. Evidently the captors were not stupid enough to go straight across. The best that Taya could tell, they had traveled upstream for several hundred feet before exiting the stream on the same side and hiking even further upstream before attempting to cross.

As it was Rift scouted the far side of the stream for traces of anything, and Taya and Firebane stayed on the near side until the scent was recovered. They caught a break when they came across the trail upstream, because once the target had made his way across, he was immediately joined by several others. Apparently, the kidnappers expected whoever might be tracking them to have given up by now, or else decided that the odds anyone would track them this far were low enough. In any case, the trio made their way through some very dense undergrowth.

This made tracking a little more difficult as multiple paths began to crisscross, but the assurance that they were nearing the home base was encouraging.

The next sign that indicated they were closing in was the appearance of a guard who was standing watch over a small clearing near the steep slope of the ravine wall. While not surprised by his appearance, the fact that his three dogs immediately picked up their scent and alerted him to their presence forced their hand.

Firebane had directed Taya to dispatch the guard, which she did effortlessly. This had the unfortunate effect of the guard releasing the dogs who were already growling and yipping uncontrollably. The guard dogs charged into the woods toward them.

Rift stepped out into the open drawing the attention away from Firebane and Taya. The young dogs instantly surrounded him and growled viscously.

Firebane took advantage of the distraction and tossed Taya up into the tree. He then darted behind a large dead tree and readied his sword.

Rift twisted his head side to side as the three dogs circled their prey, waiting for the opportune moment for the kill.

"Come on, which one of you is going to be first," Rift said still in his old weak form.

The three dogs continued their dance around Rift until finally a tall black hound faced Rift straight on.

"Ooouuu!" howled the black hound preparing for the kill.

"Oh, that's not bad," Rift chided, "for a pup. Now my turn." That's when Rift dug his paws deep into the soil and arched his back. Lifting his head high, he began howling his transformation prayer.

Taya remembered hearing that for the first time back at the church, and the sound here even in the open spaces still seemed to echo and shake the forest around them. She looked down from her vantage point and saw the three guard dogs back up slowly as the battle wolf morphed and grew into a creature more than three times his original size.

"Come and get me," Rift's now massive voice taunted the now tiny dogs around him.

The lead dog in front of Rift decided that he still had the advantage at three to one and snarled and charged straight at the battle wolf with its mouth open wide ready to take a bite right out of Rift's neck. But he never quite made it that far, for Rift simply swatted the dog away as a mature dog would a playful puppy. The black dog sailed through the air and slammed into the side of a tree with a thud. He let out a whimper and collapsed on the ground.

The two remaining dogs wasted no time and lunged at Rift's front shoulders simultaneously from both sides and sunk their teeth into his iron-like fur. While more annoyed than hurt, Rift growled in response and began to shake like a dog that had just gotten wet. The dog on the left side did not have nearly as good a hold as it needed and went hurtling through the air, landing directly in front of Firebane. Firebane reacted by striking the dazed pooch on the head with his staff, rendering it unconscious.

The remaining dog held on for dear life, his teeth tearing through Rift's fur and his paws searching desperately for something solid that it could brace against. Rift dropped to his left side and rolled twisting his head around and grabbing the attached dog with his own giant maw.

With a snap of his massive head, Rift tore the dog free from his shoulder and slammed him down on the ground with a smack.

Rift jumped back up on all fours and studied the last dog as it struggled back to its feet determined not to give up. After regaining its bearing, it charged toward Rift in a vicious assault. With a similar motion as the first, Rift batted the dazed dog with his paw and sent him sailing into a tree. This time, there was a sharp cracking sound as the last dog's spine was snapped in two. It slid to the ground, lifeless.

Rift turned his head and howled a mournful howl. He had not intended to kill any of the dogs as they were only doing as they had been trained. The sound of the howl reverberated throughout the woods and up through the ravine.

"Rift," Firebane called out, "there's nothing you can do about it except exact justice on the people that trained them to this life."

Rift slowly made his way back behind a fallen tree. Taya looked down at the massive creature and marveled at the stirring emotion that she had just witnessed.

* * *

Guntharr heard the second howl from Rift and could tell by the tone that something happened that had not been planned. This caused him to panic for a moment, wondering if either Firebane or Taya had been hurt or worse. For a moment, Guntharr's pain was gone as he considered the possibility that something had happened to his ward. Then he considered the situation for a moment. Rift, as battle hardened as he was, wouldn't mourn the death of Taya or Firebane so quickly, not without roars of vengeance first. No, something else has happened; Rift's killed something without intending to.

A new bandit came running into the cavern where Guntharr was being held. "Manni, the dogs. Someone's approaching the hideout."

Manni's head snapped and stared over at Guntharr. "Arm up," Manni said, "looks like our guests have found us. Let's not spare any expense and give them a welcome to die for."

Guntharr pushed down the pain for a moment so that he could get in a breath. "It doesn't have to go this way," Guntharr whispered through his clenched teeth. "Let me and Arnethia go, and no one else has to die."

Manni found this statement amusing and laughed out loud. "No, the only ones dying today will be you and your friends if they try to step one foot into this place." Manni turned to the others, "Come on!" They turned and left to prepare the defenses, and Vandor carried with him Guntharr's war hammer.

Guntharr struggled against the ropes that held him and pushed off the wall with his good leg, arching his back as he pulled. He could feel the muscles in his back and shoulders strain against the bonds, but again to no success. Exhausted, he collapsed as far as the ropes would let him. He no longer tried to remain upright, but slumped forward instead.

Arnethia moved toward Guntharr as far as her chains would allow. "Your friends have come to help?"

Guntharr struggled to lift his head, "More than that, they're family."

She smiled and a tear ran down her face as she thought of having a family again. "You are a very blessed man, to have ones that would risk their lives for you."

"I know," the thought generated a new surge of life in his pain riddled body. "And you will meet them very soon."

"I hope so," she replied softly. "Manni has many men, and they all fight savagely. I fear for your loved ones."

"Do not fear for them," Guntharr's voice grew stronger, "for they have the power of the One True God with them. Instead, pray for Manni, that he will see his error and surrender before they send him and his brood to the grave."

"Manni does not concern himself with such things," she responded. "He instead relies on treachery and minions of the dark."

Guntharr bowed his head, not in defeat or exhaustion this time, but in prayer for his friends.

* * *

Firebane glanced over at Rift who looked as if he were ready to take on an entire Talicron army. He was pacing back and forth and occasionally stopped to study the air. Looking over his shoulder, he saw Taya intently staring down at the two of them from high up in the tree.

"What do you see?" he whispered knowing that her elf ears would easily pick up what he said.

Taya lowered herself down several branches so that she could be closer to the two. "I see four bowmen guarding the entrance to the cave. They're all in black, so they're almost impossible to see. There's a dim light coming from the entrance to the cave and two big burly guys standing at the mouth of the cave. They've clearly been alerted to our presence."

"Indeed," Firebane waved a hand upwards in an effort to direct her back up the tree.

Manni and Vandor stood at the cave entrance scanning the darkness of the trees surrounding the clearing in front of the cave.

"What's your plan?" Vandor inquired, still holding onto Guntharr's hammer.

Manni leaned into him slightly, "We find out how many there are, and lure them out and then crush them."

Vandor was happy with that arrangement. Manni's plans were often very complex and sometimes unnerving, but this one was pretty straightforward.

"Hello," Manni called out to the darkness, "I know you're out there. Why did you attack us?"

Firebane listened to the stranger and considered what had just happened. Could it be that they had provoked the attack by not seeking the truth first? Could they have misinterpreted the situation surrounding Guntharr's disappearance and in fact reacted foolishly? He looked over at Rift.

"I don't like this," Rift directed toward Firebane.

Firebane decided that he would engage in conversation to try and learn more. "A friend has gone missing and we traced him this way. We suspected wrongdoing. Your man with the dogs reinforced our suspicions."

Manni smiled as he now knew there was at least two others here. "I am a very private man and I don't like to be disturbed. I hire men like him to keep people out of my business. Is that a crime?"

Firebane considered his answer, "No, so long as your business doesn't involve kidnapping."

"I assure you it doesn't," Manni lied. "Please, come into the light and we can discuss your missing friend."

Firebane looked over at Rift who was shaking his head back and forth. "What's wrong?" he asked the battle wolf.

"It just doesn't smell right. There's something else, but I can't tell what it is," Rift replied.

"How can we trust you?" Firebane called back.

Manni laughed loud enough so that he was sure that the strangers could hear. "You can't," he added. "You trespass on my privacy, and therefore don't deserve my trust. However," he looked in both directions, "I will have my guards stand down." Manni nodded at the bowmen on either side of him and they all relaxed their stances and returned the arrows to their quivers.

"Firebane, don't trust them," Rift walked over next to them. "I smell something else besides the six of them and us. It's very distinct, but it's nothing I've ever smelled before."

He reached over and laid his hand on Rift's back. "I don't," he nodded, "that's why you're coming out with me."

Rift snarled in disapproval but knew that arguing the point was a waste of time. And time, if Guntharr was hurt or in trouble, was something they didn't have in abundance.

"I've offered a gesture of trust," Manni called out with just a hint of frustration, "now show yourselves."

Rift looked over at Firebane and Firebane looked up into the dark branches overhead searching for Taya's outline. Whispering so that only she could hear, "You stay put. Whatever you do, do not reveal your position. You will know if I need you to do something."

Taya heard Firebane, but was still worried. In response, she made a soft clicking sound like that of a snapping twig.

Firebane heard the sound and figured that Taya was acknowledging his command.

Taya focused hard through the branches and leaves to see everything. The light coming from the cave made it hard for her to decide to use her day or night vision. She decided she wanted the advantage of her night vision since this allowed her to make out the figures even through the foliage. She turned her eyes off to the right for a moment so that they could focus in the dark. As she slowly concentrated on the dark, the last vestiges of light caused a movement to catch the corner of her eye. She focused even harder, but realized that it must have been a trick because she was seeing no residual heat in the direction she was looking.

Firebane and Rift slowly made their way around the dead trees that had acted as their barricade, and stepped forward just enough so that the light streaming out of the cave ahead illuminated their figures.

Manni was clearly surprised at the sight. He had expected to see men, while not specifically Firebane but men in general, but the sight of Rift completely caught him off guard. "That's an amazingly beautiful animal you have with you."

Taya heard this, "Rift will never let us forget that, "she thought.

"Indeed, he has his moments," Firebane tried to be conversational. Out of the corner of his eye, Firebane could see the corner of Rift's long mouth open up in a smile.

Still drawn to the magnificent sight of Rift, he took a step forward away from the cave. Vandor, not wanting to leave his side, matched his step. "What type of creature is that?" Manni couldn't help but ask.

This time Firebane choose to laugh. "Now you're trespassing on matters that don't concern you."

"But surely you could at least tell me where you got it," Manni continued.

Firebane shook his head. "After you help us locate our friend, then we might consider having a social conversation. But now the more important matter is finding out if you or anyone of your men have seen a lone warrior come through here. He would have been wearing a studded leather shirt, high black boots and carrying a large warhammer, much like your associate there." Firebane emphasized this last part by pointing at Vandor who had casually slung Guntharr's warhammer over his shoulder as he glanced back and forth.

Taya shook her head. Firebane purposely pointed out the warhammer. She decided close her eyes and let them use the light again from the cave to study the hammer.

"Was he a tall fellow?" Manni asked.

Firebane nodded, "Yes, he is definitely above average height."

"What say you?" Manni looked to the men on his right.

The two bowmen merely shook their heads.

Manni looked up at Vandor, "And you?"

"No, my lord." Vandor replied with little emotion.

Manni turned to his left. "What about you? Have you seen a tall warrior come past here this evening?"

The two bowmen on his left responded identically to their counterparts on his right.

"There you have it," Manni spread out his arms, "my men have not seen anything that resembles your lost warrior."

Firebane crossed his arms and leaned forward on his staff. "My lord has not answered the question for himself," he asked pointedly.

"Indeed," Manni bowed his head slightly, "I have been all evening inside tending to," he paused for a moment, "my business."

"I see," Firebane looked down at Rift for a sign, but he was sniffing with his eyes half shut. "Well, we should be on our way then. Again, our sincere apology for the," Firebane looked over at the body lying just a few steps away, "little misunderstanding."

"Misunderstanding," Manni tried to sound offended, "sir, you and your beast have just killed an employee of mine. I believe you owe me the courtesy of sitting down and discussing some restitution."

"Beast," Rift said through clenched teeth, "I'll show him a beast."

Firebane reached down and patted the wolf on the head. If these guys were in fact innocent of any direct crime to them, then restitution for an accidental slaying was within reason.

"I'm not going in there except to bite their heads off," Rift muttered.

"Did you say something?" Manni called out.

Firebane looked down at Rift and back up again, "My friend here is getting a bit restless and I was just trying to calm him down. Of course, you are well within your right to ask for restitution."

Taya had tried to identify the hammer but the guard that was standing next to the leader had held it over his shoulder for the last few minutes. As Firebane took another step forward, he brought the weapon around holding it open so that Taya could clearly see it. There were markings on the head. She shouldered her bow which had been at the ready so that she could lean out over to get a closer look.

It was Guntharr's, she was sure of it. They had been lying. What should she do? Firebane was going to walk right into the den with them.

"The hammer is Guntharr's!" Taya cryed out.

Firebane and Rift stopped still. The bowmen immediately reacted and readied their bows. The two on left scanned the tree line behind Firebane and Rift with drawn arrows looking for the source of the voice and the two on the right had beads on them.

"Who said that?" Manni questioned.

"Who said what?" Firebane challenged, knowing that Taya's voice was fully audible and there was no hope of bluffing him.

Taya realized that she may have made a big mistake, but she felt like she had to let them know. This is clearly a trap and it was about to be sprung. From the corner of her eye, again a slight movement was detected. She turned so that one eye could focus but her other stayed on Firebane and Rift. There was something definitely moving out there, but it was too far away to make out.

"I am not a man to be trifled with," Manni spoke sternly. "You have violated my premises, you have violated my good faith, and now you are about to violate my patience. And when that happens . . ." he let his words trail off as he looked both ways at the two sets of bowmen who now trained all four arrows onto Rift and Firebane.

Firebane heaved a sigh and at the same time touched Rift slightly on the ear signaling him to be ready. "Very well," he stated. "I will be honest with you."

"That would be refreshing," Manni sneered.

"I'm very sorry for your loss," and with that Firebane lunged forward in a roll toward the two bowmen on the right.

Rift shot forward, covering half of the clearing in two giant leaps.

"Get them," Manni called out, and immediately fell back to the mouth of the cave.

Because of his quickness, the left side bowmen shot wide of Rift. The bowmen on the right, stunned at the charging priest, fired square on; however, Firebane anticipated the shots and dropped and rolled well under them. He then sprang back up and closed in. One of them stepped back to reload while the other dropped his bow to pull out a short sword holstered on his hip.

Taya reacted like lightning; loading and unleashing an arrow at the far left bowman in a flash. The one near to Rift was partially obstructed by a branch, and so she needed to hop from one limb to another. As she did so, the new limb, which was slightly smaller, bent under her weight, which caused her to delay readying the new arrow.

Rift charged Vandor, who eyed the wolf with excitement. Rift sensed no fear from this one, but was determined that he would know fear very, very soon. As he neared Vandor at full speed, he decided to try a diving attack to knock the large man off his feet. Vandor, feeling confident with his new found weapon, stepped up as the Rift leaped toward him and swung a fierce swing with the warhammer. He connected solidly with Rift's shoulder and sent the wolf hurtling toward the archers on the right, knocking them down in a mess of arms and legs.

Firebane engaged the bowman turned swordsman with his priestly staff. The exchange was a well choreographed dance between the two fighters, and Firebane paid careful attention to keep the swordsman between him and the other bowman who had stepped back to try and get in another shot. Firebane could tell that the swordsman was competent but not a real match for him, so he decided to drive the attack. He pressed forward with blow after blow forcing the swordsman to step back under the barrage of strikes. Closer and closer the two danced their way to the bowman when suddenly, Firebane spun a pirouette around the swordsman and slammed his staff into the side of the startled bowman's head, sending him sprawling unconscious.

"One down," Firebane said as he faced the approaching swordsman.

Rift reeled from the strike. No matter how tough the fur was, a blunt strike like that was felt all across his shoulders. But he had been hit many times before and by better warriors. He rolled to his feet and stood on one of the bowmen with his hind leg. The bowman struggled to get up and Rift was determined to get the one who had just knocked him a good one. With the strength of a horse, Rift dug the nails of his rear foot into the man's chest. He let out a cry as he did so, and Rift kicked with all his might and sent the bowman colliding with a rock upside down. He slid down the side of the rock, his chest torn open from force of Rift's paw.

Taya finally steadied herself in time to see the second bowman climb to his feet and draw back on his bow, almost at point blank range of Rift. Taya aimed quickly and fired, sending an arrow through the man's bow-side shoulder, causing him to drop the bow as he released. The arrow sailed straight into the ground just beneath Rift's furry midsection. In the cave entrance, Taya saw the leader return, holding a mace in one hand and a figurine of some sort in the other. He appeared as if he was speaking to the figurine while he watched the guard carrying Guntharr's hammer circle around to receive Rift's next attack.

Rift circled Vandor, who started swinging the hammer wildly. Rift knew he dared not charge him again and face a second possible strike on his now weak shoulder. He couldn't get up enough of a charge to flash past him and get him from behind, because there was not enough room on either side. His only hope was to time the swing of the hammer and either go under or above it, and hope he connected.

Vandor pressed the attack, sensing Rift's hesitation and general fear of the warhammer. A step forward caused Rift to match that step backwards. He was definitely not wanting to take another hit from the hammer.

"What's the matter, you mangy fur ball?" Vandor taunted. "Scared of a little hammer?"

Rift growled in response. He so much wanted to drive his front feet through Vandor's chest. "You'll think mangy, when I'm standing on your chest with my claws sticking out of your back."

Vandor was caught off guard by the talking creature. Rift took the moment of surprise and made a mad dash at Vandor's weapon hand. Vandor reacted to Rift's sudden attack and took a step back. As he did so, he raised the warhammer up in defensive position.

Firebane's opponent also heard Rift speak and instinctively turned to see where the strange voice came from. This made Firebane's job easy. He stepped forward unleashing a flurry of attacks with his staff. The swordsman frantically parried the succession of blows, trying desperately to maintain a forward stance. Firebane swung up hard, knocking the sword up and away from his opponent, leaving him vulnerable. Without hesitation, Firebane spun around brought up a kick to the swordsman's chest sending him back against the rocks. Spinning again, Firebane brought his staff around and into the guard's dazed head, sending him to the ground unconscious.

Rift's charge took him beside Vandor and with mouth wide open, he bit into the guard's forearm causing him to instantly drop the warhammer. Rift's momentum caused them both to go down, which was exactly what he had hoped for. Rift jerked his head back while standing on Vandor's chest causing his teeth to tear through the muscles in Vandor's arm.

With blood pouring down the man's crippled arm, Rift stared down at him, "Now, about that mangy crack," and Rift began to flex his claws.

Taya saw it coming but couldn't get the words out in time. Manni had come up from behind Rift and swung his mace at Rift's head. "Behind you!" She yelled.

Rift had sensed someone coming up behind him, but Taya's words came too late for him to dodge the blow completely. Fortunately he was able to turn his head enough so that the impact slammed into his side. Unfortunately, it was the same side that had already sustained the blow from the warhammer. The mace also had sharp spikes which tore gashes into his side.

Taya saw Rift fall over, dazed and wounded from the attack. Realizing that she had to do something, she knocked an arrow quickly and let it fly at Manni. Because he was hopping over Vandor to close in for the kill, her shot went wide. Rift lay on the ground, struggling to get up so he could face his new opponent, but his right shoulder wouldn't move.

Manni lifted the mace over his head and swung hard downward for the kill, when Firebane's staff sunk deep into the ground beside Rift's head causing Manni's swing to be deflected into the ground just missing the battle wolf. Manni looked up to see Firebane snap forward with a two-fisted attack. The blow caught Manni just below the neck and sent him backwards, stumbling over Rift. The mace in his one hand slipped out and the figurine flew through the air into the edge of the brush as he tried to catch himself before he hit, half landing on the wolf and half on the ground.

Rift let out a yelp as the bandit's weight pressed down on his injured side. Instinctively, he turned his head and snapped at whatever body part was reachable which happened to be Manni's leg.

Manni reached frantically for the dropped mace when Firebane stepped on his wrist and looked down at him.

"I really don't think you need that," Firebane call out just as Vandor slammed into his side sending them both tumbing across the ground.

Taya hopped down from her perch to come help get the bandit off of Rift, when she felt a strong rumbling in the ground beneath her.

Firebane sprang back up to his feet and pivoted, ready to grapple with the attacking guard, when he too felt the vibrations.

"What was that?" Taya asked as she stepped out of the woods just into the clearing, revealing herself.

Firebane reacted by waving her back into the safety of the trees. "Go back, girl!" he shouted.

She turned to dash back into the trees as instructed, when a large object moving toward them caught her eye. It was more than three times her height and it looked like a big pile of rocks, but it was more than that. She blinked her eyes once then twice because she'd never seen anything like that.

"Crush them!" Manni ordered.

The lumbering pile of rocks didn't exactly have a form, but clearly was held together by some magical force for it managed to move forward by restacking itself in front of where it was.

"What do I do?" She asked Firebane.

"Make for the cave," Firebane replied just as Vandor landed a solid punch into his jaw.

Firebane staggered backwards, refocusing on the problem at hand which was Vandor.

Taya darted across the clearing and narrowly made it across the path of the shambling rocks before it started dropping its heap into a new pile. Manni stretched out his arms and tried to grab the girl as she sped past him. Rift, trying desperately to keep him from reaching her, pushed with his hind legs with all of his might while he held Manni's leg still tight in his mouth and drug them both away from the opening of the cave.

Rift's teeth dug deep into the muscles of Manni's leg and Manni let out a cry as the stress of being drug across the ground increased the damage done by the wolf's razor sharp teeth. He began to kick with his free leg but he was unable to make contact. He then attempted to roll to one side, but Rift just tightened his hold on his leg, causing Manni to submit under the pain.

Firebane noticed Vandor's damaged arm hanging useless at his one side, but Vandor, undeterred, beckoned him to come and get him. A glance to his side showed that the shambling stones would be on them very soon, and subsequently, rain down boulders on both of them. He decided to press his advantage and charged forward with a pattern of punches and kicks that Vandor struggled to avoid completely. Several of Firebane's blows landed and caused his opponent to stagger.

Circling around to press the attack on his weak side, Firebane sidestepped a wild swing and connected with an open handed thrust to Vandor's face, smashing his nose and sending him backwards into the path of the living rock pile which had just completed restacking itself. Vandor steadied himself against a large rock before realizing what it was and stared up as the first rock began unstacking itself and drove him to the ground, crushing him instantly.

Firebane cringed at the sight and realized that the tumbling rocks were headed toward Rift.

Taya turned after seeing the guard get crushed and ran down the tunnel, not sure of what she'd find. She weaved her way through a stretch of various winding passageways until she came to a large central cavern. In the middle of the room was a fire with a boar on a spit. Several make-shift beds lay scattered around, as well as an array of chests and tables.

A quick scan indicated that there were three passages out of the cavern. Knowing she didn't have time to wander up and down all three passages, which themselves could branch out further, she decided to do something dangerous.

"Guardian!" she yelled as loud as her soft voice would allow.

At the end of the passage nearest to her, she faintly heard a reply, "Taya?"

Without responding, she took off with all the speed and agility of a cat in the direction of the voice. Seconds later she came to a tiny, dimly light room at the end of the passage. On one side of the room a woman stood straining against chains that held her from coming any closer.

"Over there," Arnethia directed Taya to an inset on the other side of the room where she saw Guntharr hanging by his hands.

"Guardian," she cried as she rushed over to his side.

Guntharr lifted his pain-filled face, and for a moment, he forgot all about the pain and struggled to smile. "It's good to see you," he whispered hoarsely.

"What happened?" she asked.

"Later," he replied.

"Over here," Arnethia called, "the dagger."

Taya spun around and spotted the dagger that Guntharr always wore and ran across the room toward it.

"He's very lucky to have friends like you," Arnethia whispered.

Taya reached down and picked up the dagger. She stood up and turned to rush back over to the guardian, but stopped a moment then turned to the woman.

"We'll get you out next, once I cut him down." Taya smiled then moved across the room.

Guntharr struggled to stand on his good leg, but the combination of wounds and the position that he'd been in for the last several hours now had caused him to lose a lot of this strength.

Taya climbed up the wall beside Guntharr and hung gracefully by one small toe hold and her free hand, holding tight to the ring of iron that had been pounded into the rock that the ropes were attached to.

She cut feverishly through the ropes wanting desperately to free Guntharr.

"Easy does it," Guntharr started to say as he felt the ropes begin to loosen, and then he fell in a heap on the ground as his weight caused them to give way suddenly.

Taya dropped from the wall and landed beside the guardian, who was face down in the dirt. She frantically lifted up on his shoulder to roll him over. As she lifted his head and shoulders, she could hear a subtle laugh coming from Guntharr.

"Thank you," he gasped, as the movement caused by her lifting him up caused agonizing pain through his shattered leg.

"What did they do to you?" Taya asked, nearly in tears.

"His leg is shattered," Arnethia answered. "Vandor took the war hammer and hit him with it."

"Where are the others?" He asked, ignoring his current state and trying to lift himself upright with his arms, which were still numb from being hung up.

Taya had to think for a second. "Rift is hurt, and Firebane is fighting off the two remaining bandits."

Righting himself slowly, Guntharr managed to roll himself upright completely now, and he lay back carefully against a rock. "Rift," he took a deep breath, "how bad?"

"He took two solid blows to his right shoulder," she looked up at his face. "I think it's broken."

Guntharr nodded in understanding. "Just two bandits left?"

Taya nodded in response, then stopped and shook her head. "Oh, but then out of the woods came a big heap of tumbling rocks."

Guntharr studied her face for a minute, considering if he had really heard what she had just said. "What was that?"

Taya stood up to emphasize her point. "It's a towering pile of large rocks as tall as the ceiling in this room," she pointed up. "It seems to fall and then restack itself."

"It's the mountain shambler," Arnethia added. "It's an elemental creature that can be summoned by anyone who holds the enchanted figurine."

"Is it alive?" Taya asked.

"No, it's just magical pile of rocks that attempts to carry out whatever command it's given," Guntharr injected.

"Taya!" a faint call echoed through the cavern.

"Firebane," Guntharr reacted by trying to stand and immediately fell back.

"I could use your help!" Firebane's voice continued.

"How do we stop it?" Taya asked.

"It will only respond to commands given by the person that activated it," Arnethia said.

"Does the bandit that had the figurine still have it?" Guntharr asked.

"That would be Manni," Arnethia added.

Taya shook her head, "No, it disappeared into the woods when Firebane hit him."

"Go to Firebane," he waved her away. "Quickly, find the figurine and have Manni order it to stop."

Taya didn't hesitate, but took off back through the tunnels to the cave's entrance as quickly as she could.

"Guntharr," Arnethia hesitated at his name, "Manni will die before he orders it to stop."

"Then what option do we have?" Guntharr inquired.

Arnethia shrugged her shoulders, "Destroying the figurine might work."

Guntharr started to call after Taya, but the crashing sound of rock grew louder as the mountain shambler neared the cave entrance. There was only one thing he could do.

Taya reached the entrance of the cave and slid to a halt as she saw, towering just outside the mouth of the cave, a teetering mountain of stones.

"Get back," Firebane yelled as he struggled to pull Rift clear of the path. Manni lay off to the side unconscious or dead.

The shambler wobbled, trying to anticipate Taya's next move. Taya stepped outside the cave mouth as far away from the shambler as she could, then spun around and ran toward the shambler. The shambler reacted to her first motion and began the stacking process where she had first looked like she was going. As stone after heavy stone rained down into a new tower, Taya ducked under the arching rocks as they fell and skirted around to meet up with Firebane and Rift.

"I need you to help me pull him clear of this thing," Firebane instructed.

"Why doesn't he just shrink back down?" Taya asked trying to find a hand hold on the wolf.

"I can't," Rift growled. "Wounds are too bad. If I return to my normal size now, my body won't be able to sustain the damage." He struggled a minute to help them but was unsuccessful. "I need some patching first if I'm to survive the change back."

Taya stopped trying to lift the giant wolf and dashed off into the woods where she thought she saw the figurine fly.

"What are you doing?" Firebane called as the shambler nearly finished its current stack. Just one more stack and then the rocks would be falling on him and Rift.

"I've got to find that figurine that the bandit had," she called from the woods.

Firebane was puzzled, but decided not to argue the point. "Over to your left more," he called out.

The shambler had started the stack near enough to Rift that once it began to tumble, it would crush Rift for sure and him if he didn't get out of the way.

"Found it!" she shouted and ran back into the clearing holding out the figurine.

"Now what," Firebane yelled still struggling to slide the wolf. "Come on you big, fat puppy dog, help me out."

Rift's anger flared at the insults and he growled and pushed with his hind legs as best as he could. The combination of Rift's surge of effort and Firebane pushing on his hind quarters moved him enough to buy them one more stack.

Taya ran over to the bandit known as Manni and began trying to slap him awake.

"You killed him," Taya declared after she received no visible response.

"I didn't try to," Firebane shrugged. "After the big guy got crushed, I decided that I needed him out of the way so I could try to get Rift free of the walking stones. So, I rapped him on the back of the head."

"Great," she sighed, "now what do we do?"

"Destroy the figurine," Guntharr's faint voice echoed out of the cave.

Firebane heard the instructions. "Don't go anywhere," he said jokingly to Rift and immediately ran over and picked up Guntharr's fallen warhammer.

The shambler had only a few more stones to stack before it would be ready to start falling again and this time it would be on top of Rift.

"Taya, the figurine," Firebane called running in her direction.

Taya tossed the figurine into the air toward Firebane who had twisted full around with both hands on the hammer. Swinging with all of his might as the figurine flew toward him the impact of the hammer on the figurine caused an explosion sending shards of the figurine in every direction.

Taya and Firebane stopped to look at the towering rocks as it swayed in the night air. For a minute, the two thought they were sure it was going to start falling again, but the tower slowly stopped moving and stood completely still.

Chapter 11

The first thing to attend to was to try and get Rift bandaged up enough so that he could safely transform back. He was already very weak from holding his form for as long as he had on top of the damage he had sustained. Fortunately, Firebane was able to locate a bottle inside the cave mixed in with all of the junk, that contained enough magical ointment to stabilize Rift's wounds. He couldn't stand, but the bleeding had stopped and the gashes had closed.

A weak howl indicated that Rift had started his transformation back into the scruffy old wolf, who now had some severe injuries to overcome. As soon as he was back to normal, he immediately fell unconscious from the stress and fatigue.

"Will he be okay?" Taya asked Firebane.

"Maybe, but we'd do better if we could find some more of that Naffer ointment," he indicated the empty container.

Taya nodded in understanding, and headed back inside the cave to look. When she arrived in the central cavern, she saw Guntharr stretched out on one of the bunks and Arnethia tending to the fire.

"Would you care for some of the roast," she asked softly extending a wooden plate full of the meat. "I understand it was your kill."

Taya smiled meekly and took the plate. "How is he?"

Arnethia, tried to give the young girl a reassuring smile. "He appears to be pretty tough. It will take a while, but I think he'll pull through."

"What about his leg?" Taya asked.

"While you were out tying up the bandits, Firebane and I lifted him up on the cot." She stopped and looked over at him for a moment then back at Taya. "Firebane checked his leg and its completely shattered, he'll likely never walk again without assistance."

Taya began to cry softly. She set the untouched plate of food to the floor and lowered her face into her hands to try and hide the tears.

Arnethia stood up and moved over to her. She put her arm around her to try and comfort her, but Taya threw off the comforting touch and ran over to the guardian and knelt beside the cot.

Softly she began to sing quietly an elvish prayer that Guntharr at taught her to the One True God.

> Healer, you are the healer.
> Healer of the broken, the wounded and lost.
> You alone have the power,
> For you alone have paid the cost.
> Come, O mighty healer
> Come to me this hour
> Heal me or I die
> Your healing touch I trust.

Arnethia listened as Taya sung the verse over and over again. She marveled at the girls beautiful voice and her near perfect pitch. Though she didn't sing loudly, the music echoed throughout the chamber and caused a calming and soothing feeling to descend, even on her. She imagined that it was just the events of the past several hours had left her emotionally drained, and for the first time in as long as she could remember, she was free.

But, Guntharr began to stir on his bed. Taya didn't allow the movement to interrupt her as she finished the verse and then started into a chorus.

> I am alive,
> I am alive,
> I am alive because of you.
> I am healed,
> I am healed,
> I am healed because of you.
> Your love knows no bounds,
> Your power knows no limits,
> You alone can heal
> I am healed because of you.

As she completed the last phrase, she bowed her head in silence and Guntharr awoke and slowly sat up in the cot.

Arnethia's eyes struggled to understand just what had happened.

"Guardian," Taya smiled.

He nodded, and slowly turned putting his legs over the edge of the cot, letting them down to the floor softly.

Arnethia moved across the room to stand beside Guntharr who was now sitting upright on the edge of the bed.

"Well, it looks like Rift is going to be okay," Firebane spoke out as he strode into the cavern seeing the two girls standing on either side of Guntharr who was sitting up in bed. "Are you insane, man?" Firebane hurried over to Guntharr who was about to test the strength of his shattered leg. "At least let me find some Naffer ointment to regenerate your leg."

Guntharr starred down at the ground, cautious at first as he lightly pressed down on his foot. "I don't think that will be necessary," he said confidently as he stood.

Firebane and Arnethia's eyes both nearly popped out of their heads.

"How is this possible?" Arnethia spoke. "I saw the hit you took! I heard the bone shatter."

Firebane looked over at her, then at Taya. "A very good question indeed."

"I told you earlier, not to underestimate her gifts," Guntharr reached down to the kneeling Taya and laid his hand on her head approvingly. "How long before Rift can move again?"

Firebane looked back in the direction where he left Rift to rest then back again. "With the help of the Naffer and a good night's rest, he'll probably be able to move again tomorrow. Although, he's not going to be up to fighting again anytime soon."

Guntharr nodded, "Nor will I. I can stand and walk, but it will be a few days before my strength returns."

"We don't want to stay here, what about Silverfoot, Nightfury and Angel Dance?" Taya looked worried. "We just left them back at the camp."

Firebane looked at the state of the crew and shrugged his shoulders, "I will go fetch them." He thought for a moment about how to get back to their location. It was nearly dawn now, and the hope that no one had spotted them or stolen them was foremost on his mind. "It will take me a while to find a safe way down into the valley."

"I can help you with that," Arnethia spoke up. "I've lived in these parts all my life. I know this valley and there are only a couple of paths safe for horses to decend into the valley."

Firebane studied her for a moment then turned to Guntharr for reassurance.

Guntharr in his familiar ways, tilted his head down a fraction of an inch, to indicate approval.

Firebane turned and started out of the cave, "Very well. You two try to get some rest, we'll be back as soon as we can."

With that, they left the cave. Guntharr sat back down on the cot and patted a spot next to him for Taya to join him. She obediently sat next to him waiting for his next instruction.

"Thank you, for what you did for me," Guntharr spoke quietly.

Guntharr could see the color in Taya's cheeks turn from her normal pail white color to a soft red. "You are my guardian, there is nothing I wouldn't do to help you."

The two sat quietly for a moment before Guntharr broke the silence. "Your gift is every bit as powerful as I had imagined, but we must be careful about who knows this."

"I will obey," she replied, "but I would like to understand why you make this request."

He stood on his newly regenerated leg and started to walk over to the semi-charred boar and tore off a piece and smelled. "You have a noble heart, as I have taught you to have and that your father would have wished. As such, you will be compelled, even forced to the point of death to use your gift where it may not be God's will."

"I don't understand," Taya pulled up her feet and sat on them.

Guntharr took a bite of the meat and chewed for a moment. He looked at the remains still in his hand and tossed it into the fire. "The gifts that you and I have. The gifts that we all have are not gifts of ourselves, but they have been given to us by the One True God to use for his purposes. Those who are evil also receive gifts but use them to fulfill a purpose of evil. As a servant of the God of light, he will only allow our gifts to further his purpose, so if challenged by evil to use our gifts for evil, they will fail. And when they do . . ."

Taya eyes showed understanding. "Then I would be at risk," she completed his thought.

He turned slowly, "you continue to amaze me at how quickly you understand some of the more difficult things of this world."

Taya smiled. "Thank you. I have a good teacher."

"At times." Guntharr turned his attention to a small barrel containing a variety of fruits. He reached in and pulled out a green Lincor fruit and began to eat it.

* * *

Firebane and Arnethia encountered nothing unusual as they left the cave. Rift lay at the mouth of the cave snoring loudly. The two surviving bandits were bound to a large boulder outside, and the large mound of stones that roamed around earlier, remained piled high and unwavering.

The journey back to the original camp took some doing as the dawn had not quite arrived and the thick darkness that hung over the forested valley made it difficult to travel, even with his light staff. Firebane conversed casually with Arnethia, trying to learn more about her and how she'd come to be imprisoned under the bandits that they had just dispatched. The conversation was very one sided as Firebane asked a lot of straightforward questions and Arnethia, if she answered, gave very simple answers usually consisting of "yes" or "no" without any elaboration. Still her attitude was not one of deceit or guile but more along the lines of caution or reservation.

"Do you have a family?" He asked trying to break the ice.

"No," she replied her eyes focused on the path ahead.

"How long had you been held captive?" He asked next, but got no reply.

"Were you being ransomed?" He tried a different angle.

"No," she stated.

"What is your favorite food?" He decided to pick something completely innocent.

Again she did not answer, almost as if she didn't hear the question.

Firebane began to get discouraged. "You do eat don't you?" He asked jokingly.

"Yes," she replied with a slight chuckle realizing that he was just trying to be kind.

Finally, he was getting through. She had obviously built up quite a wall during the time she had been down in that dark cave as a prisoner. Still, Guntharr had trusted her and had not given any indication that she should be a concern. He even had blessed her on this find-and-retrieve operation. Granted, Firebane could manage three horses and their packs, but with her help and knowledge of the paths and valley, the trip would be much shorter.

"Guntharr is a very strong man," she commented.

Firebane nodded, "Indeed he is. He has to be, he's a guardian of Fairhaven."

This announcement seemed to connect several things together in Arnethia's mind. She stopped for a moment which caused Firebane to stop and turn. "How is a guardian way out here getting captured by a group of local thugs? Did the Governor send him out to finally assist the people of Falcon's Roost?"

Firebane could see that this revelation intrigued her, but he felt like it was best for Guntharr to reveal the whole story. "Guntharr will be the one you need to ask that question," he replied. "It is a fairly long story and he is a much better story teller than I."

Arnethia stamped forward. "You're hiding something."

Firebane caught up with her and helped her quickly avoid a large tree root that was jutting out across that path that she nearly stumbled over. "I'm not hiding anything from you, I'm stalling. There is a difference."

The two managed to locate the area of the ravine where Guntharr had been captured. "Okay, we need to head up that way," Firebane pointed in the direction of their camp.

"This way, then," Arnethia replied and led him away from the steep slope that they had slid down earlier. "There is an easier way to the top further down."

Firebane led out in the direction that she had indicated with his light staff. After working around several large clusters of fallen stones they came to a narrow path that wound its way steadily up the side of the ravine.

"Is it this narrow all the way to the top?" He asked.

"Yes, mostly,"she replied as they started up the path.

"It should be safe enough to bring the horses down in single file, I think," he added.

"It is your only shot on this side, otherwise we would need to travel hours around the rim to find a wider, steadier path," she replied.

As they reached the top and started through the woods to the clearing, Firebane put a hand out to halt Arnethia's progress. "What's that smell?" He asked in a whisper.

Arnethia sniffed the air. "It's just the smell of a campfire," she whispered back.

"Exactly," he agreed. "We left here many hours ago. There's no way that fire is still burning unless . . .," he let his words trail off as he caused the light from his staff to dim so as to not give away their position.

Quietly, they inched their way toward the clearing. As they neared it, the soft glow of a fire illuminated the center of the clearing. The three steeds stood quietly to one side, the firelight outlined their forms.

"That's a relief. They're still here," he whispered off to his side.

Firebane stood through several seconds of silence expecting a "yes" comment to come back from Arnethia, but when he turned she was no longer there. "Hey," he whispered loudly, "Arnethia, where are you?"

He looked forward to see if maybe she had taken off out into the clearing, but he didn't readily see her anywhere. He squatted down to assess the situation and a slight poking sensation hit him in the middle of his back as if he'd backed up against a limb. He instinctively turned to see what it was that was now seriously starting to hurt.

"Don't move," a raspy voice hissed in his ear.

"Okay, you got me," Firebane said disgusted that he'd been surprised so easily. "Can I at least stand up?"

The sword which was hitting him just above the center of his back pressed into his skin slowly.

"Drop the glowing stick and you can stand," the voice replied.

Firebane, not knowing how many where behind him, figured the staff would be of no use to him. Reluctantly, he dropped it and the pointy thing sticking in his back relaxed slightly indicating he had permission to stand up now. From the corner of his eye, he could see a small dark clad figure reach down and snatch his staff. He started to turn around but the point was immediately shoved back into its position, only this time it was just below his ribcage.

"Move," the voice instructed and the point encouraged, so forward he went into the clearing.

"Let me guess," Firebane asked, "you must be friends of the dark goblins that stormed my church back in Brittle and your angry that we kicked their butts."

"Vang not angry," the point's owner said. "Vang just doing his job."

This accidental bit of information made Firebane stop suddenly.

"Move, or Vang will see how far it is to your heart," Vang's sword now penetrated Firebanes robe and dug into his skin.

Firebane began to move again but tried quickly to think of what this could mean. Unsure what to say next instead he ran through the different options in his mind as they approached the fire and the animals. For the most part, everything was as they had left it, with the exception that the fire had dwindled but was still alive and a large sack had been tossed over near Nightfury. Something was in the sack, something alive because he could see the sack move, or maybe it was the flickering of the fire that gave it the illusion of movement.

Since Firebane was sort of leading Vang and whoever was behind him, he decided to move closer to the sack and investigate it. Angel Dance, Nightfury and Silverfoot all raised their head at Firebane's approach and whinnied with approval. "Hi guys," Firebane spoke to the three steeds. Angel Dance tried to respond by pawing at the ground but struggled. Firebane looked and noticed that her front hoof had been chained and the chain staked into the ground.

"That one is a bit of a challenge," Vang spoke up, "strange seeing a pegasus with one wing."

Firebane was now close enough to reach out and touch her. "Easy girl, I'm here now." He studied the rest of her to see if she'd been injured in anyway and was relieved to see no signs of trauma. "What is it you want, really?" He asked slightly annoyed.

The sword point released itself and there were sounds of scurrying feet around him and three dark goblins came into his vision and positioned themselves in front of him and to either side of him. The two on either side had bows drawn, and the third directly in front of him held a small sword, which he judged had been gouging him in the back just moments ago.

"As Vang said," the same voice said from behind Firebane.

Firebane spun around to see who this voice was. Now, standing in front of him was another dark goblin, but this one was a little taller and dressed in red wearing a headband with many colorful feathers and some miscellaneous teeth.

"So, you must be Vang," Firebane asked.

"Yes," Vang replied.

"And your three colleagues?" He asked, waving a hand at the three guarding him from behind.

Vang shook his head, "Vang not need to tell you."

A rustling sound came near the horses, but at quick examination Firebane didn't notice it coming from either Nightfury or Silverfoot. Curious as to the source of the sound, Firebane traced it with his eyes to the sack near Nightfury. From this distance, he could see something sticking out of the end of the sack. As his eyes focused, he realized that whatever it was had feathers all over it, then his mind remembered that the hawk lord that Guntharr had sent on ahead had disappeared.

"Raskin," Firebane called out loud enough for the creature in the sack to hear. The sack responded by shaking even more. "Where did you find him?" Firebane asked Vang.

"Not where, but how. Vang has gifts that hawk lord find hard to resist." Vang grinned showing a mouth full of grisly teeth.

Firebane stepped toward the sack to see closer, but his three body guards stepped to within arm's reach, each with their weapon trained on him. Firebane froze in his position not wanting to push his luck when he heard a different rustling coming from behind Silverfoot. The guard with the sword heard this too and started to pull away to investigate, so Firebane acted like he was going to try again to get to the sack. This had the desired effect and immediately drew the swordsman's attention back to Firebane. The sword in the guard's hand once again jabbed him in the ribs.

In the next instance, a small hand attached to a long slender arm reached around Silverfoot. In a single swift motion, the hand grabbed on to the back of the nearest bowman's head, and with a yank, caused him to stumble backwards in the direction of the attack. He released an arrow wildly into the dawn sky. Reacting to the commotion, the other two near Firebane turned to see what happened. Firebane quickly reached out and grabbed the center of the sword and pulled creature and all toward him. He brought around his free hand down in a chopping motion onto the creature's neck sending the creature crashing to the ground.

"Firebane!" Arnethia called out.

Seeing the second bowman targeting Arnethia behind Silverfoot, Firebane spun around and kicked at the dark goblin. Missing the creature, he was able to clip the end of the bow which sent it and the arrow into the ground directly in front of the assassin. Arnethia turned and saw the first bowman return to his feet and put a new arrow onto the string. She took two huge steps and lunged toward the assassin who was drawing on her. She reached out as she sailed by and wrapped her arm around the creatures neck. Spinning in mid-air as she fell, she drove the bowman's head into the ground.

Vang uttered some words in a strange language and a bolt of bluish-white energy leaped from his hand. Firebane turned just in time to see the bolt splatter hard on his chest. The impact was so magnificent that it picked him up and hurtled him into the side of Nightfury. The warhorse whinnied at the sudden impact that nearly caused him to lose his footing.

"You like Vang's gift?" Vang said.

Firebane lay frozen on the ground shivering and unable to move anything. "Nnnot, vvery much," he mumbled through chattering teeth. He tried to look around to see where Arnethia had disappeared to, but he was unable to spot her.

The dark goblin made a clicking sound with his mouth and shook his head. "Vang sorry you not impressed. As soon as Vang finds the female assassin, she will get to try out another, more toasty, gift Vang has."

The remaining bowman crossed over Firebane, careful not to touch him and made his way back over to Vang.

Vang mumbled something in a goblin tongue and the bowman simply shook his head.

"What do I do?" a soft voice touched Firebane's ear.

"Knnnnife. Sadddle. Sack," he chattered as he spoke.

Arnethia stood still beside Nightfury her form blending into the horse out of sight of the goblin shaman and bowman. She understood about the knife and the saddle, but what had Firebane ment by the sack. She slowly reached up and felt around the saddle. She felt in several different spaces before she found a small stub protruding from a slit in the saddle. She pulled slowly and the stub was attached to a small blade. Contemplating her next move, a rustling sound emitted from the mysterious sack laying in front the white pegasus. Understanding what her next action should be, she studied the situation for a moment. She could just make out the voices of the goblins and their general direction. Daylight was slowly appearing through the trees which would make it harder for her to blend in with the darkness.

After toying with several different plans, she settled on one that would buy her one chance at getting to the sack and freeing whatever it was that was in it. She picked up a rock and carefully aimed it at the backend of Silverfoot. With one movement she threw the rock as hard as she could and jabbed the knife into the butt of Nightfury.

Both horses let out cries and took off in the general direction toward the goblins. The goblins reacted just as she'd hoped they would and began to panick at the sight of the stampeeding horses. While the goblins ran for cover she quickly ran over toward the sack. The goblins in the meantime had started screaming at each other. She knelt down and immediately noticed the feathery head sticking out of the top of the sack. Rolling it over she could tell it was some kind of bird, but the massive beak had been bound. With a quick stroke of the knife she severed the binding and the bird let out an immense squawk. Without looking, she hopped over from one side of the sack to the other just in time for an arrow to thud into the ground, just inches from where she had been kneeling.

She could tell the bird was struggling fiercely against the sack, and a quick examination revealed that there was a rope synching it closed tightly. She sawed frantically at the rope as she faintly heard the goblin shaman begin to utter another one of his magic spells. In an explosion of cloth and feathers, Raskin's mighty wings ripped apart the sack as the rope snapped free and he immediately took to flight crying with a terribly angry cry.

Vang finished his recitation and a glowing ball of fire shot forward out of his outstretched hand. Arnethia seeing it coming dove sideways but the fire smashed into her feet. The simple boots she had been wearing burst into flames and she cried out as she desperately tried to kick them off.

"Vang think you can hit that target, can't you?" Vang chided the bowman who was struggling to aim at the rolling target.

Overhead another cry from Raskin indicated that he was near. Firebane was able to tilt his head enough to see the shadow of the hawk lord in the dawning sky. He was diving fast toward the goblins.

Arnethia finally kicked off the other boot and at the same time swooned from the searing pain in her feet and legs. The bowman drew back and started to take aim, but hawk lord's talons ripped into his shoulders. At the same time, Raskin used his momentum to lift the goblin bowman off the ground. The arrow released and completely missed its target. With wings spread wide, Raskin assended higher and higher. The goblin cried in pain and fear but was unable to free himself as the hawk's nails had severed the muscles from his shoulders to his arms.

"You'll never bag this hawk lord again," Raskin said and he pulled his feet up causing the goblin to slip off the talons and sent him falling through the air and crashing into the ground.

Vang eyed the circling hawk and began preparing his next attack. With both arms reaching up toward the hawk, which was now diving fast again with wings drawn in toward the shaman, he spoke the last of the spell and round stringy ball rocketed toward the hawk.

Raskin had been prepared for this and spread his wings out full which caused his decent to stop and his direction to change dramatically sending him safely away from the magical webbing.

With a spin he retracted his wings and began to drop almost straight down. Without time to prepare another spell, the shaman took off running away from the hawk. Dawn's rays shown down through the trees as Raskin lowered his feet as he neared his prey. But rather than spread his wings back out to catch and carry his victim as was normal, he instead drove the dagger like nails deep into the shamans back with such force that the shaman fell flat on the ground and skidded across the ground with the hawk standing proudly on his back.

With the shaman's death, the effects of the freezing paralysis that Firebane was suffering immediately dwindled away. Wasting no time, he jumped up and ran over in the direction of Arnethia. The smoldering remains of her boots lay to one side of her unconscious form. He knelt down and gazed at her feet and legs. They were burned alright, but not as bad as he'd seen before. She would be in pain for a while, but they would heal up in a few days.

"Arnethia," Firebane whispered as he tapped the sides of her face.

She began to stir. "Ow, my feet hurt." She immediately recalled her feet being set on fire by that fireball spell and sat up quickly to see that her feet, though red and somewhat blistered, were still there.

"Easy, they'll hurt for a while, but I think you'll be okay," Firebane tried to reassure her. "You handled yourself very well," trying to distract her from the obvious.

"I can be useful," she fell back into the grass. "I don't think I can walk back to the cave, though."

"That's okay," Firebane replied. "I'll gather the horses and we can ride back."

With the sound of fluttering wings, Raskin landed softly next to Arnethia and looked down with his hawkish eyes. "Raskin, thanks you for freeing him."

Arnethia's eyes grew widdened as she realized that the voice came from the hawk. "You're a hawk lord?"

"I am," Raskin tilted forward slightly which was his version of a bow. "I am Raskin former lord and captain of the clan Featherstorm, and I am bound to the lady Taya and her guardian."

"A guardian, a battle wolf and now a hawk lord, now this is a family I could get use to," Arnethia said with a smile.

Chapter 12

The next day was fairly boring to Taya as she, Guntharr and Rift spent it waiting for Firebane and Arnethia to return with their transportation. Rift mostly rested as he had taken a good beating during the fight and his older normal body didn't react to that very well. Guntharr, thanks mostly to Taya's healing ability, was about scavenging supplies from the den they were occupying.

When Arenthia and Firebane returned that afternoon, Taya saw Raskin riding on the back of Nightfury. Her heart was overwhelmed with joy. She beckoned the bird to hop down from the tall warhorse, but when he refused knowing what was coming, she instead climbed up on the back of the horse and gave the bird a massive hug which was stunningly similar to the snugness that he felt while being kept in the sack.

"Easy," Raskin squawked, "I'm not as solid as you think."

Firebane dismounted Angel Dance and went over to help Arnethia down from Silverfoot. Taya immediately noticed as she hopped down that her legs nearly gave way and Firebane caught and steadied her. Taya jumped down and ran over to see what was wrong.

"Are you hurt?" Taya asked.

Arnethia did not respond directly but a glance down at her bare feet gave Taya all of the information she needed.

"Oh my, what happened?" She looked up at Firebane.

"Help me get her into the cave and I'll tell all of you at once," Firebane supported Arnethia on one side and Taya ran around and helped provide support on the other as they walked in together.

Close behind, Raskin waddled slowly into the cave.

Guntharr, hearing the commotion stopped digging through one of the remaining trunks and turned to watch the group enter. Seeing Arnethia supported on either side validated his assumption he had made earlier that they had encountered some kind of trouble. "What kind of trouble did you run into?"

Firebane and Taya guided Arnethia to a cot, and she eased herself down to take the weight off her blistered feet.

"It would seem that our dark goblin friends decided to take up camp back by the steeds and ambushed us as we approached." Firebane looked over at Arnethia who turned her head sideways.

"You got ambushed," she corrected, "I snuck away just before you were captured, and then came and saved your hide," she ended with a wink.

"Are you in a lot of pain?" Guntharr asked Arnethia.

She tried to put on a smile, "Only when I stand."

Taya knelt down beside her, "I think I can help with that."

"No," Arnethia responded gruffly. She paused for a moment as she took in the startled reactions from Taya and Firebane. Guntharr did not seem clearly startled but merely raised an eyebrow. "Thank you," she tried again. "However, your gift should not be casually taken advantage of whenever it is convenient. My wounds while painful are tolerable and I will be okay in a day or two."

Guntharr crossed over to get a closer look at the burns that spread from her calves to the bottom of her feet. "She is correct," he added. This caused even more surprise from both Firebane and Taya. "Something you must learn about the gifts that God gives to us is that we must use them to fulfill his purpose and not our own purposes."

"But, I wasn't trying . . ." Taya stopped at Guntharr's raised hand.

"Hear me out," he interrupted. "You have a powerful and miraculous gift that few are ever blessed with. Just as we have discussed before, you cannot go around brandishing your gift like an everyday walking stick. God prefers you to use his gifts for His purposes. Misuse can lead to trouble or even loss of the gift. In this case, her wounds are neither life threatening nor impeding her from fulfilling God's purpose."

"How will I know when it's okay to help people?" Taya asked.

He reached over and put his arm around her shoulder. "You will learn, in time. For now, trust me and Firebane. He's the one who can help you more on how to best refine and strengthen your gift."

She smiled and nodded in response.

"These are pretty nasty burns. Taya, you can help by running out to the woods, don't wander too far. Look for some arnica or comfrey leaves. I can use those to mix up a salve that should help reduce the swelling." Guntharr instructed.

"I saw a patch of confrey about one thousand paces up the main path," Arnethia commented.

Taya took off like a deer on her quest.

Guntharr waited to make sure that Taya had left the cave before continuing. "These are not normal burns. You encountered magic, didn't you?"

Firebane nodded, "One of the dark goblins was a shaman."

"He webbed me as I was scouting," Raskin injected as he waddled into the room. "The fall nearly killed me."

"I had suspected that you'd encountered some problems along the way, since we hadn't been able to contact you," Guntharr added.

"I took a shot from a paralysis spell, and Arnethia just missed getting torched with a fire ball," Firebane said.

Guntharr closed his eyes. "It would seem that whoever has been tracking us, is starting to get serious. They have either figured out who we have, or they're growing impatient and they're trying to force us into our next move."

Arnethia waved a hand from her cot to get the two men's attention. "I'm new to this, what is it that you have that's brought on this savagery?"

Guntharr opened his eyes and studied her for a moment before looking over at Firebane. The two made eye contact and Firebane

The Silverwood Chronicles

could tell Guntharr was seeking reassurance of her trust. Firebane responded with a nod, but it wasn't a confident nod.

"Before I tell you," Guntharr directed his focus on Arnethia, "you must know that by me telling you, you put your life in peril. Firebane indicates that he trusts you, and I must admit your demeanor has shown you to be honorable. However, this information cannot leave this group. So, by asking, you commit yourself - for the time being - to our quest and ultimately to my leadership. " He paused to study her reaction before continuing. "As of this moment, you are free to do as you please. We will tend to your wounds as best as we can and provide you transport back to Falcon Roost. There we can part company as friends and no burden will be yours."

"Or?" she inquired.

"Or, you can commit to our quest and become a part of our little family with all of the burdens and protections that come with it," Guntharr offered watchfully.

She looked down for a moment, not wanting to stare into those eyes that radiated with a commanding fire. It had been so long since she'd had any kind of a family. She knew that even back in Falcon Roost, there was nothing for her there. Still, the events of the last day seemed frightening and exciting all at the same time. Was she ready to commit to that in exchange for having a place to belong?

"Guardian," she looked up and met his eyes with a renewed fire of her own, "I have nowhere to call my own and no one to call friend or family. You, Taya and Firebane have shown me more trust and compassion than I have seen in such a long time. I want to be a part of that," she paused for a moment to take a deep breath. "I therefore pledge my honor to support you . . ."

Guntharr raised a hand cutting her off. He listened intently at an approaching sound. Seconds later, Taya's hurried footsteps announced her return.

"It was right where you said it was, Arnethia." Taya handed over a clump of the leaves to Guntharr.

Guntharr nodded in approval. "Do not pledge to me," he said to Arnethia, "pledge to Taya, the Heir of the Silverwood."

The expression on Arenthia's face indicated that all of the pieces started to come together for her. She stared at Taya for a moment, who was at a loss.

"What did I miss?" Taya asked the guardian.

Arnethia pushed herself off of the cot onto her knees. "I pledge my life and honor, Taya of the Silverwood, to see you safely on your quest, and to help you in whatever means I have at my disposal to that end."

Taya was overwhelmed by the show of submission this total stranger had offered to her. She stood looking at Arnethia's kneeling form trying to fathom what would cause her to be so giving. The whole idea of being someone special beyond what Guntharr had been teaching her, seemed odd to her. She had always identified herself as being a child under a great warrior's protection and tutelage, not a person of rank or privilege.

Guntharr sensed that Taya was struggling with this. "As her guardian, I, in return, will pledge my protection to both you and your honor whether by my life or death."

Arnethia looked up. Tears ran down her face. She had not felt accepted in such a long time. Taya seeing the tears, ran up to her and gave her a hug, then helped her back to the cot.

"How far away are we from Falcon Roost?" Guntharr asked Arnethia, trying to get back to the matters at hand.

She thought for a moment before responding, "About a half day's journey."

"Hmm, too late to head out today. We may as well rest here for one more day, and then we can head out first thing in the morning." He wandered over to a corner where he set a mortar and pestle down. He placed the comfrey leaves in the bowl and began crushing it slowly.

The remainder of the evening was spent in preparation for the journey the next day. Guntharr and Firebane decided to take the two criminals that had survived the fight into town to face whatever punishment the local council deemed appropriate. They also collected all of the money that the bandits had stashed away so that they could return it to the town.

The night passed without incident as Guntharr, Firebane and Taya all took turns at the watch. In the morning, after snacking on some dried fruit that had been kept in the den, the group set off toward Falcon Roost. The two captives were pulled along behind Guntharr who was on Nightfury. Taya and Arnethia road together on Silverfoot and Firebane remained paired with Angel Dance.

Rift, while only two days out from taking a substantial beating, refused to be hoisted attop Angel Dance and instead walk beside them. Taya even offered to let him ride in her place on Silverfoot, but Rift pointed out that battle wolves were not designed to ride horses.

Raskin resumed his place in the sky, careful to stay within sight of the group at all times.

Nothing terribly exciting happened between the thieves' den and Falcon Roost. At one point along the trail, the captives saw an opportunity to escape and started to pull against the warhorse. Guntharr sensed the effort and gave Nightfury a slight tap to the ribs and the horse took off in a trot forcing the bandits to run behind the horse for quite some time.

After several pleas to slow down, Guntharr finally reigned in Nightfury and the bandits thankfully slowed down to a casual pace, but were still huffing and puffing.

When they arrived in the small village of Falcon Roost, Arnethia guided the group to where she remembered the council was housed. It had been a long time since she'd been back on the streets and it felt really strange to her. Nothing had changed much. The trees had gotten a little taller and the buildings had gotten a little older but everything seemed to be where it had always been.

Since it was mid-day, the town was bustling with activity. Merchants were out on the streets selling their goods, and women and children were scurrying about. Needless to say, the strangers got their fair share of stares. In part, because they had the prisoners who were tethered to the warhorse, but mostly because Angel Dance was a creature that could not be ignored easily.

In the sun, her silver coat and golden tipped wing demanded that the casual observer stop and take notice. Guntharr's focus was on getting through the town as quickly as possible, but Taya and Arnethia took in the attention like they were on parade. Whenever a child would stop and look up at the two, Taya would smile and wave.

Firebane tried to smile casually as the strode along, but several of the more curious folks walked up near to the Pegasus and started to touch her. He decided to give them a show so he tapped Angel Dance on the neck and brought his heel up to her side. With a blast from her nostrils she kicked up on her hind legs and spread her good wing out to its full extent causing the curious ones to step back in awe.

Rift had to dodge the event in order to avoid getting crushed by Angel Dance's front hooves.

"Sorry about that, Rift," Firebane called down at the annoyed wolf.

"Was that really necessary?" Rift replied.

Firebane smiled. "No, but it was fun."

Rift gowled and took off to catch up with Nightfury.

"I've never seen her extend her wing clear out like that before," Taya marveled to Arnethia.

"It's truly a pity that she doesn't have both wings," Arnethia replied. "Did Firebane ever tell you what happened to the other one?"

Taya shook her head. "Not really. I don't think he really knows."

"Still, she is a beautiful creature," Arnethia added.

Guntharr had stopped in front of a prestigious looking building that stood alone. There were simple gardens surrounding the walkway to the front of the building and several tall trees cast their shade over parts of the walk.

"This is it," Arnethia confirmed as Silverfoot maneuvered up next to Nightfury.

Guntharr dismounted. "Stay here, I'll fetch the authorities."

"Palident is who you're looking for," she instructed.

Reaching into one of the saddlebags where he had stashed the coinage retrieved from the thieves, he made his way up the path, then disappeared inside.

"So this is where you lived?" Taya asked innocently.

"Yes," she said softly. "More specifically, my family used to live over there." Arnethia pointed off into the distance to an overgrown area where a few scraggly trees stood, but nothing else much except brush.

Taya studied the area in the direction she had pointed, but could not see any kind of dwelling or structure. Straining to look even further she was unable to find anything this side of a large field filled with almost ripe wheat. "But, I don't see anything over there."

Arnethia dismounted and landed softly on the ground. Her feet were now wrapped up with cloth and snuggly inserted into some larger boots. She stepped slowly over toward the area she'd indicated.

Taya followed after her. She stood beside her staring into a vacant empty area. "It's gone, isn't it?"

As she nodded, she couldn't help but tremble at the emptiness. "It was here. My family. My mother and father, two sisters and a brother. It was a simple house, much like all the rest in this town. Over there," she pointed at a small tree. "My father had just built us a pen where we were raising Kriken birds to produce eggs. But, they took it all away from me."

Taya struggled to understand. How could anyone be cruel enough to do something like this to anyone? "Why?" she finally asked.

"Because of me," Arnethia turned tears now visible in her eyes. "They came for me, and Manni and his thugs killed them. I tried to stop them. I pleaded with them to just let them take me, but my father and brother stood and fought." She fell to the ground her hands resting on her knees. "They weren't fighters. They had no training. One by one he killed them all right in front of me."

"I know we cannot replace them, but we are here," Taya got down beside her.

"You," she turned suddenly, "you have a wonderful gift. A beautiful gift. And I, I have this curse."

"You're not cursed," Taya tried to reassure.

Arnethia dug around the ground and pulled up a broken piece of pottery. "So you think, what is this?" She held out the pottery for Taya to see.

"It looks like an old pot," Taya guessed.

"Do you know where it was, who held it last, what happened around it?" she asked in a challenging voice.

Taya looked confused. "You know I can't know those things."

"Well I can." She wrapped both her hands around the shard and closed her eyes. "All I have to do is concentrate on this and I can see the people that have touched it and what was going on all around it." She fell silent for a moment, and then suddenly let out a scream.

Taya jumped not expecting this. Arenthia's eyes snapped open and she quickly dropped the shard onto the ground. She began sobbing uncontrollably.

"What was it?" Taya asked.

"I saw them. I saw it all over again." The tears flowed heavily down her face. "This was my mothers, she struck one of the bandits with it trying to free me just before they killed her."

Firebane dismounted Angel Dance and jogged over to the girls. "Is everything all right?"

Taya looked up at Firebane, "This is where Arenthia's family was killed."

Firebane bowed his head and began a silent prayer for the dead and the living.

A whinny from Nightfury caught everyone's attention. When they looked the two prisoners had managed to scramble onto the horse and were trying desperately to get him to move.

"That's a warhorse," Firebane called out to them. "He doesn't take orders from just anybody."

About that time, some commotion originating from the building Guntharr had disappeared into, indicated that he was returning. Two armed guards followed alongside him they made their way back to Nightfury.

"Come down off that horse!" One of the guards demanded.

The two were reluctant to dismount and continued to try to encourage the horse to make a run for it. in In an effort to exert their authority, the guards struggled at pulling on the bandits' legs, but that only resulted in them getting kicked repeatedly in the face.

"Allow me, gentlemen," Guntharr motioned the guards to step back.

"Nightfury," Guntharr commanded the horse's attention. He then made several clicking sounds. The horse responded by rearing up on his hind legs sending the bandits toppling to the ground in a heap.

The guards secured the rope that had the two prisoners bound, then one turned to Guntharr and tossed him a pouch that contained some coins.

"Here is the reward we discussed," the guard said.

Guntharr nodded his approval without checking the contents of the bag.

Taya, Arnethia and Firebane walked up as the guards led the prisoners away who were making less of a commotion now that the guard had drawn his weapon.

"How did you do that with Nightfury?" Taya asked.

Guntharr stroked the beast in affection. "While you were napping back at the church, Firebane gave me a quick lesson on some of the tricks that Nightfury knows."

"Does Silverfoot know any tricks?" She asked.

This time Firebane held up a hand to silence Guntharr. "None that you need to know about at this time," he chuckled.

"We must be off," Guntharr mounted the massive warhorse. "There is a smithy on the far side of town who may be able to provide us with some items that could be of use to us in the next phase of our journey."

The rest of the troup mounted their steeds and they all headed off in the direction given to Guntharr by the councilmen. Halfway through town, Guntharr spotted a merchant that specialized in attire for women. Stopping he turned to Taya and Arnethia. Arnethia was still wearing the remnants of a tattered dress that she'd been in for who knows how long. On her feet she was wearing some make-shift boots that they had found back at the bandit camp.

"Taya," he called out. "You and Arnethia stop here and see about getting her some new clothes that are fit for our journey. There is also a cobbler just up the street, see about getting some boots that are more appropriate." He reached into the pouch he'd received from the authorities and pulled out several silver coins. Taya guided Silverfoot up beside him and took the money from him.

"Thank you, my lord," Arnethia smiled.

"Keep in mind we have a lot of riding and, assuredly, there is bound to be more fighting coming our way." He paused. "I will do my best to avoid your involvement . . ."

"I do not fear the battle," she cut him off. "So long as I have my family beside me, I have nothing to fear."

"Indeed," he nodded. "You know the way to the smithy?"

"Yes," she replied.

"Then we will meet you there." Gunthar, Firebane and Rift trotted off down the street.

Taya started to guided Silverfoot over to the merchant, but Arnethia reached up a hand and touched her on the side of the arm. "I will not be able to find anything appropriate here."

"The guardian wants you to get some new apparel," Taya argued.

"Guntharr needs me to be prepared for battle, these are clothes that a commoner or plan folk would wear. I need something I can depend on in a fight and that are more suitable to my skills," Arnethia replied with an air of mystery.

Taya started to respond but decided instead to scan the street vendors, but all the obvious choices, Arnethia rejected with a shake of her head. "Where can we find what you want?" She asked, finally.

* * *

Shortly after sending the girls off to do some shopping, Guntharr, Firebane and Rift arrived at the smithy to do a little shopping of their own. As they had been told, he was the last merchant at the edge of town and for good reason. He had an open area where he worked on crafting various weapons as well as tools for the locals. A respectable forge was located toward the back billowing smoke and large pots of water sat around a central anvil where the burley owner was busy beating a piece of iron into shape.

The two dismounted and approached the smithy who did not take his attention off of the task at hand, but did manage to acknowledge their presence with a gruff snort. Begging their indulgence for a few minutes, he completed the work on what looked like the end of a pike. Dropping his hammer, he approaching the would be customers.

Discussions ensued, and many different specimens were shown and demonstrated by the multitalented smithy. Seconds into their discussion a loud squawk over head signaled that Raskin was coming in for a landing. The smithy surprised at first to see the hawk lord, quickly returned to his 'show and tell'.

Guntharr pointed at Raskin and made some quick inquiries. The stunned smithy studied the bird that stood half as tall as the man and pushed his fingers through what little black hair he had left. Guntharr then rattled off a series of other requests. A few received immediate nods or shakes of the head. Then as Guntharr was asking about some bracers for himself, without warning, the smithy spun around and dashed inside a small little building that must have doubled as the man's house.

Firebane looked over at Guntharr confused. Had something they'd said frightened the man off? Both looked around in sudden concern that maybe they were being ambushed, but no threat was found. Almost as quickly as the smithy had disappeared, he reappeared laughing stoutly. As he neared them, he held out a small vest of chainmail that looked like it might fit a young child.

Guntharr held out his hand and measured the weight of the shirt. It was amazingly light.

"What material is this made of?" Guntharr asked.

The smithy smiled. "Its Conical from the Winding Sea, very tough."

"How tough," Firebane asked.

"Tough enough to stop an arrow shot from all but close range," he puffed out his chest.

Guntharr looked over at the hawk lord. "What do you think, Raskin?"

"I'm willing to try it, but I don't see how you're going to get it on me," he replied.

"We'll take it, but it must be fitted immediately," Guntharr commanded.

The smithy reacted by holding out an open hand and showing a toothy grin. Guntharr sighed at this and reached into his pouch and pulled out a single gold coin. The smithy was not impressed with this, instead, he wiggled his fingers to indicate that he needed to see more.

"Ah, come now sirs," the smithy mocked them, "this is shirt of Conical mail almost made to order. There isn't another shirt like this within a month's journey of here, I'd wager."

After settling on three gold coins, the smithy whistled and a young lad who appeared to be the smithy's son, came running around from where he had apparently been stoking the forge. The smithy whispered into his ear some instructions and the boy in turn began fetching several of the other items that had been requested.

The smithy immediately set out measuring Raskin's chest and wing size then set to work altering the Conical armor to fit the hawk lord.

A couple of hours later, Taya and Arnethia arrived to find Guntharr and Firebane seated, their backs against a tree examining the new toys they had just procured. Rift was on his back, legs extended in mid air, taking a nap next to Firebane. Raskin, who was perched on Nightfury, was apparently holding a conversation with Angel Dance.

Taya was the first to dismount. "What did you find?" She asked as she approached the two men.

"Arnethia," Guntharr began to speak but stopped when he looked up from the sword that was in his hands to watch the newly clad Arnethia dismount the horse. The black leather tunic extended from her shoulders down to just above her knees. The sides of the tunic were lined with ring mail that extended down from under her arms to the hem of the tunic. The ring mail had a dull, mat finish so as to make it barely noticeable. The full length boots of the same color sported several buckles extending up the side. On her hands, she had short-cropped leather gauntlets that fastened snuggly with a similar buckle style as the boots. The gauntlets were black and fingerless.

"What do you think?" Arnethia asked.

"Not what I was expecting," Firebane replied, "but it will do."

"Guardian, do you approve?" Arnethia spoke directly to Guntharr who appeared to be slightly distracted.

"Satisfactory," he replied finally. "It seems to be more functional than what I had originally envisioned for you, but I'm glad you chose what you did."

"Thank you," she said as she came nearer. "Is that for me," she asked as she extended her hand?

Guntharr looked down at the sword that he was previously admiring before extending the hilt of the blade to her. "As a matter of fact, it is."

With precession, she pulled the blade free of his hands. With careful movements, she swung the sword in several large arcs before stopping with the blade perfectly straight up and down. She studied the feel of the blade. She tipped the end over till the blade was nearly flat to her eye.

"Impressive," she remarked. "Although, this is not something I envisioned the local smithy of fabricating."

"Agreed," Guntharr replied. "He had acquired it from a group of travelers who appeared to be down on their luck and didn't realize what they had in their possession."

She brought the hilt close and studied some of the engravings that had been skillfully etched in base of the blade. "Did the smithy know what he had?"

"Did he?" Firebane let out a chuckle, "He took us for nearly half of what we had in our reserves."

"Nonetheless," Guntharr continued, "blades like that are not easy to come by. Do you know of its origin?"

Arnethia dropped down to the ground beside Guntharr and Firebane almost stabbing Rift who still lay snoring peacefully. "Not specifically, but I'm going to take a wild guess that it's elvish."

Taya rushed over. "Did you say elvish?" She asked.

"Correct," Guntharr extended his hand to receive the sword again from Arnethia. "Specifically, this bares the seal of the royal house of Krestichan and the personal stamp of Jimla his personal smith."

"How can you know this?" Arnethia asked, curiously.

"The guardian served my father for a time, isn't that correct?" Taya stated.

Guntharr stood to his feet and stroked the blade slowly across his hand. "Smooth as the day it was made. Yes, I studied at Lord Krestichan's side and later fought beside him before he was killed."

"And you would give this to me?" Arnethia asked in surprise.

He nodded. "I would and I do. I would have my companions equipped with the finest resources I can provide them; for then, only their lack of faith or passion can get in the way of success."

Firebane handed Guntharr the belt and scabbard that came with the sword. He in turn sheathed the weapon and handed it reverently to Arnethia. "May it serve you well as you fulfill your pledge to Taya."

She took the weapon and strapped it to her waist. After making some slight adjustments she drew the blade quickly from its scabbard and held it up so the light of the mid-day reflected like a blazing fire from its polished surface. "What are we waiting for? Let's get going."

Chapter 13

Naranda woke up in the middle of the night to a glowing statuette at her side. For several days, she had been away from her home that sat just outside the walls surrounding Fairhaven. While not opposed to sleeping in strange places, she ultimately enjoyed the peace and security that the estate, that she had inherited from her father, Duke Ambelhand, brought her.

She got up from her warm plush bed and crossed over to the cabinet where the figurine sat. Picking it up, she focused her energy into the face of the figurine until it slowly morphed and turned into the image of Scrag.

"Ah, mistress, you are there," Scrag sounded relieved.

"This had better be good, Scrag," she said in a angry tone. "You just woke me up from the first good night's sleep that I've had in days."

The tiny head on the figurine that looked like Scrag drooped slightly. "Scrag apologize, mistress, but they're gone."

She walked across the room to the little table that served as her private dining table and pulled up a chair. She just knew this was not going to be a quick conversation. "Who is gone?" She asked.

"Ah, the guardian and the elf girl, mistress. We lost them," he reported sadly.

"How?" Naranda growled. "What happened?"

"Scrag sent teams out from Brittle in different directions to make sure he not lose them," he added. "Vang's team captured the hawk lord near the Clearwater brook and followed them toward the mountains."

"Who is Vang?" Naranda asked not recognizing the name.

"Vang is a shaman of Rotu," he replied.

"Rotu, god of decay?" Naranda enquired trying to remember her goblin lore.

"Yes mistress," he replied. The figurine with Scrag's face smiled. "Would you like me to tell you more about Rotu?"

Naranda shook her head. She should have known better, "No, not now. Please continue your report. What happened to the guardian and the elf?"

"Near the valley of Hazelbark, they made camp, but something strange happened. First the guardian disappeared, then the rest of them took off, " he stopped.

"Any idea what happened? Did they come back?" Naranda tried to push the conversation.

"Well, Vang went into their camp and waited thinking maybe they come back to gather the horses. Vang wanted to try and capture them to bring them to mistress," he mumbled the last part knowing what her reaction would be.

"He did what?" she shouted at the figurine. "I told you to follow them for now, not engage them. How many was with Vang?"

"Only three," Scrag replied. "When Scrag went to stop Vang, he found Vang and his team dead. The horses were gone and so was the hawk lord."

"And no sign of where they went?" She shook her head in unbelief.

"Scrag tracked them down into Hazelbark valley, but we lost them at the river," he said.

Naranda reached up with a hand and pulled her fingers through her long dark hair. She took in a deep breath and then noticed a cold metal object touching her throat.

"Even pretend to start a spell, and I'll relieve you of your head," a ghostly voice from behind said. "Nod if you understand."

Naranda nodded carefully so as to not push the blade into her throat any further.

"Mistress," Scrag's voice came from the figurine still in her hand. "Why are you nodding?"

Naranda knew it was no good to say anything to Scrag, because he would only see a representation of her through his figurine. He wouldn't see her visitor nor the knife stuck to her throat. So she decided best to not provoke the stranger.

"Get rid of the goblin," the stranger demanded.

Naranda slowly took a hand and placed it over Scrag's face for a moment and the glow from the figurine disappeared. "So, Scrag was right, there was someone back at Dravious' hovel."

"I don't know what you're talking about," the voice whispered. "I don't know anyone named Dravious, but the person I do work for told me about you. Where I could find you and that I needed to be careful around you."

"I'm flattered," she replied dryly. "What is it you want? It's bad enough that worthless assassin can't even keep track of a few vagabonds, then he has to wake me in the middle of the night. Now, I'm being threatened by a hatchet man. Can we get on with this so I can go back to bed?"

The stranger grabbed her by the shoulder and spun her around to face her directly. His long scaly fingers replaced the blade by wrapping themselves around her throat.

Naranda stood in total shock. What she saw was something that even she had not expected. It was hard to tell in the dark, but there was enough light streaming in from the moon outside to make it almost certain. The creature in front of her was nearly half again as tall as she was. His skin was dark green and scaly all over. The eyes glowed an eerie red even in the darkness. He had fins on the sides of his head and all up and down his arms. There was no question about it, she was standing face to face with a Talicron. "What are you doing here?" She demanded.

"I've come to warn you," he spoke. "You have threatened the life of someone my master needs, and he wants you to stop."

"What are you talking about?" She spoke with slight agitation.

"The elf girl," he growled. "You and your assassins have been hunting down the elf girl and her guardian for several weeks. My master needs the elf girl to complete his mission."

"Your master is crazy," she said. "That girl is the heir to the Silverwood - the kingdom your people destroyed nearly 14 years ago. The longer she lives, the greater the chance that she can reunite the realms and drive back the Talicrons and all dark creatures into the shadows."

The Talicron squeezed slightly at the perceived insult. "Watch your tongue, human. The master has use for you, but he told me not to hesitate to kill you if you proved uncooperative."

"If your Master's goal is to somehow restore the throne of Silverwood, then you might as well kill me now," she spat.

A trill of sounds resonated from the Talicron, this Naranda perceived to be a laugh. "I am permitted to inform you that your suspicions couldn't be further from the truth," he added. "In fact, one has to wonder why you have tolerated the continued existence of the elf. You have had ample opportunity even with your pathetically inept hirelings to kill her and thus eliminate the threat. But you haven't. Why?" He paused. "You seek something."

Naranda narrowed her eyes at the invader in anger.

"The master will be pleased to learn this, I'm sure," he flexed his arm and flung her back into a waiting chair at the table. Stepping closer, the Talicron started to position his dagger in a threatening position, but Naranda was already a step ahead.
Flinging herself onto the floor, she rolled once then twice away from the Talicron. At the completion of the second roll, she lay facing the Talicron with the quickest spell prepared that she could utter. Her extended hand caused a flash of bright white light to radiate out from her hand causing the Talicon to throw up an arm to shield his sensitive eyes.

"Ah," the Talicron said in frustration. "Your resistance will cost you dearly."

Naranda scambled back to her feet and began preparing a quick attack. At the end of her formula, she reached back and grabbed at the hair and pretended to throw something at the unwelcomed visitor. This motion triggered a small trunk that was behind her to go sailing through the air. The Talicron responded by effortlessly grabbing the big chair that he had thrown her into and swung it wildly at the flying trunk. The impact of the trunk and the chair caused a loud crashing sound as the two collided and fell to the floor. This impact was strong enough to knock the Talicron backwards, and he caught himself from falling over completely by grabbing onto the edge of Naranda's bed.

Naranda took a few steps back and came up next to her wardrobe. Keeping her eyes on the Talicron she felt along the side and found the staff she normally kept there. Wiping it around, she pointed it directly at the Talicron, who made his way back on to his feet and was nearing the table in the middle of the room.

Calling out several words, a ball of red flame leaped out of the end of the staff and hurled its way toward the intended target. In a desperate attempt from being scorched, the Talicron dropped to the floor. The fireball exploded just above him showering him with molten fragments that burned his skin. In a wave of anger, the Talicron kicked with his massive legs and sent the table sliding across the room toward the sorceress. Naranda unable to dodge the skidding table threw her arms up in panic to block it. But the weight and momentum of the table slammed through her relatively weak arms and pinned her back against the wardrobe. Her staff was knocked free from her hands and went bouncing across the table and onto the floor.

With several smoldering holes in his skin, the Talicron stood up and grabbed the dagger which he had dropped as a result of the chair-trunk collision. With several cautious steps, he neared the sorceress. "I'm impressed," he hissed. "You handle yourself pretty well against a single Talicron. I'm sure I wouldn't be so impressed if there was more than just me here."

"You're in my house," she scoffed. "I'm not going to blow up my own house just to impress you. I'm trying to minimize the damage. Good carpenters are hard to come by."

The Talicron spotted the fallen staff and decided that two weapons in his hands might put him in a little better position. Once he picked it up, Naranda smiled and began uttering several commands. An instant later the staff flashed and flames enveloped the Talicron's hand.

He immediately discarded the staff and shook his hand frantically to get the flames off of his hand. Naranda continued uttering commands and suddenly the table that had her pinned tight to the wardrobe started scooting toward the distracted Talicron. Like an uncontrolled bronco, the table barreled right over the Talicron knocking him down and raking its pedestal across his body. The ancient table did suffer some damage as one of the feet snapped off as it dug itself into the Talicrons chest.

"Now you see what you did?" Naranda mocked. "That table has been in my family for over two hundred years, and now it's broken. Who am I ever going to find to repair it?"

The Talicron lay unresponsive on the floor. Dark purple blood leaked out of the gash across the creature's chest. His breathing was still; almost non-existent. Naranda walked slowly toward the fallen enemy and reached down to retrieve the staff. With an air of victory, she stood over the creature.

"That will teach you to come barging into my house, uninvited," she muttered.

A swift kick by the Talicron sent the staff flying across the room. He spun and brought his other leg around and quickly knocked Naranda off her feet. In a single leaping motion, the Talicron straddled Naranda's stunned body with his immense hand grasping her throat again.

"Enough!" A familiar voice came from the doorway.

Naranda turned to see the familiar voice, and saw in the doorway the outline of a chair being held by two more creatures that looked like Talicrons.

They moved the chair into the room. "Tagaroth, release her. You were sent here to warn her, not destroy the place."

Tagaroth, the Talicron, slowly relaxed his grip. With reluctance and a growl, he stood to his feet and moved away from the woman.

"Dravious?" Naranda croaked trying to regain her breath.

"Now go tend to your wounds before you bleed on something worth more than your miserable life," Dravious barked.

Naranda stood to her feet and watched as Tagaroth left. He weaved his way around the Talicrons that carried the chair where Dravious was seated.

"Put me down, and go help him," he commanded. The two Talicrons silently obeyed and left the room.

"Did you send that, thing?" Naranda asked indignantly.

"No," the sorcerer replied.

"Then why is he here?" She asked.

"As I said, to warn you. His master is concerned you may prematurely disrupt his plans," he said.

"I was cordial when I sought your help," she walked slowly toward him. "Now, you're in my home and I will not be trifled with here."

He chuckled lightly, "Please, I am not here to start anything with you. Besides, your powers are no match for my own."

"Are you willing to test that theory," she uttered a command and stretched out her arm. The fallen fire staff flew from the corner of the room and she caught it bringing it swiftly to bear on Dravious.

"Must we be so melodramatic?" He responded. "Let me show you something. Shall we have a little more light?"

"Be my guest," she replied not taking the staff nor her eye off the sorcerer.

With a upraised palm, the candles inside the room instantly lit and glowed. Naranda squinted for a moment until her eyes readjusted to the sudden illumination.

"Do you know what this is?" he asked pointing to the artifact that hung around his neck.

"An amulet," she replied.

"Ah, it's more than that," he wiggled his finger at her. "This is the Talisman of Alterian."

"Impossible," she shot back.

"I assure you it is," he calmly replied.

"How is this possible?" She asked. "Where did you come by it? How did you survive putting it on?"

He settled back in his chair as much as was possible. "Fourteen years ago, I led a group of Talicrons in an attack on Spire Tree. We had been looking for opportunities to take out Krestichan, but we'd been unable to due to their persistent defense."

"But what changed," she inquired.

"Word got out that a festival, a celebration was to be given in honor of all of the master warriors who served. This included a special regiment of guardians from Fairhaven that had been training with Krestichan for several months." He paused for a moment and closed his eyes to relive the events. "That night, at the height of the celebration, we snuck in through a hidden entrance and made our way into the heart of Spire Tree. We were able to strike at the heart of the company where they were grossly unarmed."

"How did you find out about the hidden entrance?" She asked.

He shook his head, "Some things are better left unknown." He clasped his hands together as he continued. "I chased Krestichan back to where I knew he kept the talisman on display. He never wore it except on rare occasions. There, I struck him down before he could gain access to it and its power."

She pulled up a chair and sat down in front of him. "How did you manage to put it on, and survive?"

"As you know," he lowered his voice, "no one actually knew what would happen if you put it on, because no one had ever attempted to do so that wasn't in the royal line."

"And here you are," she added.

"There was some consequence," he continued. "As you can see, I've lost all but very limited use of my hands and legs. And the talisman," he stopped.

"Go on," she prodded.

"Cannot be removed," he groaned. "It's a prison of sorts. The power sustains me, nevertheless I am confined and unable to go about on my own; it is almost a curse."

"I feel real bad for you," she sneared.

"Don't you see? To be so close, to have all of the power this talisman generates and then to be caught short. It is more torment than one can imagine," he sighed.

Naranda stood back to her feet and paced around the room waving the fire staff around. "Why come to me?" She asked. "What could I possibly do to help you? For that matter, why would I?"

"Because," he reached out with his power and pulled her toward him. "You're as interested in this power as I am, and I think there is a way to unlock it."

"You're kidding, right?" She started her casting her own spell to resist the force, but Dravious flicked his wrist and released her.

"Around my neck, the talisman has only one stone in it. You see?" He pointed to the central white stone.

"Yes, how can I not see it?" She replied.

"There are four others that form a cross. They are missing," he struggled to point to the empty sockets.

"I see," she said studying the talisman more closely. "Where did they go? Were they not there when you captured it from its former owner?"

He nodded. "They were, but in my haste to put it on, I failed to realize that there was a trap set for anyone who put it on. The four gems, black, red, blue and gold, which gives the talisman power over every aspect of known reality, vanished. They have been hidden somewhere among the five realms."

"Sounds like you've got an awful lot of looking to do then, but I'm afraid I can't help you," she scoffed.

He raised a hand slightly, not to pull, drag or constrain, but to plead. "You can, simply stop hunting the guardian and the elf girl, and allow me to capture them. If she is of the royal line, I can use her to locate the missing gems," he paused for a deep breath. "Once I have them, you can be assured that her destruction will occur."

She walked up to Dravious and slammed both her hands down onto the armrests of his chair. "And what's in it for me?" she commanded.

Dravious leaned forward, "Power," he whispered. "A return to the old ways, where chaos reigns supreme. Do you want to sit on the throne of Spire Tree? I can give that to you. Or, if you'd rather see it burned to the ground, I can make that happen too."

"You really think I believe you?" She stood up straight. "You honestly think that I would be dumb enough to believe that you'd offer me a share, just for staying out of your way?"

"A lord cannot reign without masters," he muttered. "Your initial cooperation is just a start, as we search for the missing gems, I'm sure that a priestess of your abilities would be very handy."

She stared down at him with a glare of doubt on her face.

"Naranda," he cooed. "Do you not think I could have just as easily let that Talicron goon throttle you on the floor? You were doomed and I intervened. Does that not count for anything?"

Naranda turned and walked back over toward her bed. "Be gone," she waved a hand. "Seek me out once you have captured the elf girl, and I will assist you so long as you keep those beasts away from my home." She sat down on the edge of the bed and waited for her guest to leave.

Dravious raised a finger and the door behind him opened to reveal the two Talicrons that carried had him there. "Let us take our leave of the Lady Naranda," he commanded.

The two stepped forward and grabbed the poles that supported the chair and lifted. Turning him about slowly, they navigated their way out the door. "We will be in touch," he chimed.

"Don't forget to turn the lights . . ." her words drifted off as the candles instinctively responded by dimming themselves into darkness.

Chapter 14

The trip from Falcon Roost to the edge of the Silverwood was largely uneventful. It had taken them nearly two weeks via the route that Guntharr had chosen, but he deemed it wise to come into the area without going through Fairhaven. This made Taya a bit sad, as she had missed the little place that had been her occasional home for the last fourteen years. Guntharr promised that they would be returning there soon, and that once they got there, he assured her it would be for a while this time.

Overall, encounters were few and far between compared to the earlier part of their quest. No dark goblins or bandits managed to block their paths. One night while they were resting, Taya was taking the watch, and a large bear-like creature waddled into their camp. Taya didn't want to kill the creature so she did her best to scare it away by waving a torch at it. That didn't work very well. Fortunately, Rift's keen hearing and smell picked up on the intruder and he awoke. At Taya's request, Rift did not actually attack the creature, but instead morphed into his battle wolf form long enough to make the bear reconsider. Regrettably, the wolf's transformation howl woke the entire crew up.

The first part of the trip was largely focused on the discussion of where Arnethia learned to handle herself as well as she had. Through much prodding and reassurance from everyone, she finally confessed that she had been training at the local thieves guild for the last couple of years. Not to become an actual thief, she emphasized, but rather to learn the craft so that she could better protect herself and eventually join up with a group that could use someone to help spy and gather information.

"So in a way," Taya marveled aloud. "You're picking up where you left off?"

"Of sorts," Arnethia replied. "You see, it was while I was training in stealth and various spying techniques that I discovered my gift. At first, everyone thought it was simply a parlor trick and they all laughed it off. Then I started to develop it. It got so I could dig deeper and deeper into an object's past. This caused amazement as everyone still thought I had just mastered the art of spying and infiltration, and was selectively playing jokes on the other members."

"But then," Firebane prodded.

She bowed her head slightly. "I got irritated. No one thought I had a true gift. No matter how deep I went into someone's past, it was just credited with my investigative ability."

"Why didn't that make you happy?" Taya asked.

Arnethia's expression was sad. "One thing to know about thieves and spies, they think everything is about them. And I knew that this was something that I had been given. I knew that I had been blessed with an amazing gift, and I just wanted them to realize that even spies can have gifts from God."

"So what happened," Firebane prodded again.

"Well, someone brought in a new candidate for us to evaluate for guild membership," she paused.

"Let me guess," Guntharr interrupted, "Manni."

She nodded. "I didn't know who he was at the time, but I quickly learned what he had done in the past. I decided I would show off and went first. I asked for one of his gloves and then began to read the history."

"What did you see?" Taya asked.

She shivered. "I'd rather not say, it was awful. Needless to say, I picked up something from way back in Manni's past, that there was no way I could have dug up through normal means. When he acknowledged what I said was true, the guild members stood starring at me with thier eyes wide open."

"Did the guild accept him?" Firebane inquired.

"No," she answered bluntly. "Manni, as you could see, was too erratic, too vile even for the guild. He was ushered out that night screaming and cursing at us all. He, of course, threatened me personally, but I didn't think anything of it."

"Why?" Taya prodded.

"Because, I had been training. I knew how to handle a sword. I could hold my own in a fight. I never dreamed that someone could be so cruel." She reached up and rubbed her eyes.

"That's when he came for you," Guntharr added.

"A few days past, I had all but forgotten the incident. I had just gotten home from a routine training session, drained and exhausted when his thugs surprised me at the door." She closed her eyes for a moment seeing once again the terrific event replay itself in her mind's eye. "They had been there long enough to subdue my family. I tried to fight them off, but they killed them. I wasn't prepared to handle that at the time. I couldn't believe that anyone could be so evil."

"There is a lot of evil out there," Guntharr replied. "Unfortunately, we're getting ready to ride right into the heart of it for this realm."

"You have my word, guardian," she replied, "I will follow you and the princess to the end."

He held up a hand to indicate she needn't go on. "Your word is good with me. But soon, we will need you to exercise your gift."

This caught Arnethia by surprise. The expression on her face indicated that she wasn't exactly sure how she would be able to help.

"Does this trouble you?" Guntharr asked in response to her expression.

"No," she stumbled, "I'm just not sure how I can help."

"Let me explain," he replied coolly. "I'm sure Taya could elaborate on the fact that while I can sometimes be generous, I usually have more of a motive behind my actions than just pure and simple kindness."

Her expression went from concern to confusion.

"I have to side with Arnethia on this one," Taya spoke up. "I'm not sure I understand what you're saying."

The edge of Guntharr's mouth curled up slightly which indicated he was having fun. He frequently enjoyed being mysterious at his friends expense and this was going to be one of those times. "Let's take a look at a practical example, shall we?" He paused to allow them time to react. After a moment, with no response, he decided to continue. "The exquisite sword that we found for you back in Falcon Roost," he gestured toward the weapon at her side. "How much did the smithy rightly milk us for it, Firebane?"

Firebane still freshly and painfully aware of the cost of the sword blurted out, "One hundred gold coins, which I'm still not sure . . ." his words trailed off and Guntharr redirected his attention back to the girls.

"You have to admit, for a sword with no real magical ability, that would appear to be a bit extreme. For me, I have seen similarly crafted swords not bearing the elvish crest, obviously, go for a single gold coin," he stopped again to allow for some obvious questions.

Taya was the first to speak up, "So, why did you get it?"

"We have time," Guntharr was savoring the mystery. "Why don't you hazard a guess? It would do us good to hear you reason out the real purpose of the purchase."

Taya had played this game with him before and she knew there was no point playing dumb when he was in this mode. The only way to get to the point was to play along and try to work it out. "First, you knew Arnethia needed a weapon, right?"

"Fair point, but why that one?" he challenged.

"Because of the quality?" Arnethia argued.

"Not really. As I have already mentioned, I have bought as nice a weapon for a fraction of the price," he responded.

"He wanted to show off," Rift barked from behind them.

"Nice one, Rift," Firebane chuckled.

"Hardly," Guntharr sighed. "Focus on the sword itself, ignoring the price we paid for it."

"Well," Arnethia thought hard, "It was clearly from the armory of the Silverwood Rangers of Spire Tree."

Guntharr nodded in agreement.

"So, what was it doing in Falcon Roost?" She asked.

A glimmer of excitement sparked in Guntharr's eye as he could see she was getting close, "Go deeper, not what," he prodded.

"How did it get there?" Taya exploded with excitement.

Guntharr pointed a finger at her indicating that she had got it. "How, indeed? A weapon like that would not have left Spire Tree willingly, especially to end up in the hands of a smithy far away in Falcon Roost."

Arnethia's expression changed from bewilderment to amazement. "I see, so we want to know how it got out? But I'm not sure I understand why that's important?"

Guntharr nodded, this was certainly a less obvious answer. "I will forgo the games and come right out with it. We are headed into a very dangerous situation. Remember, the last time I was here, I was blessed to have escaped the Talicrons with my life and that of Taya's. I'm not so anxious to walk right in through the front doors again if I can help it."

"You think there's a more discrete way back into Spire Tree?" Arnethia asked.

"I'm counting on it," Guntharr concluded.

Little more was spoken about it for several days. Each member of the group theorized on possible ways into Spire Tree. Once they had gotten to within a day's travel of the edge of the Silverwood, Guntharr paused the journey long enough for Arnethia to settle the debate once and for all.

Knowing that the history of the weapon was long, she indicated that it could take a while for her to work her way back through time to find the answer they were looking for.

Guntharr understood.

"Anything in particular I should be looking for?" she asked.

"My guess is it's an underground passage hidden somewhere in the surrounding hills, but that's pure speculation." He emphasized the speculation part.

The group had dismounted their rides and taken up a comfortable position along a grassy hill overlooking the valley that marked the entrance into the Silverwood.

Arnethia drew the sword and sat cross-legged on the soft grass laying the sword across her lap and placed both of her hands on the blade. Slowly she moved her hands across the blade, taking in the various facets of the metalwork. As she closed her eyes, the others could tell that she was being taken back in time; through the history of the sword.

Minutes passed like hours as the waiting companions sat around silently watching not only for any reaction from Arnethia but also for any potential threats coming up from Silverwood to greet them prematurely.

Sweat began to pour down her face as she unwound the history of the sword looking for any indication of how it had been taken from the armory of Spire Tree and carried out of the Silverwood. She waded past the brief time that the smithy had possessed it and onto its previous owner. There it spent some time in storage and encountered only some minor activity. Further and further she dug into the weapon's past. Once again, the sword passed hands this time from son to father; and from commoner to the hand of a master swordsman or so it would appear. Fight after fight, Arnethia saw the unrecognized faces of foes that fell before the blade.

Time continued to unwind as she saw various places that the sword had been. Some she recognized as the valley around Falcon Roost and others she knew only by their descriptions such as the great city of Fairhaven. Once she arrived in Fairhaven, the scenes seemed to mirror a common pattern for a time, the owner must have been a guard or authority for sometime in Fairhaven for the images repeated, over and over with only minor interruptions or an occasional skirmish. Then something changed, the scene went from the city of Fairhaven to the forest that boardered the city and into the Silverwood. She carefully focused her attention at this part as she could only control the time stream of the sword and not the perspective for which she saw things around it. Oddly, she saw only what the object wanted her to see.

Over time when using her powers, she'd gotten use to seeing things happen in reverse, but this investigation had been tedious and long. She'd never had to delve back so far in an object's history. Time was intangible and hard to quantify when she was doing this. When looking at a scene, it could be days, months, or years and she couldn't tell. Suddenly, in the corner of the scene, she saw it, Spire Tree standing tall. The bearer of the sword seemed to be moving toward the fortress, backwards of course, at an amazing pace. Slowing the time stream down she tried to find key landmarks to help her identify where the barer was. The sword's owner was moving through open hilly terrain at the edge of the forest. Closer and closer he drew to the forest's entrance then suddenly, made a turn and ran parallel along the edge of the forest. He neared a stoned lined hill when at last she saw a large log holding up a massive rock which revealed a gaping hole into the hill beside Spire Tree.

In reality, her companions sat still and quite as they observed the stress it put upon her body. Her hair was now dripping with sweat and her breathing became shallow. The hands that once swept up and down the blade now clinched it tightly on either end. The hand that grasp the tip of the blade had a small trail of blood dripping down from it. Her body began to quiver.

"It's been over an hour," Taya whispered to the guardian. "Shouldn't we do something?"

He shook his head, "No, it is best not to disturb her during this time. I'm sure she knows her limits."

Firebane in response to Taya's concern, bowed his head and began uttering a prayer of protection and strength for Arnethia.

With a sudden final gasp, Taya saw Arnethia stop breathing. Her body reacted by slowing its shivering and began to wobble as if she would topple over. The sword fell out of her hands and she fell back onto the ground.

Taya responded immediately and ran over to her calling her name.

"Arnethia, wake up!" she cried.

A huge influx of air startled Taya as Arncthia slowly revived and inhaled deeply the fresh afternoon air. Her eyes opened slowly to look up at Taya who was cradling her head in her lap. "I think I found it," she said weakly.

"Are you all right?" Taya asked frantically.

Arnethia smiled slightly, "I think so, I've never had to dig so deep before."

"What did you find?" Guntharr asked.

Arnethia struggled to raise herself up and Taya provided some necessary assistance to get her in a seated position once again. She wiped her forehead and marveled at the sweat that she wrung out of her hair. "How long was I out of it?"

Firebane came close and handed her a flask of water. "It was right about ninety minutes," he answered.

She took a large draft from the flask and then wiped her mouth off with her forearm, not realizing that there was blood that had run down from her hand. "Oh, my!" She reacted to the taste of her own blood on her lips. "What happened?"

Guntharr spoke up, "During the last several minutes of your," he paused looking for an appropriate word, "research," he finally decided on, "you gripped the point of the sword with your hand quite tightly. Let us take a look at it."

He reached out to take the hand that had trails of blood that ran out around the fingers. She responded by stretching out the hand to see a small gash in the center of her palm. Guntharr reached into a small pouch beside him and pulled out a strip of cloth and from another he pulled out a container of salve. After carefully washing the blood from her hand, he gently applied some of the salve to her wound like an expert physician.

After expertly bandaging her hand, Guntharr turned their focus back to the subject at hand. "So what did you learn?"

She took a deep breath before beginning. "First I want to be clear that I have no good way of knowing how far back I had to travel in order to find what I did."

"What do you mean?" Guntharr asked.

"Normally, I can travel through the life of an object very quickly." She stopped to think for a second. "Even something that is several years old, I can usually scan through its history in just a matter of a few minutes."

"Give me an example, please." Guntharr closed his eyes to consider the situation.

She thought back to some of the more recent scans she had done. "For example, when I ran through your dagger back in the den," she indicated the small weapon on the side of his hip. "It only took me a minute or so to scan back through to when you left Fairhaven."

His eyes snapped open at the revelation that she had gone back that far when she had scanned the dagger for Manni. "How long ago was that anyway?" she asked.

"Almost a year ago," Taya reported.

Arnethia's expression on her face indicated that she was puzzled. "That doesn't seem right."

"It could be," Guntharr closed his eyes as he thought out loud. "Imagine if you will that an object's timeline grows denser the older it is, making it more difficult to travel through."

"You've lost me, guardian," she confessed.

"You lost me too," Taya responded.

"I've been lost ever since we left the church," Rift threw in.

Guntharr twisted his lips around then spoke. "Consider a stream for me. The longer and older the stream is, the deeper and often wider the valley is that holds the stream."

Arnethia began to understand. "So, the older the object, the more it takes to travel the same amount of time because of the history?"

"That's a theory, anyway. It could also have to do with the number of events or actual action that occurs. Much like a river will dig deeper and faster than a slow flowing stream, an object that has gone through a number of wars or battles - such as your sword and my dagger - would seem much harder to go through, a simpler object such as a tapestry that possibly has little or no encounters may be much easier to go through." He concluded.

Arnethia looked down at the sword laying in her lap, "That would mean one of two things, this sword is really old or it has been involved in an amazing amount of activity."

Taya reached over and tapped the hilt, "Or it could be both."

"Correct," Firebane blurted out, "if Guntharr's theory holds true."

"I can assure you, that the sword you are holding in your hand is no less than fifty years old," he remarked.

"How is that, guardian?" Taya asked.

"As I had indicated before, I met briefly the smithy in your father's court that produced this weapon as well as most of the weapons that your father's rangers used." He replied. "During our discussion, he elaborated on what some of the symbols meant on the blade, and he indicated that he always marked his work in respect to the generation of weapons that it was. We discussed, the different markings he had used over the last fifty years and none of them resemble the generation this weapon belongs to."

"So this means that whatever I saw in regards to the opening, could be long gone." Arnethia said disappointedly.

Guntharr did something he seldom did which was shrug his shoulders, "We'll soon see. Now, tell me what you saw."

Chapter 15

Two lumbering Talicrons carried Dravious' chair through the dank empty hall where his journey with the Talisman had started. Once they arrived in the great hall where Lord Krestichan had held his feasts and celebrated life with his people, Dravious held up a hand and the Talicrons stopped.

"Leave me," he ordered.

The Talicrons carefully sat the chair down and moved toward the exit where several heavily armed Talicrons stood guard. Leaving the room through two massive doors, the sound of the doors closing had barely finished echoing through the hall when Dravious detected footsteps coming up beside him.

"Did your meeting with Naranda prove successful," the newcomer inquired.

Dravious chuckled slightly, "She ultimately saw reason. It wasn't without negotiation, though."

"Explain," responded the man behind him.

"I thought to scare her by sending in a Talicron during the night to deliver the arrangements. She didn't take to that too well," he reported.

"Did she kill him?" Dravious' associate asked with fake concern.

"No, but she could have. She's far too in love with that house of hers to risk blowing it up, so she went easy on him. I jumped in after I heard the commotion start and figured things were getting out of hand." Dravious paused to allow for additional questions, but none came. "So why did you bring me here?"

There were footsteps as the associate moved about the room, outside of Dravious' vision. "This is where it all started, is it not? I thought you might enjoy coming back to where you had accomplished your most notable feat and at the same time condemned yourself to a lifetime of immobility. Killing Krestichan and ushering in the fall of Silverwood was something few thought possible."

"As much as I'd like to, I cannot take all of the credit, someone from the inside told me of the events of the evening. I was given detailed descriptions of where men would be stationed and how to sneak in without getting clobbered before we ever made it here," he replied hoping to learn more about the figure he was bound to serve.

"Ah yes, the inside man," the voice behind chided. "You still hold that you received help from someone within Krestichan's inner circle? Who was this traitor?"

Dravious slapped a hand against the arm rest of his chair. "Are you mocking me? I don't know who it was, I never met the informant. All I know is that he got paid well, and I ultimately got what I wanted and what you needed."

"And that was?" He questioned.

"The end of the elvish influence over the five realms. The ability to take control of the realms one by one and make them our own. We would have completed that task, if I hadn't underestimated the talisman." Dravious looked down at the symbol of power bound to his neck. "Why won't you come around where I can see you?" He craned his neck around to look upon the mystery voice.

"Klock-no vuma," the voice uttered at Dravious' attempt to locate him. The words instantly caused the talisman around Dravious' neck to exude a searing heat that shot directly into his chest.

"All right," I yield. " Stop it!" Dravious begged.

"Nostelium," the voice commanded and the talisman cooled as quickly as it had gotten hot. "Do not challenge me. My ability to stay anonymous protects you as well as me. The moment that anonymity is compromised, I will have no more use for you."

Dravious bowed his head in surrender. "As you wish. What would you have me do next?"

"Stay here and protect Spire Tree," the voice replied.

"From what?" Dravious asked confused. "We already have a small army of Talicrons here to keep anyone from getting in. Why keep me here?"

There was no response but footsteps. Dravious listened as they moved off into the distance then stop. "Because, I suspect 'he' will be arriving soon to try and find clues as to the whereabouts of the Talisman. If he comes, you must capture the girl. The others, you can do with as you wish."

"Where will you be?" Dravious asked, but the footsteps had started again and disappeared into the distance leaving him alone.

*　*　*

Guntharr listened intently to Arnethia's description of the sword's exodus from the Silverwood. The clues led them to the edge of the Forest of Dunemoore. To the south, a small range of tall hills butted up against the forest and it was in this area that the proximity of Spire Tree was nearest to the edge of the forest. The hills seemed to bury themselves into the woods until the forest gave way to an open area between the forest and Spire Tree itself. This area was known as the Ring of Death. It was called this because the massive limbs of Spire Tree extended high above the ring, elven guards would position themselves high above the ring and monitor any approaching enemy. A small squadron of elvish rangers could easily take out a small army before they could cross the ring.

It was at the edge of the hills that the group came to an abrupt halt. The area was littered with stones that could easily hide an entrance into a secret cavern.

"If I've interpreted your geography correctly," Guntharr dismounted Nightfury, "this should be the place."

"How will we ever find the entrance?" Taya asked hopping lightly off of Silverfoot.

"Exactly what I was going to ask," Firebane remarked still sitting on Angel Dance.

Raskin settled gently on one of the stones near them. "I'm afraid I can't be of much help," he cooed.

"Actually," Guntharr turned and looked at him, "I think you can. We may be here a while, and we haven't exactly been subtle in our approach. Would you make a quick circle over head to see if we have any nearby threats, then head over to Spire Tree to get our bearings. Remember to stay high when you approach. It's not just the elves that like to sniper things from the trees."

"I'll be back before Rift can utter a reasonable complaint," Raskin said as he took off into the air.

"That sounded like a challenge to me," Rift wandered over toward Guntharr who was studying the hillside and the numerous possibilities. "I don't suppose you or Firebane have any prayers that can help us, you know like a 'seek and you shall find' type of prayer?"

Guntharr furrowed his brow in a look that Taya had never seen him make before. "I really don't think we need anything that sophisticated."

"You don't?" Arnethia responded surprised.

Firebane dismounted and walked over to join the group. In the process, he knelt down and rubbed behind Rift's ears which he didn't seem to object to. "I think Guntharr has something more practical in mind."

"Sometimes the best tools to get the job done, are the ones that God provides us naturally." Guntharr held out his hands.

"You really think we're going to go around and pick up every one of these rocks?" Arnethia questioned.

Firebane laughed. "You're starting to sound like Rift."

"Well, that's what I would have said if I wasn't currently preoccupied." Rift tilted his head in toward Firebane's hand indicating that he wanted him to rub harder.

"Rift," Guntharr turned his attention to the wolf, "let's use your nose to see what we can find."

Rift stiffened at the sound of his name and the suggestion that he use his nose. "I think you over estimate my nose's ability. There is no way I can detect the scent of somebody that may have ran through here fourteen years ago."

Guntharr tilted his head. "Who said anything about hunting the scent of someone whose not been through here in more than a decade? I was going to suggest that you sniff around the base of some of the more potential stones. You see, the cavern under one of them will still have air seeping out of it, and most definitely it will be distinctly different than the clean forest air that we're breathing now. Find the leak, and you find the entrance."

Rift nodded without argument and went to work. He first started around a small rock that couldn't possibly be hiding a hidden cavern to try and get a baseline for the scent of the ground. He then moved on to the big rock that Raskin had landed on. A few minutes of circling around the edge and he looked up at the group. "Well, I hope you're not expecting me to howl or anything dramatic, but I think Raskin picked the right one without knowing it."

Guntharr looked amazed. "You really think that's the one?"

"Hey, it was your idea," Rift replied. He bent his head down and studied the seam between the stone and the ground a little more. "I can't be certain, but there is definitely something different going on under this rock."

"It's huge," Arnethia pointed out. "How will we move it?"

"I have a theory," Firebane spoke up as he walked over to the rock. "Give me hand," he called out to Guntharr.

The two dug their fingers under the edges of the rock. With knees bent and backs straight, Firebane counted out, "one, two, three." When he hit three the two of them strained to pick up the stone. Even as strong as they were, Taya didn't think there was any way the two of them could lift a boulder of that size. But as they straightened their knees the edge of the rock lifted steadily off the ground.

The horses let out a snort of approval and Taya clapped her hands. Beneath the stone, they saw a dark entrance to a cave.

"That's it!" Taya cried.

"Quick, find a stout branch or limb to prop the stone up," Arnethia commanded. The two rummaged around the edge of the forest and came up with a recently downed limb.

They brought over the stud and made a prop to fit under the edge of the stone that Firebane and Guntharr were holding up.

"Thank you," Firebane sighed. "It was starting to get heavy."

"Starting," Taya wondered. "I still can't believe you two picked it up."

"Lord Krestichan had to have known this tunnel was here," Guntharr said. "The stone has been magically altered to be much lighter than it should. While still very much a broad heavy stone to the casual onlooker, once you put your mind to it and a little muscle, it can be moved."

They secured the three steeds and set them up with plenty of food and water. Firebane then offered a prayer of protection for them while they were gone just as Raskin returned.

"Report," Taya asked as he landed upon the up raised stone.

His head twitched for a moment from one side and then to another before speaking. "Nothing immediately nearby. The edge of the forest was easy enough to see through, but the closer you get to the ring, the denser it gets."

"How well guarded is Spire Tree?" Guntharr asked.

Some more twitching then, "there were guards roaming the base of the tree and a few scouts out on the greater limbs, but no one seemed to be bothered by me."

Arnethia nodded in approval. "It would seem we're not expected."

"Agreed," Guntharr concurred.

Raskin twitched once more. "Did you find it yet?"

"What?" Taya asked.

"The entrance," Raskin sqawked.

"Look beneath you, my friend," Taya replied.

Raskin ruffled his feathers and twisted his head sideways and almost upside down. "Oh, I see."

"Maintain a watch over the horses, Raskin, for the caverns are not a place for you," Guntharr directed. "Every hour, circle round to the far side of Spire Tree. Look for the largest opening near the great lower limbs. This should be the windows into the great hall. If you see light, you know were there and probably need your help."

He stretched out his wings slightly and flicked them up and down, almost in a nodding fashion.

"Firebane, we're going to need some light," Guntharr remarked.

Reaching into his bag which now hung around his neck, he pulled out the light crystal and secured it to the staff. One by one, they filed slowly into the mouth of the cave. Seconds later, Raskin was alone with only the company of Angel Dance and the other two horses. With a quick hop, Raskin leaped from the stone onto the saddle of Nightfury who was standing near Angel Dance. Within a moment, the two were engaged in an inaudible conversation.

Firebane and Rift led the way through the cavern with Taya in the middle and Arnethia and Guntharr in the rear. Just inside the cave, a small stash of ancient torches lay waiting to be used. Deciding to take one along, Guntharr grabbed one and lit it for good measure.

While the passage was roughly hewn, the care and skill by which the makers used to carve it was evident. This was no naturally occurring cavern, but rather it was made on purpose. The downward slope of the path was steady. After a very short while, the path turned and angled in the direction of Spire Tree.

"Why is this here?" Taya asked.

Guntharr shrugged. He really had no clue as to the reason for the tunnel's existance.

"Silverwood wasn't always a loved and cherished place, Taya," Firebane said. "There was a generation before your father that suffered and fought many battles to maintain control of this realm. It's likely that this was built as an emergency escape route should the king's life and the fall of Spire Tree seem eminent."

"So, you don't think Krestichan had this built?" Arnethia asked.

"Not likely," Guntharr replied. "To be truthful, I don't think he even knew of its existence."

"Is that possible?" Rift asked.

"I suppose," Firebane said. "You knew him better than any of us," he said to Guntharr.

"If he did, he never shared it with me," he said softly.

Time passed and the passage leveled off for a while. Nothing exciting could be seen in any direction.

"This would explain a great many things," Guntharr muttered.

"Like what?" Arnethia asked.

"Like how the Talicrons managed to sneak into Spire Tree without alarming the rangers," he concluded.

Taya's head started to play tricks on her. She was used to the dark, but this was different. The dark combined with the shallow direction on either side and the seemingly never ending tunnel ahead caused her to second guess her steps.

"We've started going up," Arnethia anounced.

"We must be nearing the base of Spire Tree," Firebane remarked.

"Be on your guard," Guntharr cautioned. "Arnethia, can you go up ahead and scan for traps? I don't anticipate any, but one cannot be too sure."

Arnethia smiled, "Finally, something I can handle," and she trotted up ahead of Firebane and Rift. She paced herself just at the edge of the light that radiated from his staff.

Guntharr moved up alongside Taya.

"Don't worry, I'm ready," she answered before he could ask.

Their pace slowed as the path's incline increased dramatically. Combined with Arnethia's delicate search of the way ahead made time seemed to slow to a crawl for Taya.

"What have we here?" Arnethia's voiced rang out from ahead.

"What is it?" Guntharr asked.

"We seem to have reached the end of the road," she replied.

"You mean a dead end," Firebane approached holding the light up so they could clearly see the solid rock wall that stood before them.

"No, just the end of this road," she stated.

"Is it possible this was added recently to prevent entrance?" Firebane asked.

Arnethia studied the wall carefully. Her fingers moved along the smooth stone work taking in every detail. "Just one way to find out," she said and then closed her eyes.

Minutes passed as the group stood in silence. Her eyes snapped open suddenly indicating that she had uncovered something.

"Well," Rift prodded.

She reached down and patted the wolf on the head in a patronizing fashion. "Are we anxious to go chew up some bad, evil monsters?"

Firebane couldn't contain himself and began to roar with laughter. Taya also caught herself snickering at the gesture.

"As a matter of fact, I am," was all he could come up with without loosing his temper.

She smiled. "Well, the good news is the wall is not new and it does open."

"I assume you have bad news to go along with the good news," Guntharr said.

She nodded. "Unfortunately, the last time this door was used, and remember, I can't even begin to tell you how long ago that was, it was opened from the other side and closed automatically."

"So that means, its magical," Taya exclaimed.

"Or it has a very sophisticated mechanism built into the wall itself," Arnethia argued.

Firebane stepped up to the wall and began feeling around on it. "Based upon what we saw at the end of the cave as well as the fact that it was put in by the elves, it's probably is magical."

Guntharr stepped away and thought for a moment, closing his eyes to consider all of the possibilities. "Arnethia, considering the circumstances, how long would it take you to find a hidden triggering mechanism - assuming there is one - on this side of the wall?"

She ran her fingers through her dark hair and considered the question. "Assuming its near the door and its sophistication lives up to its design, I would say it could take an hour or so to search thoroughly."

"Do it," he ordered. "We can't risk alerting everyone in the vicinity to our presence. Not yet."

With that she set to work. Firebane kept near with the light to help her as she felt around the walls of the tunnel. Guntharr, Taya and Rift huddled together to discuss next steps.

"Rift, don't give into the temptation to transform right away," Guntharr instructed. "Your battle form is tremendously helpful, but until it seems that we've lost the surprise, I don't want to risk our position on your howl."

Rift snorted. "I guess I see your point. I'll have to stay back. In this form, I'm afraid I'm not very durable."

"Agreed," Guntharr nodded. "However, your ears and sense of smell are still superior to everyone else's, so you can help by keeping us informed."

Taya reached over and touched the guardian on the arm. "What about me?"

He turned and took her small hand in his. "You will have to be selective and watchful. Firebane, Arnethia and I will need you to watch our backs. The Talicrons are large creatures, unlike the dark goblins you've encountered. They are taller than me and very well armored. You will need to hit high on their chest in order to pierce their skin. Shots to their midsection, legs or back will most likely just bounce off."

"I found it," Arnethia called out successfully.

Everyone jumped to their feet and readied their weapons. Rift moved slowly to the back next to Taya in order to limit his exposure to attack until such time as he was needed.

"Open the door," Guntharr commanded.

On one of the stones to the left of the end wall, a small hole which looked like nothing more than a simple pore in the stone contained an intricate little triggering mechanism. Arnethia jammed her finger in tiny hole and tripped the switch with a clunk. Almost immediately a grinding sound of rock against rock could be heard. Part of the wall separated and opened up just enough that one person could squeeze through.

"I'll go first," she offered as she pulled out her sword.

The ambiant lighting in the room was only slightly brighter than the light produced in the tunnel by Firebane's staff and Guntharr's torch combined. Looking around, she saw no apparent occupants in the room, so she slipped in low and slow to the ground. She concentrated for a moment to listen for any sounds, and was unable to identify anything. On the far side was a heavy door with bars in the window.

"It looks clear," she whispered back through the doorway. One by one, the group entered the room. It was basically empty except for the one door leading out.

"We're in the dungeon," Guntharr indicated. "This is one of the prison cells on the lowest level."

"How convenient, a perfect escape route in a place where no one would expect there to be an escape route," Rift said.

Arnethia moved over to one side and quickly located the other triggering mechanism. "Just in case we need to go back the way we came, here is how you would open this back up." As she said this the door automatically closed back, disguising itself as a perfectly solid stone wall.

Guntharr moved up to the cell door and checked it. It was unlocked. Slowly he pushed it open and peered out into the hallway. The cell they were in happened to be the last one in a long row of cells, so there was only one way to go from there. Seeing no guards or signs of life, he pushed the door open further and stepped out into the hallway.

Cautiously, the group made their way through the rows of vacant cells until they reached a final door. Looking through the bars, they could see remnants of an old table and chairs and a winding stairway on the other side.

"Rift," Guntharr whispered back.

Rift stepped forward and sniffed the air and listened carefully. "Nothing's alive in there as best as I can tell," he decided.

Guntharr pushed the door open slowly and quietly. Years of neglect and no use made the second part harder than it should have been. After taking almost a full minute to open the door, he glanced through the crack and Arnethia jumped in. One by one the companions worked their way inside.

"So, what is it exactly we're looking for in here, besides trouble?" Arnethia paused and asked.

Guntharr drew close to her so as not to have to raise his voice much higher than a whisper. "Ultimately, we need to find the Talisman of Alterian. The few times I saw it not with Krest it was in a hidden vault adjacent to his private quarters."

"How well hidden?" She wondered quietly.

"Very few even knew the vault existed. Only people within his inner circle would even know where to look for it," he concluded.

"So there's a chance it might still be there?" Arnethia asked.

He nodded once. "There is a remote possibility."

With that, Arnethia bolted up the stairs in such a quiet manor that even Taya was impressed. The next serveral levels were repeats of the previous - long rows of unused prison cells. The final level of what appeared to be the prison section contained two sets of stairs on either end of the long corridor. Instead of cells, the center was divided into several rooms that use to be the home for guards and officials watching over the prison.

Guntharr directed Arnethia toward the stairs at the opposite end of the corridor. With a surge of energy that resembled a trapped creature being set free, Arnethia crossed the length of the corridor and carefully assended the stairs to the next level. The rest gathered together and started to ascend slowly when she returned. "Looks like we've hit the cellar."

They all arrived on the next floor which was evenly divided by a long passage. Part of the floor was devoted to storage of food and drink.

This area seemed to have seen some attention recently as there were several new casks of wine and crates of grain and various foods. The other half of the floor was at one time dedicated to storing various treasures and valuables. The bared gates hung open and the large cavernous room stood empty with nothing but some busted pottery and broken shelves.

Moving on, they managed to climb two more floors which were mostly vacant staff quarters. It wasn't until they reached the ground floor, that they saw their first signs of life. The base of the tree had been carved out into a large courtyard which had entrances on both ends to the Ring of Death. Two sets of Talicrons were stationed at either entrance, but fortunately they were busy watching outside of the tree.

Guntharr was now on familiar territory. He knew they needed to only go up a few more long narrow flights and they would be at the great hall. From there it was another long flight to the residence level where the king's family would reside along with their personal assistents. Between the great hall and the residence was the kitchen and eventually the armory.

The group started across the courtyard. Rows of empty stables lined the courtyard on either side that once housed some of the finest battle ready horses in the five realms. Quietly, as they crossed, the group kept careful eyes to see that the guards kept their backs to them at all times. Once they arrived safely on the other side, the group ducked into a corner behind a sweeping staircase that led up into the heart of the tree.

"Well, at least we know we're not alone," Firebane pointed out.

"Are there any other ways up to the area we need to get to without taking the wide open path?" Arnethia asked.

"Once we get up to the next level, there are less open stairs to the other levels, but we have to get up this stairway and down past the Ranger's hall before we get that option." Guntharr pointed off in the direction they needed to go.

"Do you think there's anyone up there, now?" Firebane asked.

"No question about it," Rift spoke in low growl.

Arnethia reached up and grabbed the edge of the ledge of the staircase that curved up above their heads. "I'll check it out." With that she hoisted herself up and onto the stairs.

Rift responded by crouching low. He was prepared to move quickly if needed and the others stood with their backs tight against the wall. A moment passed and Arnethia's head poked over the top of the stairway. "It's clear for the moment," she whispered.

One by one, the group filed around the corner and onto the stairs. Guntharr brought up the rear and was last to arrive at the landing.

"Okay, which way now?" Arnethia asked.

Guntharr pointed and led the way quickly down a wide sloping corridor carved out of solid wood. On either side, rows of compact rooms lined the corridor. This is where many of the rangers lived when the Spire Tree was occupied by the elves. The corridor started to rise slowly as it curved around following the shape of the tree.

"I thought you said that once we got to the end of this corridor, there would be a stairway we could take to get out of the main traffic area?" Firebane asked.

"And there it is," Guntharr pointed out directly ahead of them at the far end of the tree. "The corridors at this level wrap around the tree.

This one wraps on the inside of the tree trunk, the other way takes you on a more outward sweep of the trunk."

As they approached the door that would take them out of this seemingly vacant part of the palace, the clicking sound of the next to the last door to the stairway indicated that someone was coming.

"Oh great." Firebane declared.

Just then two large Talicron guards stepped out of the room both with swords at their sides.

"It's them, sound the alarm," the taller of the two called out to the second one.

With that, the second one took off toward the stairs trying to get out to alert the rest of the guard.

"Taya, drop him!" Guntharr ordered.

Still trying to recover from the shocking sight of the large creatures, she quickly knocked an arrow and let it fly. Regrettably, she'd forgotten to take into consideration what Guntharr had told her regarding their built in armor and the arrow glanced off of the Talicron's lower back causing not much more than a scratch.

Guntharr reacted immediately and took off toward the escaping Talicron. The big one stepped in his way and pulled out his sword. Guntharr put his head down and lowered his shoulder. Running at top speed he collided with the Talicron who swung uselessly at the shrunken target. Guntharr's shoulder plowed into the Talicron's side sending the guard off balance and up against the wall. Spinning, Guntharr took off up the stairs after the other one. Firebane and Arnethia stepped up and, as the dazed guard pushed himself off the wall, parried a strike from Firebane's staff. Arnethia taking advantage of the opening thrust forward and rammed her sword deep into the guard's mid-section.

Startled and dying, the guard fumbled for the sword as she pulled it out. Stumbling forward he tried to take a swing at her, which she easily dodged. Firebane quickly brought his staff around and stuck a blow to the back of the guard's head, sending him face forward onto the ground.

Taya and Rift moved forward and she looked down marveling at the creature's size. "Is he dead?" she asked.

Rift sniffed, "close enough."

The four ran to follow after Guntharr up the stairs, but as they reached the door to the stairs, it flung open to show Guntharr standing there.

"We need to hurry, I couldn't catch up to him. We need to get to the royal residence and then get out of here before they can rally a sizable group and find us." He started to turn and lead them on up but Taya's voice stopped.

"I'm sorry I missed, guardian," she said sadly.

He paused a moment and looked at her. "It happens. We'll be okay, but we have to hurry now." He turned to Rift, "At the sign of the next Talicron, do your stuff."

When they stepped into the stairway and looked up, the group was amazed at the site. The stairway wound its way up, but instead of being a single staircase with a single destination, the stairway wove itself up through a large hollow opening of the tree itself and branched off in many directions landing at various points within the tree.

Guntharr led the way and began trekking his way up the stairs. At the first junction, he turned one way and then continued on past several more. Below them, sounds of soldiers could be heard gathering together and the sounds of orders were echoing up through the tree. The stairs began getting steeper and harder to climb. Guntharr took a junction and headed off toward a rather ornate looking part of the inside of the tree.

"That must be the royal quarters," Taya said to Arnethia who nodded in agreement.

As they approached the landing that lead into that section of the palace, the doors swung open just beyond and out stepped several Talicrons.

Taya stopped, and fetched an arrow. She wouldn't miss this time. "Down!" She shouted. On the stairs the three companions and even Rift crouched low at her command. She let fly the arrow which struck precisely where it needed to, embedding itself just below the base of a Talicron's neck. The Talicron's head snapped back then forward, and he tumbled forward falling off the balcony and down through the many floors to the lowest level of the tree.

Rift was the first to jump up from stairs and he started to howl his prayer of transformation as he jumped over the others. The sound echoed throughout the tree causing an almost deafening roar that grew as his body morphed and grew into its' battle form. Taking the stairs four at a time, the now fully grown battle wolf sprung into the air at the guard who had stepped up to take the place of the one who Taya had dropped just seconds ago.

Unpreparred, the Talicron threw his arms up as Rift collided with him, paws and claws first. While his claws made little more than a dent in the Talicron's outer skin, the force of the impact sent them both crashing into the back wall of the balcony.

Guntharr stood up and tried to make it up the remaining steps before a second Talicron entered through the door to take a swing at Rift. "Rift needs cover," he started to call out still several steps from the top. As he did, a missile of some sort whizzed by just missing his head and embedded itself into the neck of the target. The throwing dagger hilt was all that stuck out of the Talicron's skin and the guard fell back into the oncoming guard.

Guntharr took a moment to look back at the source of the dagger. His eyes first fell on Firebane who was nearest to him. Firebane looked blankly at him before pointing back at Arnethia. He directed his gaze at her who momentarily smiled at him and then called out, "Don't just stand there, Rift is a sitting duck."

Rift, recovering from the crash, hopped on top the Talicron who was struggling to grab his sword that he had dropped. The Talicron turned his head at the sensation of the massive creature standing on his chest as Rift drove his fang filled maul into the Talicron's face.

"Hmm, crunchy," he called out in his deep massive voice.

Guntharr, Firebane, Arnetha and Taya continued up the steps. Guntharr saw the next Talicron come out of the doorway and looked around. Spotting the group ascending the stairs, he drew his sword and started down to meet Guntharr. After taking several more steps, Guntharr planted himself and awaited the first move from the descending Talicron who now had not only a natural height advantage, but also an advantage from the stairs.

The swing from the massive sword came down while the guard was still three steps away. Prepared for the strike, Guntharr crouched and swung the warhammer up to meet the sword in a incredible clash that sent sparks flying. Using the height to his advantage, the Talicron stepped back up a step and swung again at the top of Guntharr's head. Doing the only thing he could, Guntharr dropped prone on the steps to avoid the swing putting himself in a dangerously weak position.

Looking up, he expected to see a downward cut that would force him to either roll to one side or the other and hopefully not fall off the stairs to certain death. But instead of seeing a sword swinging down, the Talicron himself came tumbling forward with the feathers of an arrow sticking just outside of his mouth. Bracing himself, the heavy creature crashed on top of him pining him to the stairs. With a groan, Guntharr pushed up with his arms sending the body rolling off of him and down into the bowels of the tree.

Firebane and Arnethia came up alongside and helped him up the rest of the way and the four finally reached the top of the stairs. Rift, by now, had encountered the next Talicron and was trying carefully not fall off the balcony while staying clear of the massive sword that was being swung at him.

With the Talicon's attention focused on Rift, Guntharr was able to reach the attacking guard and swing hard at the Talicron's weak side. The blow landed square in the Talicron's back with a distinct snapping sound. A cry of pain from the Talicron and his legs buckled underneath him and he fell to the floor.

"Are we having fun yet," Rift asked Guntharr who ignored his comment and headed into the royal residence hall.

Inside the two massive doors off the balcony, the group found themselves standing in a beautiful hall. There were columns that stretched from the floor to the ceiling carved out of the living tree and polished so smooth that they shimmered almost as if covered in gold. A large table was arranged in the middle of the room with seats decorated with ornate cushions along each side. Several doors lined the each side of the hall.

"What's in there?" Taya asked as they carefully made their way through the now empty room.

"Those were the attendants quarters. Your father treated his attendants better than he treated himself in most situations," Guntharr pointed out.

Several chairs that lined the table had been thrown to the floor, and remnants of food lay scattered on the table itself. Toward the back of the room a very fancy door led off in one direction. Guntharr stopped at the sight of the door and just stared remorsefully. The memories of past times spent in this room with Krest flashed through his mind. It wasn't far from here that he'd lost his friend, and at the same time where he had discovered Taya.

"We have incoming," Firebane called wheeling around to face two Talicrons coming through the doors toward them. Behind them, coming up the stairs a line of more Talicrons were nearing the balcony.

"Rift," Guntharr called out. "get those door closed, now!"

Rift took off back across the hall in a dead run. The two guards seeing the oncoming battle wolf spread apart to force the wolf into a pickle, but Rift kept running right up the middle. With a nod, the two opposing Talicrons leaped toward the approaching battle wolf in a kill strike, but as they came down with their swords, the wolf disappeared and the swords came crashing down onto the ground. Near the doors, he skidded to stop, and reaching out with his paws, he slammed the two doors shut, just as the first Talicron reached the balcony.

Arnethia, jumped up on the table and ran toward the Talicrons who were looking around trying to find out where the battle wolf had vanished to. The one nearest the table looked around to see Arnethia swing her sword at his head, just a moment too late.

"I can't exactly bar the door," Rift barked out from the other end of the room.

"Just lean on it," Firebane yelled back. "I'll be right there to bar it."

Rift looked at the human he had known for a long time and tried to determine if he was really serious or not. Sounds from the outside indicated that the lone Talicron had waited for another to join him before approaching the door. Rift decided he would take Firebane seriously so he maneuvered himself against the door and dug his claws into the wood floor as the first blow from the Talicron hit the door. The impact vibrated through the wolf's recently healed shoulder and caused him to shift slightly. He knew this wasn't going to work for long as the second, stronger blow hit the door.

"You better hurry," he barked back.

Firebane struck hard at the armored warrior but was unable to cause any lasting effects. The warrior came back with a sword thrust that he had to parry to avoid getting impaled. Guntharr arrived by his side. "I got this one, get up there with Arnethia and bar that door," he ordered.

Arnethia had reached the door and was has helping Rift hold it closed as the Talicrons outside now threw their bodies at it. "He's not kidding, somebody get up here and help me lift this bar!" she shouted.

Firebane took off around the Talicron. As he circled around, the Talicron followed him to try to get in a parting shot. Guntharr took advantage of the distraction and swung low at the soldier crashing the warhammer into the back of the knee. The knee gave way, but as the Talicron started to fall, he used the momentum to spin and drive his fist holding the sword into the side of Guntharr's head, sending him toppling against the table.

Guntharr lay dazed against the table trying to get his bearings as the Talicron used his sword as a walking stick. He struggled over to the incoherent guardian and raised a fist to bring it down in a blow that would certainly kill him.

"Oh, no you don't," Taya's voice challenged as she slid across the table.

The Talicron looked up to see the small elf girl just as she unleashed an arrow at near point blank range. Dropping his sword, the Talicron fell over, dead.

Taya jumped off the table and landed next to her guardian. Helping him back to his feet, he shook his head to clear the stars that were swirling about. "Are you okay?" she asked.

He nodded, "I am, thanks to you."

She smiled back at him as Firebane, Arnethia and Rift made their way back to them. "We got the door barred. That should hold them for a while," Firebane reported.

"Satisfactory," Guntharr acknowledged.

Arnethia walked up beside him and wiped the blood off of the side of his head where the Talicron had opened up a sizable gash. "You're going to tell us that there's another way out of this section of the palace, right?"

He turned and made his way toward the back of the room. "First, we must find the Talisman. Krest's quarters are this way. Inside, there is a hidden anti-room that only a few of his closest friends knew about."

The group quickly fell into lock step as the pounding of the Talicons against the large doors continued to reverberate through the chamber. Guntharr was the first to reach the door. As he did, he immediately flung it open and they entered.

Chapter 16

Inside the royal chambers, Taya marveled at the splendor of the decorations within the room that even after fourteen years of neglect still appeared in magnificent glory. Arnethia and Firebane also stopped and gazed around at the grandeur that once was the Lord of the Elve's resting place. Guntharr, however, was not taken aback by the pomp but rather ran to a section near the dressing area of the room. He fumbled around the edge of the massive wardrobe that stood against the wall until he was able to trip a hidden lock and the dust covered cabinet swung open to reveal a room beyond.

"What's in there?" Firebane asked.

"Nothing, I suspect," Guntharr replied. "Taya, come with me. The rest of you look around for anything that might give us some clues to the where the Talisman might have been stored."

Taya followed Guntharr into the room. Inside was a spacious nursery whose furniture looked as if it hadn't been touched in years.

Guntharr pulled Taya close to him. "This is where I found you. Apparently, your father kept you hidden away immediately after your birth until he could determine what threats would be placed on your life."

"How did you know I was here?" she asked.

"It was the last thing he told me, before he died," he replied.

She walked around and pictured what it must have been like when the palace was full of life. A small shelf held several handmade dolls. The dim light that filtered down from the numerous small holes that had been carved through the tree allowed her to see only the faintest of details of the soft figures.

"I wanted you to see this, because I know it helps to know where you came from," he spoke softly. "One day, you'll be able to return and reclaim all of this, but now we must be off."

"Oh, please, just a moment longer," she begged.

He nodded and left her alone in the room. She reached down into the cradle that had been fashioned of the finest wood. Inside a thick layer of dust covered the otherwise white bedding that had at one time been thrown aside and never replaced. Taya took her hand and gently ran it over the dusty covers in the spot where she'd laid the last time she'd been in this room so long ago. Tears formed in her eyes as she tried to image what it would have been like to have grown up in a world where her father was still alive and Spire Tree stood tall as a symbol of God's righteousness and grace.

She crossed over from the bed to the shelf containing several little toys that had been made for her. She picked up a doll that resembled a miniature elf girl with silver hair, much like hers. She blew the dust off and wiped some cobwebs away before pulling it close to her chest and hugged it tenderly.

"Taya," Guntharr's voice echoed into the room.

"Coming, guardian," she replied in a tear filled whisper. She carefully stuffed the souvenir inside her belt and looped a lace of leather around it to hold it fast. She then backed out of the room one step at a time. Scanning each aspect of the room and committing it to memory as best as she could before crossing back out into the main room.

Guntharr was there to meet her and gave her a light hug as he pushed the wardrobe back in place to protect the sanctity of the room.

"Guntharr," Arnethia called over to him. "I think I found something."

Guntharr and Taya ran over to her. As they did, she pulled pieces of an ornate box out of a pile of rubble. The pieces were part of some trash had been piled up in the corner of the room, apparently by looters after they had taken over the palace. "This looks significant," she held them up so they could see. "My guess is this was holding some very important jewelry to warrant such a magnificent box. Not to mention the fact that it's been smashed open by something other than traditional means," she added.

Guntharr studied one of the small fragments she handed him. "I remember this box, but I don't recall Krest ever putting anything in or taking anything out of it. How do you know it was opened by means other than just dropping it?"

"The fragments are unbreakable. The material this box is made out of is magical in nature. I tried to snap one of the smaller splinters and was unable to even bend it." She held up a small splinter of wood.

"So, whatever was in there, was worth protecting, is that what you're saying?" Firebane asked.

"My guess is the Talisman is gone," Arnethia said sadly.

"I hate to interrupt this fascinating discovery, but it sounds like they've brought something up to bash their way through the door," Rift said.

The group all listened carefully and a much deeper pounding sound could be heard coming from the end of the residence hall.

"We need to move," Guntharr directed the others out of the personal chambers and back into the main hall.

"But we can't go back that way," Taya said.

"Indeed, we'll have to try the other way out," Guntharr replied and then headed off toward one corner of the hall.

Hidden in plain sight was a narrow hallway that curved up and behind the attendant's quarters and then changed into stairs.

"Where does this go?" Firebane asked.

"This comes out in the kitchen attached to the great hall. Before we get to the kitchen, we'll pass the place where I found Lord Krestichan dying," Guntharr said as he started up the stairs.

"Is going to the great hall a good idea?" Arnethia asked. "Surely whoever is running this place will be running the show from there."

"I don't know that we have much choice," Firebane replied as he followed close behind.

At the top of the stairs a small room opened up just outside the kitchen. As Guntharr crossed the room, he paused for a moment and stared at a particular dark spot on the floor where he last saw his friend lying.

"What is it?" Taya asked detecting something wrong.

"Nothing," Guntharr said turning his head toward the kitchen. "We must hurry."

As they entered the kitchen, smells of recently cooked food and the site of dying fires indicated that it had recently been used and abandoned.

"What's the plan?" Arnethia reached up and put a hand on the door that Guntharr reached for. This was the door that would lead them out into the great hall.

Guntharr studied Arnethia for a moment. Deep inside he knew this was a trap and at this point he regretted bringing them here on the slim chance that they would actually find the Talisman. Now, they faced a monumental challenge of getting through the next room alive. The largest, most open, and probably well guarded room in the whole palace.

"The plan," he said at last with determination, "is to get through the Great Hall and escape through a corridor off the far end. If we're attacked, you, Firebane and Rift will make your way to the exit while I try to hold them off."

"I should stay with you," Rift growled. "You and me can take out just about any army they can throw at us," Rift's showed a toothy grin.

Guntharr nodded in appreciation.

"I'm with Rift, I think we should all fight our way through. We work really well as a team," Firebane argued.

Guntharr shook his head, "Taya must be protected at all costs."

Firebane started to challenge his friend, but a quick read of the guardians expression indicated that it would be wasted breath and time.

Guntharr looked over at his ward. The last several years had gone by so quickly, and now he was sure that this would be his end. "There is one thing you can do when we get inside."

"Yes," Firebane responded eager to help.

"Light up the room. As bright as you can," Guntharr pointed at the staff. "It's a huge room, so push the staff for all it's worth. Talicron's are inherently dark creatures and hate the light. I'm sure the change will catch them off guard and may buy us a few extra seconds."

"Understood," Firebane responded somberly.

"I'm not going to leave you," Taya tried to argue.

Guntharr knelt beside her so she was forced to look down slightly into his face. "My dear, Taya. I have foolishly jeopardized your life by trying to restore it. I made a vow to your father that I intend to keep."

"But," she started to speak but Guntharr held up a gentle finger to her lips.

"Arnethia and Firebane are good people. If, and I do mean if, something happens to me. They will protect you and see that what I meant to have done will be finished, and you will be restored to your father's house. But you must be brave, and follow their lead. Understood?" He asked.

She nodded slowly then threw her arms around him in a giant hug. Guntharr responded by slowly wrapping his arms around her and squeezing her softly.

Pulling away slowly, Guntharr stood up and reached for the door before turning around. "Remember, when we go through this door, don't stop for anything. I . . ."

"Don't forget me," Rift interjected.

"We," Guntharr corrected himself, "will push them back away from the exit. Once you've made it through, we'll fall back ourselves and meet up with you at the edge of the secret tunnel."

No one spoke a word, because the sounds coming up from behind them indicated that they had been tracked from the royal chambers and were in danger of being surrounded.

Flinging the door up, Rift shot out of the door first and into the Great Hall. The massive room was lined on both sides with massive columns that again were carved out of the living tree. High above the main floor on either side, a pair of balconies ran along each side the full length of the hall. Below and above the balcony on the nearside wall, in the center of the room was a large window that opened up to the outside of the tree. Jutting out below the window was a massive limb large enough that a pair of horses could ride on it. Just off to the side of the door they had entered, a raised platform holding a throne carved out of the tree. Near the throne sat a wrinkled old man in a chair with a make-shift carrying system. Surrounding him were twenty towering Talicrons. At the far side of the room, another twenty Talicrons lined the far wall guarding the exits.

At the sight of the invaders, the Talicrons broke away from the old man and charged toward them with swords drawn. The group at the far end of the hall split and half of them made their way across the large open floor to intercept them.

Rift let out an ear splitting howl as he charged head long into the twenty Talicrons coming right at them from the center of the room. Guntharr followed close behind and he let out a resounding battle cry.

"It's a trap," Arnethia called out.

"And you were expecting something else," Firebane replied jokingly.

The two along with Taya took off straight across the hall as Guntharr had directed, trying to steer wide of the Talicrons that were approaching from the center.

Firebane uttered a prayer and the staff blazed with light reflecting off the polished wood causing the room to glow brightly. This caused the Talicrons to pause briefly and shade their eyes. During this time, Rift charged forward smack into the middle of five partly blinded Talicrons. With no intention of stopping, he pushed forward as he made impact sending the bodies sprawling in either direction. Guntharr, still several paces behind Rift, took aim at the nearest Talicron who was starting to regain some vision. Heaving in mid-run his hammer at the Talicron, the mightly warhammer slammed hard into its chest sending him backward and knocking down three others who were still trying to open their eyes.

Taya decided she wasn't going to simply just run, so she grabbed an arrow from her quiver and loaded her bow in mid stride. With careful stride and aim, she let fly an arrow that flew brilliantly across the wide room striking one of the oncoming precisely in the neck sending him falling face forward.

As the three neared the center, the group of nine Talicrons that were approaching had slowed their pace as the light from the staff drew nearer and caused the area to be brighter. Shielding their eyes from the light that radiated from the staff and now reflecting off the floor and columns caused them to almost stop completely. This gave Taya an opportunity to knock and fire another arrow. This one was off just slightly but still managed to pierce the Talicron's shoulder causing him to drop his sword in pain.

Rift spun around, sliding slightly on the polished floor with nails digging small gashes into the near perfect wood. The two lead Talicrons that he hit first, were out cold. The other three were still trying to pick themselves off the floor. In the meantime, three more broke off and started toward the battle wolf.

"That's right, come and get me," Rift mocked them.

This caused two more to take notice and follow close behind. Rift waited until the three almost reached him, then he spun and hurried across the center to the opposite line of columns. The five Talicrons now chasing right doubled their pace and called back for assistance.

Guntharr reached his hammer and picked it up as a Talicron that had finally recovered his sight stepped up to take a swing at him. Rolling to one side and springing back on his feet, Guntharr swung back around behind himself slamming home into the slower Talicron's midsection causing him to double over. Continuing his motion, he swung down and around in a sweeping motion and connected with the Talicron's lowered head sending him flying backwards.

Half way across the hall, the eight Talicrons started closing in on the three. Arnethia and Firebane as they reached the center of the room, slowed and took up battle stances. They were going to have to fight these guys after all.

Off to one side, a high pitched squawk grew in intensity as the massive form of the hawk lord shot in through the central opening.

With claws down, he buzzed just over the heads of four of the Talicrons tearing huge gashes into each of their heads and sending them to the floor.

The other four scattered at first sight of the oncoming hawk lord and and just narrowly avoided the razor sharp talons that were reaching for them at the speed of an arrow. Spreading his wings, Raskin soared into the towering expanse of the great hall. Quickly assessing the situation, he circled around the large room trying to build up enough speed to make another diving attack.

Taya took advantage of the distraction and fired a shot, sending one of the remaining eight stumbling backwards with an arrow sticking out of his upper chest.

Arnethia and Firebane, glad to see their friend, stepped up to engage the other four.

Rift stood by one of the columns watching as now six Talicrons chased after him. He was just about ready to charge toward them when out of the corner of his eye, he saw activity at the door where they had just recently come out of.

"Guntharr," he called loudly, "incoming."

Turning his attention to the incoming attackers, Rift crouched to take off again. A fluttering sound overhead caused Rift to look up to see a massive net falling from the balcony overhead. Unable to react fast enough, it fell on top of him, pinning him to the ground. In frustration and warning, he howled loudly.

Guntharr was busy parrying blows between two Talicrons when Rift's howl alerted him to trouble. Diving to one side, he rolled and then sprung up in a run heading through the center of the room toward his captured friend. With his free hand, he whistled loudly trying to get Raskins attention. Two more Talicrons quickly stepped into his path as he ran. Fading to his right, he just missed the swing from one of the two as he ran past. Swinging around, as he ran, he was able to catch the one Talicron square in the back with a familiar snap.

Raskin circled around and made another massive diving attack near the six Talicrons who were standing around laughing at the pinned battle wolf. One of the six saw the descending hawk lord and tried to alert the others. Raskin's talons sliced open the first three Talicrons with expert precision. The next two were able to dive for cover avoiding the attack. But as Raskin neared the sixth Talicron who first caught sight of him, he parried the dive and swung out with his sword. With the flat side of his blade, the Talicron made contact with Raskin, knocking him out the air and sending him tumbling across the floor. As he rolled to a stop, the hawk lord lay there unmoving.

Rift growled ferociously and struggled with all of his might against the weighted net, but was unable to free himself. As he wiggled, he quickly became more intangled in the net. Snapping viciously, he tried chewing his way through the thick rope that made up the net.

Arnethia and Firebane lined up against the four incoming Talicron and began sparing with them in a series of movements that took on the form of a dance.

Taya pulled out another arrow from her quiver and waited for an opening shot on one of the Talicrons that was sparing with Arnethia when a large hand reached around her and causing her to fire wildly and nearly hit Firebane. Letting out a scream, Arnethia, Firebane and the four Talicrons they were battling paused and turned to look at the struggling elf girl now held captive by a large Talicron that had run in from the kitchen entrance.

Guntharr turned and at the sound of the scream and instantly headed toward the source when a wall of Talicrons stepped forward to block his path. Extending their swords, they formed a wall that would be impossible even for him to penetrate.

Firebane and Arnethia were distracted long enough for the soldiers they had been dueling with to restrain them.

"Please, do not make this any more difficult," the crackly old voice called from the chair. "Bring them!" he commanded.

Firebane, Arnethia and Taya were escorted back toward the center of the room where the old man sat waiting. Two Talicrons dragged Rift over inside the net. He was still growling and thrashing with little success. Guntharr was also being escorted at sword point by five of the Talicrons that made up the wall. One other Talicron carried an unconscious Raskin over and tossed him carelessly in the middle of the gathering with a thud.

"You do that again, and I'll personally bite your head clear off," Rift barked at the heartless act.

The Talicron reacted to the snapping sound that Rift made from under the net and took a step away from the impassioned battle wolf.

As the group gathered around the central figure in the middle of the room, additional soldiers filed in to watch the spectacle. All total, more than a hundred Talicrons now surrounded them and blocked every exit.

As Taya neared the guardian, she rammed her elbow into her captor as hard as she could surprising him and causing him to relax his grip. As he did so, she took off toward Guntharr. The Talicron quickly reached out for her and managed to grab the little doll that dangled from her belt. In an effort to pull her back, he yanked hard but only succeeded in ripping the doll off her belt.

Taya stumbled and fell into Guntharr's waiting arms. Helping her back up, two more Talicrons grabbed her by the arms and pulled her away from the guardian and brought her to the old man.

In disgust, the Talicron that had lost Taya threw the doll onto the ground and brutally kicked it across the floor. Guntharr noticed for the first time the little treasure that Taya had scavenged out of the room. The thought that this monster had so carelessly treated something of value to his ward made the anger within him boil to a new level he had not felt before.

"What, no warm word, no clever phrases?" The old man asked. "Surely you haven't forgotten me? I know it's been a long time, but I would think in these surroundings you would surely recognize me."

Guntharr studied the man's face for the first time. "Dravious, is it really you?" He asked knowingly.

"Ah, at last. He does recognize me," the old man clapped slowly with a pleased smile on his face.

"Guntharr, do you know this guy?" Firebane asked.

He nodded. "Yes, Dravious was the man that led the assault on Spire Tree that led to the ultimate downfall. He was there the night Lord Krestichan was killed."

"Now, full disclosure, please, not only was I there the night he was killed," Dravious chuckled, "I was the one who killed him."

"You killed my father," Taya responded in a fit of rage as she struggled against the much stronger Talicrons that held her next to Dravious' chair.

"Indeed, I did, young lady." Dravious turned his head to look at Taya. "And, had I known at the time that you existed, I would have killed you that night as well." He paused, and then turned back to face Guntharr.

"I see you found the Talisman of Alterian," Guntharr pointed to the beautiful talisman resting on his chest.

"Oh, I didn't think you'd notice. How do you like it?" He asked trying to sound witty.

Guntharr studied the talisman as if trying to honestly assess the mad wizard's question. "You've lost four of the gems, how?"

Clapping his hands, Dravious let out a brief laugh. "You are an observant one, are you not? Yes, it seems that when a non-heir of the Silverwood puts it on there are some, let's say, complications that occur before one can invoke the full power of the Talisman."

Arnethia stepped forward to stand beside Guntharr who had a large Talicron still holding onto his upper arm tightly. "You didn't answer the question. What did you do with the missing gems?"

Dravious looked down and studied the empty sockets for a moment. "They've been hidden. The stones immediately vanished the second I put it on. Also, as a result of the talisman, I have been rendered immobile. I've lost almost all ability to move except for the small movements I can make with my hands."

"Seems like a pretty high price to pay for a broken talisman of power," Firebane said.

"I must admit, it has its draw backs. However, once I have recovered the missing gems and returned them to their places, the talisman will grant me the power to rule over this realm and no one will be able to stop me," he smiled.

"So, that's why you haven't killed us yet," Guntharr reasoned.

Dravious nodded.

Arnethia looked over at him, "Care to explain?"

"Dravious, in his present state is pretty helpless. Certainly, he can't go traipsing about the five realms looking for the magically hidden gems. It would take two or three lifetimes," Guntharr explained.

"So, why not send the big green guys," Taya asked still trying to break free.

"Mostly, because Talicrons are not well received in most of the five realms and the losses he would sustain sending them out would be enormous. We would be the perfect footmen," Guntharr concluded. "Hold Taya hostage, at risk of certain death if we don't cooperate. We would then be allowed to roam the realms largely unchallenged by normal society until we could come up with the missing stones. After which, he would most certainly kill us."

Dravious looked hurt. "Now really, you think I would stoop so low?"

"Yes," Rift called out from the floor.

"I would have no reason to kill you, once I have the gems. I would be unstoppable," he said.

"Die now, or die later after we make him all powerful," Arnethia thought out loud. "I'm not liking our options right now."

"There is only one who is all powerful, Arnethia, and it will never be Dravious," Guntharr gently corrected her.

"Oh, there you go again with your faith in the One True God." Dravious waved his hand and ripped Arnethia from the grips of the Talicron holding her. Suspended in mid-air next to him, Dravious manipulated his fingers and the group could see that she started struggling for breathe.

"Put her down," Guntharr threatened straining against the grip of his captors.

"You want to see power, I'll show you power." Dravious lifted his other hand and pulled Firebane in a similar fashion next to Arnethia. Both were hovering above the floor and both were slowly being suffocated.

"Stop it, please," Taya screamed.

Arnethia's color started to leave her skin as the life was slowly being crushed out of her. Firebane however resisted and used some of his own power to push back against the dark wizard. He was able to fight against the crushing force, but only enough to prolog the inevitable. He was by no means strong enough to hold off the power of the talisman.

As Arnethia's body went limp and her head rolled to one side, Guntharr bowed his head. As the anger surged through his mind, he commanded his thoughts to be still until there were no distractions in the sea of chaos. Quietly, he prayed. Out of the corner of his eye, he caught Taya looking at him in despair. Once they made eye contact, he glance down at the ground in front of her indicating that she needed to drop. She studied his eye movement for a moment and then gave a very subtle nod that she understood.

"You see, 'guardian'. Your God has no power here," Dravious mocked as he focused more power on Firebane whose resistance was starting to weaken.

Guntharr's head snapped up at this remark. "My God has power everywhere," he replied defiantly. Taking all of the energy stored up in his anger, he hurled the two Talicrons that had been holding him to the side. He followed this with a move that can only be described as a blur, he grabbed the war hammer that had been dropped at his side and slung it from his side like he was skipping a stone on a stream toward Dravious.

Dravious who had committed all his focus on killing Firebane and Arnethia, could only look surprised as the hammer struck the Talisman directly on his chest. Whether it was the reaction of the talisman or the power of Guntharr's God, an explosion of light and power exploded out from the impact. Guntharr and Taya dropped to the ground and the power washed out in a wave over all of the Talicrons in the great hall knocking them flat. Dravious himself was flung backwards out of his seat into a pile of unconscious Talicrons, as he fell the talisman flung from his neck.

Arnethia and Firebane who was just above the exploding wave, fell to the ground. Firebane was still aware enough to land on his feet albeit unsteadily before collapsing. Arnethia, who was unconscious fell in a heap on the floor. Rushing over to her, Guntharr knelt down beside her and lifted her up so that she could breathe easier. A couple deep gasps and she was able to sit up on her own.

From the pile of bodies where Dravious landed, the free wizard struggled to right himself with his new found movement. Taya had made her way over to Arnethia and quickly wrapped her arms around her at the sight of her recovery. Guntharr stood up and surveyed their surroundings. Several Talicrons approached the great hall in response to the explosion. They looked inside and saw the floor littered with bodies and saw that only Guntharr was standing. In fear they turned and ran away as quickly as they could.

"I'll kill you for this," Dravious choked as he tried to get up, but not having used his legs in years was unable to.

"You're done, Dravious," Guntharr said as he walked over to the struggling wizard to pick up his hammer. "Go back to whatever hole spawned you and don't ever return." He then spotted the little doll that had been ripped from Taya's side half buried under a Talicron body just a few steps away. Turning aside from the seemingly helpless wizard, Guntharr holstered the hammer and walked over to retrieve Taya's treasure.

Bending down, he lifted the body off of the doll and then picked it up. With his back turned to everyone, he studied it briefly admiring the simple beauty and innocence that it embodied. With tender strokes of his finger he felt the still soft strands of silk that made up the hair on the doll's head.

Taya stood up at the sound of metal scraping across the floor. Dravious, had found a Talicron blade on the floor and was freeing it with what was left of his magic. Lifting the sword into the air he aimed the blade in line with the guardian and drew back his hand to magically hurl the sword at the unsuspecting target.

"Done indeed," Dravious spat as he conjured up enough magical energy to hurl it toward Guntharr. "We'll see who's done."

Just as he was about to release the sword for its death flight, a sharp thudding sound and the appearance of arrow feathers sticking out from his chest caused him to drop the sword in mid air. He looked for a moment in unbelief at the arrow and then looked up to see where it had come from. Standing in her battle stance, Taya was already knocking her last arrow and pulling back on the string when Dravious coughed and rolled over on his side dead.

Guntharr turned still focused on the doll and saw Taya standing there with her bow loaded and drawn in the direction of the fallen Dravious. Guntharr studied the situation and saw the sword laying out in the open pointing in his specific direction and then realized what had happened. Stepping over the bodies, he reached his ward who at the sign of no further threat, returned the lone arrow back to its quiver and shouldered the bow.

Seeing the doll, Taya's face instantly lit up in a brilliant smile. "Thank you," she said as he handed the doll to her.

"Thank you," Guntharr countered. "I guess he wasn't completely powerless after all."

"Hello," Rift's muffled voice rang out.

"Rift?" Firebane called out looking around for the battle wolf.

"Where is he?" Arnethia asked scanning the area.

"Over here," he called louder.

Everyone began looking around. Taya was the first to pinpoint the sound of his voice. It was exactly where he had been before, but now he was under a pile of large Talicron bodies. Rift struggled to get up. "I could use a little help here."

Epilogue

Back at the church in Brittle, the group sat around a table enjoying some fresh fruit and retelling the events back at Spire Tree. In the center of the table the Talisman of Alterian hung by its chain from the candle stand. Rift was back to his normal size and snoring away on the floor near the fire ring. Raskin stood on the back of a chair listening in on the conversation and occasionally pecking at some nuts that had been placed on a tray in front of him.

"Can you believe how those Talicrons just let us walk right out of there?" Taya squealed.

"Are you kidding?" Arnethia laughed, "after what Guntharr did in the great hall, I was surprised they even got close enough to watch us leave."

"Part of me wishes we could have stayed there to take back the palace and run them all out," Taya sighed.

"In time," Guntharr tried to reassure her. "We got what we went there for, mostly. We would have had to expend a lot of energy to completely drive them all out. I know it seemed like they were complacent by letting us go, but I assure you, if we started attacking them, they wouldn't have just stood around and taken it. It would most certainly have been a battle. And, even if we did manage to drive them all out, we'd never be able to hold it."

"I know you're right," Taya acknowledged. "When do I get to try on the talisman?"

Guntharr's expression turned very serious, "You cannot put it on for some time. Remember Dravious's condition?"

"Yes," she replied.

"He was trapped in his position because the power of the talisman had been broken." He reached out to the center and pointed to the empty sockets. "Because he was unworthy to wear the talisman, when he put it on, the magic built into it triggered the gems to be dispersed. This fractured the power of the talisman. So until it can be repaired . . .

"You would be trapped just like he was in a permanent position if you put it on," Arnethia reaffirmed.
Guntharr frowned at the interruption. "Yes. I'm afraid it will have to be something that we just look at and admire until then."

Rift snorted loudly and rolled over. As he did, he opened his one eye to look over the group. "Did I miss anything?" He asked with a yawn.

"No, just reminiscing," Firebane replied.

"Okay, wake me up when we get to planning something exciting, like dinner." He stretched and took in a big draw of air. "Ew, Firebane."

"What is it?" Firebane looked over at him.

Rift stood up and sniffed the air for a moment and lumbered over to the group. "You need to bury that goblin ash in the back pasture, I can still smell goblin."

"Sorry, Rift. We burned the bodies over a month ago. I suppose with your super sniffer and the wind blowing the right way, you are still going to occasionally catch a whiff of it." Firebane tried to explain.

"That sounds like it was an exciting battle," Arnethia directed toward Rift. "It could be that being back here has brought back the memories. Memories are powerful things, believe me," she added.

Guntharr turned and looked across the room, out the big opening to the hall and out the big window that led to the back pasture. For a moment, he thought he caught the glimmer of something like an eye in the corner of the window, but it lasted for only a second and then disappeared.

"Well, I don't know about you, but I need to go bed the horses down and turn in. I'm beat," Firebane turned and started to head out.

"You go ahead and turn in, old friend," Guntharr remarked. "Taya and I will take care of it."

"Thank you, I'll take you up on that, good night everyone, may your dreams be blessed," Firebane turned and walked back toward his quarters.

Taya stood up and followed Guntharr out of the room. At the window, Guntharr studied the edge of the window and sniffed the air. "Something wrong?" Taya asked.

"Just breathing in the fresh night air," he replied.

They walked quietly out of the back of the church and then across the pasture back to the stables. Taya could see that the guardian was deep in thought and choose not to say anything until they reached the back of the pasture where Angel Dance, Silverfoot and Nightfury where gathered under a tree nibbling on some grass. Grabbing the reigns, Taya lead Silverfoot toward the barn. Guntharr just whistled at Nightfury who responded obediently and simply followed him. Angel Dance took the hint and followed after the others.

Taya marched Silverfoot into her stall and then stood there and petted the mare and whispered kind words to it. Moments later, Guntharr rounded the stall door and stood next to them and proceeded to pat the horses neck.

"So, will we be able to see the Spire Tree again?" She asked quietly.

"Of course," Guntharr added. "But the next time we go, I want you to be able to stay."

"What needs to happen before we can do that?" She wondered.

"First and foremost, we need to repair the talisman. Only then can we officially establish you as the heir to the throne of Silverwood," he reminded her.

"But how can we do that? There are four gems missing, and we have no idea where they could be," she noted.

"True, that's going to be our first challenge. We need to discover what really happened to those gems. And to do that, we're going to need to do some research," he said with a wink.

"That means a lot of reading dusty old books and scrolls, doesn't it?" She moaned.

He nodded. "And I know how much you love doing that."

She shook her head much like a horse sending her silver hair flying in all directions. "Research is no fun, is it Silverfoot?" She said trying to get the horse on her side.

Silverfoot snorted in agreement and nodded.

"Well, we can hang out here for a few days, then we need to get back on the road. We can't stay in one place for too long, there are enemies out there that know you exist now, and they're going to be looking for you. So, the longer we take getting that talisman fixed, the longer you're in danger," he said in a serious tone.

Taya thought for a moment then sighed. "I see your point. I suppose the sooner we get started with the research, the sooner we can get on with finding the missing gems."

Guntharr reached up and patted her on the shoulder in agreement. "Your ability to reason things out is impressive."

"Sure," she said slyly. "So, let's get started," she said with faux excitement.

"In the morning, Taya," he replied with a smile, "in the morning."